Angel 3

Anthony Fields

Lock Down Publications and Ca$h
Presents

ANGEL 3

A Novel by *Anthony Fields*

Anthony Fields

Lock Down Publications

P.O. Box 944
Stockbridge, Ga 30281

Visit our website @
www.lockdownpublications.com

Copyright 2022 Anthony Fields
ANGEL 3

First Edition June 2022
Printed in the United States of America

Lock Down Publications
Like our page on Facebook: Lock Down Publications @
www.facebook.com/lockdownpublications.ldp
Cover design and layout by: **Dynasty Cover Me**
Book interior design by: **Shawn Walker**
Editor: **Kiera Northington**

Stay Connected with Us!

Text **LOCKDOWN** to 22828 to stay up-to-date
with new releases, sneak peaks, contests and
more…
Thank you.

Submission Guideline.

Submit the first three chapters of your completed manuscript to ldpsubmissions@gmail.com, subject line: Your book's title. The manuscript must be in a .doc file and sent as an attachment. Document should be in Times New Roman, double spaced and in size 12 font. Also, provide your synopsis and full contact information. If sending multiple submissions, they must each be in a separate email.

Have a story but no way to send it electronically? You can still submit to LDP/Ca$h Presents. Send in the first three chapters, written or typed, of your completed manuscript to:

LDP: Submissions Dept
P.O. Box 944
Stockbridge, Ga 30281

DO NOT send original manuscript. Must be a duplicate.

Provide your synopsis and a cover letter containing your full contact information.

Thanks for considering LDP and Ca$h Presents.

Dedication

This book is dedicated to Mr. David Tucker, Sr., my oldest and biggest supporter.

Acknowledgements

Someone came to me with an issue of the *XXL Magazine*. The rapper called Da Baby was on the cover. Inside the magazine, I was told a young rapper from Chicago had mentioned me in an article. Never had I heard of King Von, ever in my life. I read the article. The interviewer asked King Von what books he had read while incarcerated. I was honored when I read where King Von said he'd read and really liked *The Ultimate Sacrifice* parts one, two, and three. He didn't mention me by name, he said the books were written by "some Muslim guy." That was enough for me. Sadly, King Von was killed a month or so later in Atlanta, Georgia. Rest in peace, young king. Glad I entertained you, even if only for a little while.

With that being said, it's been almost twenty years since I started this journey. I began writing *Angel* in 2002. Shout out Shannon Holmes and his novel, *B-More Careful*. I used that book to guide me along the way. When I say I am self-taught when it comes to writing novels, I really mean it. I finished *Angel* in 2003. I self-edited, copied and mailed out manuscripts to all the leading urban novel publishers at the time.

Shout out to BlackPrint, Urban Books, Triple Crown, Melodrama and others I can't remember. In 2004, the rejection letters rolled in. And just as I thought my literary dream was over, Teri Woods contacted me. In 2005, I sold her the rights to *Angel*. In 2006, when *Angel* debuted in *Essence Magazine's* bestselling list, I was proud. I kept writing.

Next came *Bossy* with Crystal Perkins-Steel and Ghostface Killaz. Neither book did well, but I kept pushing. I went on to write *The Ultimate Sacrifice* in ninety days, then in *The Blink of an Eye*. The deal with Wahida Clark followed.

The story for *Angel 2* was inside me, so I wrote it. I tried to get Wahida, T. Styles, KiKi Swinson and a few others to put the book out, but everybody refused. No one wanted to anger the all-powerful Queen of Urban Lit, Teri Woods. *Angel 2* languished in my inmate property until 2016. Newly released from prison, I self-published.

But I never gave the book the attention it deserved, because the streets beckoned. It took for me to come back to prison to finally finish this series.

It's been fifteen years since the first book dropped, five years since the second one debuted. And now here I come, with the third installment. I sincerely hope the loyal fans of the *Angel* series (no connection to the Angel in the *Dutch* series) can forgive me for dragging things along. In this book as well as the next, I'ma forego all the name dropping and just say a few things to a few people.

To Artinis "Whistle" Winston, your nickname should be "Whistleblower." Your greatest accomplishment in life now is becoming a rat. That distinction fits you because you stay in some shit. Omar Van Hagen told me in 2011 that you were a rat, and I didn't want to believe it. Couldn't believe it. I read your statements in my appeal brief and they broke my heart.

Damn, homie! I put food on the table for your family when you couldn't. When your infant son Mason passed away, I was the first person to arrive at the hospital to comfort you and Pumpkin. When your woman couldn't pay for the lavish birthday party y'all threw at Dave and Buster's, remember, I saved the day and paid for everything. And now it all makes sense.

Birds of a feather flock together. You introduced me to Byran "Crudd" Clark, the rat who got on the stand and lied on me and my men for two straight days. He was your man. You put him in my company and look what happened. I was loyal to you. I loved you and I provided for you. And this how you repay me? If I ever get this knife out my back, I'ma keep it to remind me dope fiends can never be trusted.

Speaking of dope fiends, Abdul Kareem Samuels, aka Foots. That's how you truly feel, huh, slim? As a man, I can't respect you because you never said how you truly felt in my presence. You waited until I wasn't around to salt me down. I loved you, bruh. I trusted you. You were like a brother to me. So, naturally, when I got to D.C. jail in 2018, I called you to assist me. I said to you what I believed at the time could get you to help me. Never even paid attention to the call being monitored.

According to you, that one phone call put the ATF on your line. But how can you say that with certainty, when my phone and the burner phones in my house were taken, and your contact info was in every one of them? What about all the geekin ass text messages you sent me? All the stupid ass "Big boy, I need a whole box of graham crackers," and "Did you bake the pizza pie yet, because I need a few slices," and "Bruh, my man got a XDS nine he selling, you want it?"

You don't think all the obviously coded messages you sent to my phone could have put the people (ATF) on your line? Then you said, "Had I just copped and took my beef, that the people (ATF) would have never snatched you." Do you know that for sure? We went to trial, and we lost. That's how the game goes. You could have copped, why didn't you? And now you blame me for the punk ass eighty-four months you got? I got almost triple that, and you mad at me.

You running around talking this dry snitching stuff, throwing sea salt on a good man, but then on direct appeal, you and your lawyer file a motion to the court of appeals, arguing that I was the guilty one. All the evidence was harmful to me, my guilt was overwhelming and the only reason you got found guilty is because of your connection to me. You don't think that's some hot shit right there? I'm in the court of appeals fighting the government and you. You and your lawyers are making the government's case for them against me on appeal. We filed a motion for deconsolidation, because the law states it's unfair for one defendant (me) to have to defend himself against two opponents (you and the government.)

With the same energy you're having while slandering my character behind my back, keep the same energy and tell everybody the hot shit you doing in appeals court. And one more thing, salt kills snails, not cold-blooded men like me.

To my sandbox homie, Lonell Tucker, also known as L, I hear you loud and clear. And so has the hundreds of dudes you've told your lies to. It's been almost four years since all of this happened. So, let's be real. Tell people why you really mad. Because I read the discovery in our case and thought you were an informant. I called to the streets from D.C. jail and told all the youngins on the block you might be wicked. They ran with it. Word spread quickly that you were a rat.

Later down the line, when you were arrested and you turned out solid, I retracked my steps and my words and straightened out the bone I put on you. I tried with all my might to correct the situation. But that wasn't good enough for you. I get it. Hatred and resentment made you vindictive. So, when I got to the stand on my own behalf to deny all the allegations against me, you twisted my words and shouted on every rooftop that I had turned into Nino Brown. That I had told something. I never told anything, homie. Never told on anyone and you know that. But you had to get me back for what I'd said about you. Your ruse was crafty, slim, but ill-suited.

The men around the country in prisons everywhere know me. They know how I feel about rats. They know how vehemently I stand on the OMERTA. I'm in a federal penitentiary walking the yard, daring someone to play with me or repeat the lies you have put out there about me. You got all these young dudes who don't know me, repeating what you've told everyone at 1901 D Street, in other joints, and they don't have a clue as to what I'ma do to them if I catch any of them. While feeding them lies, you should have kept it one hundred and told them I'm a beast in this prison shit, and I'ma nail them to the concrete if I ever hear my name in their mouths the wrong way.

If you want to impress me, stop hiding out in Sweetersburg Medium. Come on up to this penitentiary, so I can really embrace your body. That's the problem with you suckas—you, Foots and Whistle—y'all talking big boy talk, but y'all hiding out in lows and mediums. And just like I just said to Foots, make sure you let everybody know about this hot ass appeal motion that your lawyer filed. Your lawyers are arguing to the appeal judges that all the drugs and guns were mine, and you are innocent. Got me fighting you, Foots, and the government on appeal. Don't leave that part out. Until we meet again.

Anthony Fields

Gotta say all praises is due to Allah. He gave me the ability to do what I do. Can't leave without saying thank you to Lashawn Wilson, Pretina Brown, Angelina Scott, Aniyah Fields, Kevin Grover, my sisters and brothers, my nieces and nephews. To Wayne Henry and Special Needs Express, I appreciate the support, homie. To all the vendors who move the product, thank you. To Wall Periodicals, Mag.depot.com and other outlets that ship books to people, thank you. To NeNe Capri who has always supported me, thank you. To Eva Lee and Ft Worth, Texas, thank you for your support. To Toni McDaniel, who started this journey by my side, I can never thank you enough. I will never forget you. Got to give out a few rest in power shoutouts - - to Thomas Ali Jr., my nephew Tyjuan, Ronald 'Mumbo Scales' Scales, Calvin 'Eastgate Fats' Wright and sadly to the woman whom I shouted out in all my books (she was a helluva typist and editor) LaShonda Johnson aka Trinity Adams (The author) who passed away from Covid-19. Rest in Power.

And even though I said I wouldn't, I can't leave without dropping a few names. To Antone White, Angelo "Nut" Daniels, Big Mac, Griff, Robert "Applehead" Barton, Donzell McCauley, Nick, Andy Daniels, Fat bug and Greg (I"ll never turn against y'all), Bernard "Tadpole" Johnson, Marcus Martin, Pretty B, Boy Wonder, Pat Andrews and Kevin Bellinger, Kenneth "Goo" Simmons, Abdul "Dulee" Fields, James "Rock" Smith, Rico "Suave" Thomas, Kevin Devonshire, Mummy, Youngboy Marco (Langdon Park), Tye, Skip, CB, EL, 88, Delmont Player, Joe Ebron, Thomas Hager, Henry "Lil Man" James, Skyler "Seven" Holley, Jugg (Ohio), MD, I.G., Tito, Jersey Keem (my Crip homie), to all the Blood homies, CB (SMM), AB, Stacks, Maino, Sauce, Ro, Rampage, Kam, Capo, Silence, Chuck, D-Rilla, World, to all the GD"s, Vicelords and others. To Antwan Holcomb, Ransom Perry, L, Flavor, Baltimore Chuck, Wood, Danny, Gutta, Day Day, Binky, to all the heartless felons in Cleveland, Ohio, to Derrick "D-Rose" Mitchell, to K. Boogie, Hov and K.Q.

Lastly, to Cash and Lock Down Publications, I appreciate the platform and support. Thanks for everything, big bruh.

And to all y'all new authors that just got in the game that's calling yourselves the GOATS, the kings of street lit, the Hov's of the game. Y'all play too much.

As always, y'all know what it is,
D.C. Stand up!
Buckeyfields

Angel 3

Prologue

Aziz Navid

Nine months earlier ...

"There's a position I want us to try, husband."

My wife Nadia lay sprawled on our bed, completely naked. Her body was a beautiful piece of art, crafted as if by God's own hand. Her golden skin tone shone with oil. Her smallish breasts poked out impetuously. The nipples dark, resembling Tootsie Roll candies. Nadia's hand found her center and compelled my eyes to follow. The landing-strip-shaped pubic hairs atop her labia and clitoris made me smile. I had suggested the trimming to my wife the day she wanted to get a Brazilian wax done. The sight of Nadia's fingers as they played in her moistness excited me. Her arousal brought about my arousal. My dick stiffened. "What position would that be, Nadia?"

Nadia removed her fingers from her center. They gleaned with wetness. She put both fingers in her mouth and suckled them. Removing her fingers, she said, "It's called the jack-hammer."

"The jackhammer? How does the jackhammer go?"

"It goes like this." Nadine took one small foot, her toenails painted white, and put it behind her head. "Now, you have to enter me, Aziz... gently, until you are laying on top of me completely. Once you've entered me as deeply as possible, you commence to pounding this pussy into submission."

I crawled down the length of the bed until I straddled my wife. "Your other foot stays outstretched?"

"No. I will wrap my leg around your middle. That allows for deeper penetration."

As I eased myself into Nadia, I asked, "And how did you learn of this position, wifey?"

"Where else? I learned it online. Now be quiet and jackhammer me, baby!" Leaning down to kiss Nadia, my hand now wrapped around the foot behind her head, I entered her deeply. Her pussy seemed to fit me like a glove. I did exactly as she requested and jackhammered her.

**

The phone beside the bed vibrated loudly. I quickly reached out to grab it off the table and answer it, before it woke Nadia. I saw the caller was Khitab Abdullah, my right-hand. I rose from the bed before saying a word. Out in the hallway, near the bathroom, I said, "Assalamu Alaikum."

"Walaikum Assalam. Sorry to wake you, Ocki, but this couldn't wait until morning."

I glanced at the time on the cellphone, 1:24 a.m. "What couldn't wait until morning, Khitab?"

"It's Muqtar, Ocki, He's dead."

"Mu is dead? How did he die, Khitab?"

"Someone killed him. Killed him and took all the cocaine he was holding."

Completely awake and now alert, I asked Khitab, "How much of the cocaine is missing?"

"All of it, Ocki. There is none left. Not one brick."

"How do you know that for sure?" I asked incredulously.

"Because I'm here at his house. Hafizah was shot but allowed to live. She called me, before calling an ambulance for herself. I was here when the police removed Muqtar's body and did their investigation. They left not long ago. I waited until they did before I checked for the cocaine. The Caravans are empty. The cocaine is gone."

"Stay right there, Khitab, I will be there shortly."

**

Yellow crime scene tape still waved in the wind as it stayed connected to the fence in front of Muqtar's home. Entering the fence, I walked around the house to the backyard and four-vehicle garage. Khitab Abdullah stood at the garage's entrance, dressed in a dark pea coat, dark pants and boots. The knitted cap on his head pulled low to stifle the cold. We embraced.

"Assalamu Alaikum," Khitab greeted me.

"Walaikum Assalam," I replied, returning it.

"I don't have all the details, Ock, but Hafizah said a man—"

"A single man? One man?"

Khitab nodded. "One man. A man named Najee ... who worked for Muqtar, came into the house, tied her up, shot her and then killed Muqtar. Somehow, she was able to free herself and get her cell phone. Hafizah said Najee took money. She did not know about the cocaine. She never mentioned it. Muqtar never told her where it was. But I know. I checked the Caravans once the cops left. It's gone."

"But, how do we know the man who killed Mu took it? Maybe Mu moved it somewhere and didn't tell anyone."

A pensive look crossed Khitab's face. "That's possible, but I doubt it, Ocki. Muqtar was a creature of habit. If he had moved it, he would have told me. I think Najee took it."

"No one man could take that much cocaine by himself."

"Maybe he was Superman," Khitab joked, but then grew more serious. "Maybe he had friends nearby. He had help. However he did it, he did it. Come in and see for yourself."

The garage was outfitted to house the four Grand Caravan vehicles, customized to hold thousands of keys of cocaine. Khitab walked me through the garage as I peered into each Caravan to see they all were empty. "Shit! Muhammad's going to be pissed if we can't locate that coke."

"I already know. It sucks to be you, Ocki. You gotta tell 'em."

I nodded my head in agreement and left the garage. The trip to upstate New York where Muhammad Farid Shahid lived would be a long drive, but the news about Muqtar and the missing cocaine had to be delivered in person.

***

Brookhaven, New York, was located near the Catskills mountains. In an affluent, gated community called the Cat's Crossing, sat Muhammad Farid Shahid's home. The house was a stunner straight out of the *Architectural Digest Magazine*. The all-brick façade greeted visitors and led you down a walkway that ended at the eight-car garage. It had a spiraling staircase, wood floors, cathedral ceilings, wall-to-wall windows that gave it a panoramic view. The entertaining deck at the rear of the house overlooked a private backyard, heated pool with a built-in Jacuzzi and a tennis court. Pulling out my cellphone at the gate near the security booth, I called Muhammad Farid Shahid to announce myself.

I stood in his study and waited for the man, the myth, the legend. Muhammad Farid Shahid had grown in stature and power steadily over the last thirty years. He was a ruthless man with a streak of unmatched cruelty. He had no compassion. Always devoid of emotion. He was insanely genuine, perceptive and intelligent. He was charismatic. A natural born leader of men. Something I recognized in him when I was a young teenager attending the Temple in Newburgh. I sought him out for tutelage. He accepted my companionship, and I never left his side.

When Muhammad left the fold of the Nation of Islam and converted to Orthodox Islam under the Ahlas-Sunnah, I followed his lead. Years later, when he outgrew the small town of Newburgh and opened the Masjid in Brooklyn, I was there. When he was introduced to Mexican Cartel members by a Mexican Muslim related to Alejandro and Jalusco Ortega, I was nearby. When Muhammad became too big for Islamic places of worship, due to the notoriety he gained because of the heroin and cocaine he bought and sold, I was there with him. Cleaning up whatever messes that came about. My specialty was killing. And he used me often.

Muhammad Farid Shahid entered the study dressed in pajamas, a robe and slippers. He stood five foot seven in height. He weighed a fit, one hundred and sixty pounds. He was diminutive, but the ferocity he showed and the power he wielded made him appear a giant. Muhammad Farid Shahid was fifty-four years old, ten years older than me, but showed no signs of slowing down.

"Aziz, it's almost five in the morning. This must be important," Muhammad Farid Shahid said.

"It is, Ocki. I knew you'd want to hear the bad news as soon as possible, so here I am. To deliver it in person," I told him.

"Bad news? What has happened, Aziz? Tell me."

"Muqtar Kareem was ambushed at home by someone. Someone who tied up his wife and shot her—"

"Hafizah? Someone shot Hafizah?"

"Yes, but she's okay. In a hospital in Newark. She called Khitab before calling an ambulance and the police. The intruder took money from Mu's safe—"

"Hafizah Kareem is my first cousin, Aziz."

"I know that, Muhammad. You know I know that. I'm sorry this happened to her, but that's not the bad news. The bad news is the cocaine Muqtar had in his possession is gone."

Muhammad Farid Shahid turned and walked to the bar in his study. He poured liquid into a glass and drank it. "How much of the cocaine was in Muqtar's possession, Aziz?"

"The entire shipment. It was at his home until it could be distribut—"

"Twenty thousand kilos of cocaine have disappeared?"

"I'm afraid so, yes."

"You said someone ambushed Muqtar. Then you said an intruder. Singular. What exactly happened, Aziz?"

"I don't know. All I know is what Hafizah told Khitab and that wasn't much."

"Where is my cousin, again?" Muhammad asked.

"At a local hospital. I'm not sure which one," I replied.

"I have urgent business to attend to, Aziz. Business that can't be put aside. I leave in the morning for Morocco. I'll be back in three days. Bury Muqtar, according to Islamic law. When I return, the money we owe the Mexicans has to be paid. Get with Anwar and have it ready by the time I return. After everything has been settled, I'll deal with this problem. Do you understand?"

"I do. I will do all you have said."

***

Three days later ...

"We commit brother Muqtar Kareem back to the earth from which he came. We ask Allah subhanallah to make the grave spacious for him. And to forgive the brother Muqtar his sins. We ask that he grant him paradise. Innal lalahi wa inna lalahi rajioon ... Ameen."

The janazah funeral service was long and interminable, but necessary. No matter how much we sin in this life, the Muslims have to be buried properly. The faithful, and Muqtar's family lined up on the musala, heel to heel, shoulder to shoulder. I joined them in the ranks. After the takbirs, the melodic recitation of the Qu'ran began. Silent, I recited the surahs along with Raguab, the Khateeb leading the prayer. But after a few minutes, my concentration was broken. I thought about the conundrum I was in.

Finding the missing cocaine was the priority, but I had no clue as to where to start looking. I thought about the three Muslims in the organization that I had been ordered to kill as soon as Muhammad Shahid returned from his trip earlier this morning. Lugman, Tasir and Dawu had made several mistakes in the past, but their deaths were ordered simply because they were close to Muqtar and didn't know where the cocaine was, why Muqtar was killed and who Najee was.

My mind drifted back to over a week ago when the shipment of kilos arrived at the private airstrip adjacent to Newark International Airport. The cocaine had been flown from Mexico, offloaded and trucked to Muqtar's home in Newark. Four thousand kilos were to stay in New Jersey to be distributed to Elizabeth, Camden, Atlantic City, Plainfield, Patterson and inside of Newark. The rest was to be shipped to New York, Connecticut, Baltimore and Philadelphia.

Muqtar Kareem and the three men that had died earlier that day were responsible for making sure all of the distribution took place. That didn't happen because Muqtar was killed, and the cocaine taken. The other three men's lives became forfeit. All because of

Najee. I made a promise to myself to find Najee and torture him. I promised myself I'd kill him slow.

I fell to my knees in sajdah, along with all the other Muslims. "Allahu akbar!" we said in unison and then pressed our faces into the ground.

***

The Gulfstream jet taxied to a stop from the hangar on the airstrip. I exited a new modeled Audi R8 driven by one of my men and joined others from our organization, gathered beside a cavalcade of expensive vehicles. The sun stood high in the sky like a mighty warrior on the sands of Rome. Rays beaming like the sword in the hands of a gladiator. As the minutes went by the air grew more and more humid. Perspiration stained the armpits of my shirt under my jaliebeeyah. No words passed between any of us. The Gulfstream jet came to a complete stop nearby. The jet's door ascended, and a staircase descended. Several Mexican men exited the jet and approached us. Muhammad Farid Shahid exited a chauffeured SUV. I went to his side.

The lead Mexican man was short and rotund with close cropped salt and pepper hair. His skin was dark, his face marked by past acne. He stopped in front of Muhammad Shahid. He offered his hand. "Muhammad, it's always a pleasure to see you, but why are you here? The delivery of money could have been handled by lesser men."

"Alejandro," Muhammad said as he shook the Mexican's hand. "I guess I can say the same thing to you. Surely, the picking up of fifty million dollars could have been done by others in your organization as well. But yet, here you are."

Alejandro Ortega, one of the leaders of the Sinaloa Cartel, smiled. "Muhammad, I forgot who I am dealing with. You are a very smart man. Such an important task should never be left to lesser men."

"I agree, Alejandro. How was your flight?"

"It was a good one. Is the money here?"

"It is." Muhammad turned to me. "Have the money loaded onto the jet."

I left to attend to the command I'd been given. The duffle bags filled with cash were all loaded onto the Gulfstream. Minutes later, the Mexican entourage returned to the jet. Not long after that, it taxied down the runway and lifted into the heavens.

I found Muhammad Farid Shahid standing in the same place where I'd left him. His eyes still on the disappearing jet. "I know what you are thinking."

"Do you, Aziz?' Muhammad asked me. "What am I thinking?"

"About the money on the jet. Money you just paid out of your pocket." Muhammad turned to face me. "You've been with me for almost thirty years, Aziz. I'm not surprised that you know me so well. And since you correctly told me what I was thinking just then, tell me, what am I thinking now?"

"That you want your money back. And your cocaine."

"Correct again, Aziz. Where is Hafizah?"

"At Beth Israel Hospital in downtown Newark."

"I need to see her, Aziz. She needs to tell me exactly what happened to Muqtar and who the hell is Najee. Lead the way to the hospital."

***

Hafizah Kareem opened her eyes as we walked into her room. Her legs were bandaged all the way to her toes. One leg had metal rods and screws protruding from it.

"Are you in a lot of pain, Hafizah?"

"They give me a lot of medicine to dull the pain in my legs and feet, but it can't stop the pain in my heart."

"I understand, Cousin. I'm sorry this whole ordeal has happened to you. To Muqtar. He was laid to rest hours ago. The service was overcrowded. His killer will be found and dealt with swiftly. But in order to find him, I need you to tell me everything that happened that night. Tell me and leave out nothing."

"I already told Khitab everything —"

"My ears work differently, Hafizah. I need you to tell me."

"Okay. I was asleep in bed that night when I was awakened by a metal object tapping my head. I opened my eyes and saw a man standing beside my bed. He was dressed in dark clothes and had a gun in each hand. I went to scream but he silenced me with a finger to his lips. 'If you scream, I'll kill you,' he said. I closed my mouth.

"I need you to get on the phone and call Mu," he told me. 'Tell him to come home. Make up an emergency but keep the words short. Try any odd messages and you die. Do you understand?' I nodded to show I did. I made the call. I told Muqtar I was sick and having a heart attack. Told him I needed him to come home and take me to the hospital. I never knew the man was gonna... that he was gonna kill..." Hafizah broke down crying.

"There was no way you could've known what the man intended to do," Muhammad said. "Only Allah knew his intentions. What happened next, Cousin?"

Hafizah composed herself and wiped her eyes. "I was told to get out of bed and then bound to a chair. It was a chair from the dining room. The man must've brought it into the room with him. After I was bound and my mouth taped up, he left the room."

"You didn't try to free yourself?" I asked.

"I was too afraid," Hafizah replied as she looked at me.

"You were smart not to try anything, Hafizah. Continue the story, please." Muhammad Shahid said.

"The man returned to the room carrying a bag of potatoes. He sat the bag down beside the chair and said, 'I sure hope Mu loves you.' After that, he said nothing else until Muqtar walked into the room a short time later."

"So, Muqtar comes home. He walks into your bedroom and sees you bound to a chair, and a man holding two guns. Then what?"

Hafizah's tears started anew. She pressed her eyes closed as if to focus, to remember. The man said, 'Mu, what's really good, son?'

"Najee, what are you doing, Ock? Whatever it is, you're making a mistake."

"First off, don't call me Ock no more. In Arabic, that means brother. And you're definitely not my brother. You may have been

fucking my sister, but we ain't brothers. And I ain't making no mistake, son. You made the mistake. All I wanna know is why?"

"Why what, Ock? Najee, what the hell mistake did I make? Talk to me."

"Oh, I'ma talk to you alright. All three of us gon talk to you. Me and these two Glocks right here. I know you probably wondering what the bag of potatoes is setting here for. Let me show you."

"He put one gun in his waist, then got a potato out the bag. He shoved it onto the barrel of the gun in his hand."

"They serve as good makeshift silencers when you need one. This is how this is gonna work. I'ma ask you a question and you answer it. As simple as that. If I don't like your answer, I shoot your wife. Since I asked you a question already and you didn't answer..."

"That's when he shot me the first time. Just pointed the gun at my leg and fired. Muqtar said, 'Please, Najee, don't kill her. She's innocent in all of this. She has nothing to do with any of this.' Najee said, 'Why did you do it, Mu? Why did you cross me?' Muqtar cried out, 'Najee, it wasn't me!' Najee put another potato on the barrel of his gun after removing the first one. Then he shot me again. In my other leg."

The story Hafizah was telling captured me. I wondered what Mu had done to Najee for him to feel betrayed.

"Hafizah, I need to know everything. Please keep going." Muhammad said.

"The man named Najee pointed the gun at me again ..."

"Don't lie to me, Mu. That's only gonna get your wife killed. I'm tryna spare her life, but you're making it hard for me. Soon, one of these bullets will be in her head. Why did you try to have me killed?"

"Najee, I - I - I -"

"Think about your wife, Mu."

"Okay, okay. I got greedy. I figured I could control things more with you out of the way."

"Was that your work yesterday, too?"

"No!"

"He shot me again. In the foot. Muqtar had tears in his eyes by then. He told Najee, 'That wasn't me.'

"It was you, Mu," Najee replied. 'I recognized one of the shooters. The one standing outside the car. He was one of the ones who ambushed me outside of Justin's. And you were the only one besides Salimah that knew I was going there.' That's when he changed the potato and shot me again. 'Where is the coke at, Mu? And the money?' Najee asked. 'What coke and money?' Mu asked him. Najee told me, 'Your husband cares nothing for you. Go ahead and make dua before I kill you. You got one minute …' Oh my God, Farid … I was so afraid. I started to recite Ayatul Kersi as Najee replaced the potato on the gun barrel …"

"Okay, just don't kill her!" Muqtar screamed. 'Kill me, not her. I'll tell you."

"He told Najee everything he wanted to know. Where the money was, the safe's combination, everything about—"

"Hafizah, let me ask you something," Muhammad said, cutting her off. "Your husband owed me several millions of dollars. There is no way possible a safe, no matter where it's made, can hold that type of cash. What Najee took from the safe in y'all's home had to be what Muqtar kept nearby. He had to have some place where he stored the majority of his money, my money, do you know where that might be?"

"All I can think of is the two storage units Muqtar kept at the storage facility on Martin Luther King Jr. Boulevard, near 11th Avenue."

"Do you have the spare keys to those units?"

"I do. The keys are on the ring where my house keys and car keys are."

"And where are those keys?" Muhammad asked.

"In the drawer of the table over there by the wall," Hafizah replied, pointing. Muhammad Shahid glanced at me. I went to the table and retrieved the keys from the drawer, pocketing them.

"Hafizah, you told Khitab something that Najee said to you before he left," I asked, leaning on the table. "What was that?"

"He told me he wasn't going to kill me."

"That was after he'd killed Muqtar?"

Hafizah nodded. "He said Muqtar had tried to have him killed twice and that Muqtar had had his friends killed. He apologized for shooting me, then he said, 'I could be about to make the biggest mistake of my life, maybe not. If you mention my name to the police, I promise you I will find you and kill you. You and all of the people you love.' That was the last thing that he said to me."

"Do you know for sure if Najee took the cocaine, Hafizah?" Muhammad Shahid asked.

Hafizah shrugged. "I don't know if he did or didn't. All I know is that Muqtar told him the cocaine was in the caravans in the garage. I was still tied to the chair, and it took me a long time to free myself. I feared I would bleed to death—"

"Najee said Muqtar was sexing his sister. Did you know about that?" I asked.

"I'm not stupid," Hafizah responded. "Muqtar was messy. He'd been having the affair with Salimah for a while. But he didn't think I knew. I went through Muqtar's phone one day and found pictures of them together, text messages. Explicit ones. I had even heard Muqtar talk to Najee on the phone several times. Sounded like Najee worked for Muqtar. I never made the connection, though. I never knew Salimah was Najee's sister."

"Do you remember whether or not Salimah's address was in Muqtar's phone?" I pressed.

"Can't recall, but I'm sure she lives in Newark somewhere."

"If I can find Salimah, chances are I can then find her brother," I told Muhammad.

"Where is Muqtar's cell phone?" Muhammad Shahid asked Hafizah.

"I don't know. I assume it was in his pocket when he was killed. I didn't see it around the house after I freed myself and called Khitab."

"If it's not at your house, and we'll check," I announced, "then that means the police have it. Did you ever talk to Muqtar on his cell phone, Ocki?"

Muhammad Shahid looked at me with contempt in his eyes. "Of course not. Why would I? He would have had to speak to Ahmed or call you. I never spoke to Muqtar directly."

I turned to Hafizah. "Have you talked to the police yet?"

"Once. Briefly. But trust me, I told them nothing. I was in too much pain."

"That was good, Cousin. Please, get some rest. My condolences about your husband. If you need anything, anything at all ... don't hesitate to call one of us. Okay?"

"Okay, Farid. Thank you for coming."

"You had to know I'd come. Get some rest. Aziz, let's go."

Outside in the hospital's hallway, Muhammad Farid Shahid grabbed my arm to stop me. He turned to face me and said, "This whole thing could have been avoided from what I heard. Muqtar wanted to control things. Ambition is always dangerous in an organization like ours. Couple that ambition with greed, and that makes it ten times worse. Muqtar grew up here in Newark. He has a grandmother who lives in an assisted living complex near Hyatt Court in Eastwood. He also has a brother incarcerated at Northern State Correctional Center.

"Find out who we have on the inside there and put them on the brother. I want both Muqtar's grandmother and brother dead before the week is out. I want you to go to those units and see if my cocaine and money is there. If it is, bring it to me. If not, so be it, find Salimah and force her to lead us to Najee. Recouping the money and coke is paramount. Either way, I want Najee and his sister dead."

"And Hafizah?"

"You already know. Kill her. No loose ends. No matter who it is," Muhammad Farid Shahid turned and walked away.

All I could do was drop my head. Hafizah was the man's first cousin, and it didn't matter at all. A plan already formulated in my head, so I went to do what I was paid to do. Kill.

Anthony Fields

Chapter 1

Angel

Present day. Where ya left off ...

February 2015

I made it three feet inside the door before I saw her. I stopped dead in my tracks and stared at the body on the floor. Tears instantly flooded my eyes as the realization of what I was seeing set in. I walked up to my mother's body and saw the neat little holes in her forehead. Every limb on my body cried out in pain. I didn't even know I was screaming. My mind never sent me the signal. I dropped to the floor and grabbed my mother, gathered her into my arms and cried. I rocked back and forth with her in my arms, until it dawned on me that my daughter was in the house.

"Aniyah!" I screamed as I laid my mother down and ascended the stairs two at a time. I ran straight to her room, praying she was still alive. I pulled open the bedroom door and turned on the light. Again, my breath got caught in my throat. I stopped in the spot where I stood and looked around the room. Aniyah's bed was ruffled, but empty. "Aniyah! Aniyah, baby, it's Mommy! Where are you? Where are ya, baby? Aniyah?"

I searched the entire upstairs and came up empty-handed. Where could she be? Who had killed my mother? The first person that came to mind was Carlos. Carlos had sent men to my mother's house and killed her. He'd mistakenly connected me to his most recent troubles with Najee. And he'd taken my daughter. An uncontrollable rage built inside me. I was on the way downstairs to search for my daughter, holding onto a glimmer of hope that she was still in the house somewhere. But then I saw something that caught my attention. It was there the entire time, plain as the nose on my face, but I hadn't paid it no mind until now. On the dresser was a mirror, a piece of paper taped to the glass. Turned out to be a letter. I snatched it off the mirror and read it.

Dear Angel,

How does it feel to come home and find your mother dead? Not too good, huh? Well, now you know how I felt. I thought by killing your mother, we'd be even. But then I remembered you also killed my father. You were always one up on me. But not today. You killed my father and my mother. I killed your mother and took your daughter. Now we're even.

Honesty

I must've read the letter a hundred times in disbelief before I realized it was real. How had I slipped and blundered so badly? Didn't I know the law?

Crush your enemies totally. Never stop halfway through total annihilation, lest they recover and come back for you ...

I couldn't believe the fatal mistake I had made. I let myself be blinded by arrogance, overconfidence, love and a nigga with a big dick. The person I had completely forgotten about had never forgotten about me. And she came back for me. Tears filled my eyes. They fell and stained the paper in my hand. I was crushed in a lot of ways, mentally, physically, emotionally. I was afraid for my daughter's life, knowing she was in the hands of my enemy.

Slowly, I moved, walked down the stairs back to where my mother lay. I stared down at my mother's cold, lifeless body and stifled a need to hurl. The desire came and left, but in seconds it returned with a vengeance. I rushed to the bathroom on the first level and reached the toilet just as my insides emptied, I dry heaved, then settled down. I moved to the sink and ran the water. Splashing water onto my face, I then cupped my hands and drank some. My throat burned as if filled with sand ... I stared at myself in the mirror.

"Honesty, bitch ... I swear by Allah, I'ma roast your ass. I promise you," I said aloud to myself.

Steadily, my resolve strengthened as my anger grew. My desire for blood was also growing. I pulled out my cell phone and found a number I hadn't dialed in ages. A face materialized in my head. The face of the person my pain blamed for my mother's death and my daughter's kidnapping. I pressed send for that number. Seconds later, a man's voice said, "Hello?"

***

The night air was crisp and cold, but I was oblivious to it. I was devoid of feeling. Numb. I stood on Mom's front porch and stared out into the dark sky. I was mesmerized by the twinkling of the far-off stars, wondered what secrets they held. Deep inside, I longed to be living there, on one of the stars so far away. My mother, my daughter and me. Just the three of us living on a star forever. Never growing old, never leaving one another. Then the sound of a car door slamming broke my reverie. A gold Lexus 500 was now parked behind my BMW. My uncle Samir walked inside the gate and headed my way. His dark-colored Thobe visible beneath a puffy Moncler coat. His dark gray New Balance 990V tennis shoes were crispy, new. Washington Redskins socks that depicted its quarterback, Kirk Cousins, pulled up almost to his knees.

"Angel, what's good? Your call was unexpected, and you said it was urgent. What's up?" Samir asked me.

"My mother," I replied. "She's gone."

"Your mother? She's gone? Gone where?"

"Let me show you." I turned, opened the screen door and entered the house, my uncle on my heels. I led him to the living room where my mother's body lay.

"Angel, what the …" my uncle started, but his words got cut off in his throat. His eyes stared down at my mother. He gasped and covered his mouth. His eyes filled with tears. Then he bellowed the word, "No," and dropped to his knees. Just as I had earlier. He leaned over my mother's body and wept. "No … no … no … no … no … NeNe … NeNe … no … no … no…"

I stood riveted to my spot as I listened to my uncle call my mother by her childhood nickname, NeNe. I watched him grovel and cry out in pain about his older sister. His only sister. The sister who had raised him. Supported him through twenty years of doing time at Lorton Correctional Complex. The sister who'd been killed because of a lie he'd told.

"This is all your fault, Uncle Samir," I said suddenly.

My uncle's eyes looked up and found mine. Tears rolled down his cheeks two or three at a time. The edge of his top lip was curled down, and a scowl was etched across his face. He looked wounded, beyond angry. "What did you just say?"

"You heard what I said. This is all your fault. The lie you told me years ago contributed directly to my mother's death. Her blood is on your hands."

Samir Nadir gently kissed my mother's face, then laid her head softly back onto the carpet where blood had stained it. He rose to his entire six-foot-one height and covered the space between us in seconds. His face was now inches away from mine. I could smell the sweet musk of his breath. "Have you lost your fuckin' mind?" Uncle Samir spat venomously. "You got ten seconds to tell me what the fuck you talkin' about, or by Allah, I'ma kill your stupid ass. Who did this to my sister? What lie did I tell you years ago? And how is my sister lying here shot in the fucking head my fault? Talk, Angel! Now!"

I took a step back before answering. "The person that killed my mother was the same person you were supposed to kill years ago. You lied and told me she was dead."

"I was supposed to kill who years ago? What do you mean, I lied?" Samir asked incredulously.

"Almost ten years ago when I was shot in my salon and left for dead, I woke up in the hospital. You were there at my bedside. I told you a young girl had shot me ..."

"I remember ... You said she was fourteen years old. Shot you because she believed you killed her father."

I nodded my head. "You asked me where you could find the girl and I told you all I knew. You told me that she was as good as dead. I believed you. Days later, you came back to the hospital and told me that it was done. That the young girl was dead because you'd killed her. I believed you. But you lied."

"I-I-I," Samir stammered.

"You lied. Why, I don't know, but you did. So, for years, I thought the girl was dead. But she wasn't and guess what, Uncle Samir? That young girl grew up, something she wasn't supposed to do."

"I hear you. I hear you, but wait, how is this my fault? You created this mess. You getting shot. Aniyah almost being killed before she was even born. Now this. How the hell am I at fault?"

"Let me break it down for you. All you had to do was tell me you couldn't kill a teenage girl. You could've told me you didn't have the stomach for killing kids. Simple as that. Had you just been honest, tragedy—avoided. I would have killed her as soon as I left the hospital ten years ago. I would have hunted her young ass and blew her muthafuckin brains out. No questions asked. Put her shit all over her bookbag and lunch box. Almost ten years ago. She'd have never been alive to do this. That's why I blame you."

Defiance faded from Uncle Samir's face and acceptance crept in. "How do you know it was her?"

I handed him the letter Honesty left taped to the mirror.

His eyes devoured the letter quickly. He looked up at me, tears still falling from his eyes. "She says here you killed her mother. Did you?"

"When I discovered she was still alive, I went after her to finish what she started. To do what you couldn't. I couldn't find her. I found her mother, so I killed her."

"And it's true she has Aniyah?"

I nodded my head, a tear falling from my eye.

"Everybody told me you were crazy. Your father was the same way. You get ..." Hearing my uncle mention my perverted father gripped me with a renewed sense of anger and revenge. I pulled the Glock from my waist.

Uncle Samir's eyes settled on the gun in my hand. "What do you plan to do with that?"

"Kill you, Uncle Samir," I answered, upped the gun and shot him. When his body dropped, I gave him the coup de grâce. Then calmly, I left the house.

Chapter 2

Honesty

I peeped in on the little girl. She was asleep in Trigger's bed as if it were her own. Closing the door back, I thought about the fact that I had went off script and kidnapped Angel's daughter. At the time, it seemed like the right thing to do. A couple of hours after the fact, I wasn't so sure. I thought about the simplicity of my act. Most children will trust a person in uniform and Angel's daughter was no different. Since Trigger and I were dressed in the security uniforms, we looked like cops. When I awoke the little girl from her bed and told her to go with me, half asleep, she never resisted. As if I had thought Trigger into existence, he appeared as if by magic. He'd been upstairs with his family since we had returned with the girl to his house.

"What the fuck are we gonna do with this kid, True?" Trigger asked with attitude.

"I don't know," I replied. "Haven't decided yet."

"Haven't decided yet? Fuck is that supposed to mean?"

"The last time I checked '*haven't decided yet*' wasn't a Sudoku puzzle."

"A Sudoku puzzle?"

"Never mind. Look, taking the little girl wasn't a part of the plan, I know that, and you know that. But now that—"

"I'm not killing that fuckin kid, True. And neither are you!" Trigger said forcefully. "So, don't even think about it."

"I never said anything to you about either of us killing that little girl. Who do you think I am? Some sorta heartless monster?" When Trigger didn't reply, I continued. "I know that I've been a bitch lately. For months, I've been kinda difficult—"

"Difficult is an understatement."

"Was your mother killed by the same person who killed your father when you were twelve?"

Trigger exhaled, took off his uniform shirt and sat down. "Come on, True, not that speech again. Heard it a thousand times. I'm sick of keep hearing that shit. It's like a broken record."

"Well, consider it the number one song on the radio because it's gonna continue to get spins. It's my truth. You feel the way you feel because it didn't happen to you."

"I'm sick of hearing this shit, True," Trigger muttered and pulled off his Nike boots. "And I'ma ask you again, what the fuck are you gonna do with that kid in there?"

"Use her to get at her mother. Angel will come wherever her daughter is."

"We talkin about a fuckin kid missing, True. That's Amber alerts and all that shit. Kids bring all different angles to shit. What if the bitch Angel involves the cops?"

I shook my head. "She'd never do that. That bitch is a real killer. She was locked up for killing a rack of people in 2002 and she never folded. Had her friend that ratted to the cops, killed. Angel is connected to Carlos Trinidad. People who fuck with him don't go to cops to solve their problems. Trust me, that bitch is looking for me as we speak. That note I left taped to the mirror in her daughter's room made sure of that. Naw, Angel ain't gon involve no cops. I still think she's the one who killed that detective who worked my father's case years ago. The one that got killed in the parking garage at the courthouse."

"Captain Sean Jones," Trigger said. "Shit was all over the news for weeks."

"I remember. It's too much of a coincidence that he gets killed, right after the dude who was her friend Fatima's co-defendant, before she made the deal to tell on Angel. It's been almost a year and none of those murders have been solved. I remember the detective well, though. He was always at our house talking to my mother. I think he was trying to fuck her."

"Speaking of detectives, have you heard anything from the ones investigating your mother's case?"

"Mitchell Bell and Able Voss. Nope. Nothing. But that's cool, because I already know who killed my mother and she ain't going to nobody's jail. Her ass is going to a grave at Harmony Cemetery. I promise you that."

"It's funny that you mentioned jail because, guess what? Neither are we. I agreed to ride with you because I love you, but I never agreed to involve my aunt and grandmother."

"We? Who the fuck is 'we'?" I spat and looked at Trigger like he was an alien. "And how the fuck is your aunt and grandmother involved in this?"

"Duh? *We* was a slip of the tongue. I signed up for this. You and me. But my aunt and grandmother become involved because this is their house, and they are both asleep upstairs. That makes them accessories to kidnapping. We should've went to your house, is all I'm saying. That way, my peoples stay out of this shit."

Trigger leaned back in the leather recliner seat he was sitting on. His eyes were closed and feet now elevated. His attitude was starting to irk my nerves.

"I couldn't take her to my house. Angel knows where I live, remember? She'd go there first. She's probably there right now waiting to see if I'll show up there."

"Even more reason for us to be there, then, right?"

"Didn't think about it like that," I reluctantly admitted.

"That's obvious. I'm starting to wonder who's the college graduate. You or me."

Going back and forth with Trigger was getting me nowhere. The impromptu decision to take Angel's daughter had me on a slippery slope with him and the end result could be detrimental to all involved. So, I needed Trigger with his head completely in the game, on my side and supportive of my every move moving forward. It was time to try a different tact.

I unbuttoned my shirt and removed it, then my t-shirt came off next. I slid out of the uniform pants and removed my socks and bra. Dressed only in lace panties, I walked over to Trigger and straddled his lap. I kissed each of his closed eyelids. "I'm sorry I took the girl without making sure it was cool with you first. I was thinking on the fly or maybe I wasn't thinking at all.

"Neither one of us even knew she was gonna be there. I knew Angel had a daughter but had no idea she lived with the grandmother. Once I found the little girl in bed… I guess I couldn't just leave her there to find her grandmother dead. That would have fucked that little girl up for life. Believe me, I know. I'm asking you to trust me. I'm gonna use the little girl as bait to get to Angel.

"In a day or two, if that doesn't happen, we'll drop the girl off somewhere. Someplace safe. I promise. And nobody's going to jail. At least, not your aunt and grandmother. You wouldn't either because I'd cop to all the charges, every last one." I kissed Trigger seductively all over his face while slowly grinding my ass in his lap. His lips parted and I quickly put my tongue in his mouth. Lifted up to unzip his pants, reached into his boxer briefs and pulled at his dick. It was definitely as hard as Chinese arithmetic.

I moved my panties to one side, rose up completely and positioned the head of Trigger's dick at the opening of my cave. My soaking wet middle. I sat down on his hard on slowly, savoring each glorious inch. My pussy became a brush fire that threatened to burn across acres of land. Trigger's cum was the only thing capable of extinguishing the flames. His eyes opened and held mine as I hit rock bottom and gyrated my hips.

"What the fuck?" Trigger muttered. "Pussy…hot as shit… wet…fuck!"

Hearing these words made me smile inside. If God had created anything better than pussy to control a man, he never revealed it to the world.

Chapter 3

Detective Mitchell Bell

Clinton, Maryland

"What's strange to me," Assistant Medical Examiner Christopher Diggs said, "is that the time of death for both victims appear to be different. They are both here together, which leads me to believe they both were killed at the same time. But science tells me differently. Unless I'm off some and I shouldn't be. I don't remember having any beers today. The female victim's body is telling me that she's been dead longer than the male. Hours maybe. If you look here, the skin has started to suppress with lividity."

Chris Diggs pointed at the woman's arm. "The blood has already congealed there. When the heart stops beating, blood stops moving. When the body is positioned a certain way, the blood will clot and weigh itself down where it is when the heart stopped beating. That is the first indicator of how long a person has been deceased. It's a little after 2 a.m. now, the body's positioning, the way the skin looks... I'll err on the side of caution and say that this woman was killed between 10 p.m. and midnight. Now, on the other hand..."

My cell phone vibrated. I glanced at the screen. The caller was Meshawn Tate, my current girlfriend. She was at my house waiting for me to come home. I ignored her call. Angry text messages and emojis came next.

"... the male victim's body tells me a different story. He hasn't been deceased that long. Maybe only an hour or two. See here," Chris Diggs said and led the way to the man lying dead on the floor. He pointed at the skin on his legs. There's no lividity in the skin. The blood has yet to fully gel or congeal. Even the temperature of his body is different. Body heat notwithstanding and the room temperature—"

"Sorry to interrupt, Chris, but I just noticed something else. Now, I'm nowhere near skilled in forensics, but doesn't the bullet entry wounds to both victims' heads appear to be different size holes?"

AME Diggs carefully examined the bullet entry wounds on both victims. After a short time, he demurred. "You're right, Detective. It's barely centimeters, but you're correct. The woman appears to have been shot with a .38 or a .380, maybe.

"Possibly a nine-millimeter. The male's wounds appear to be slightly larger. I'd say he was probably killed with a forty or forty-five caliber handgun. And I would also say the male's wounds, the number of times he was shot, tells me his killer was emotional when he or she did it. They, his wounds, appear to be inflicted from a close proximity. The woman's wounds appear more precise, methodical. Death, immediate. Two gunshots to the forehead. Tidy. Emotionless."

I wrote into a notepad everything Chris Diggs said. "Two different times of deaths. Two different caliber weapons. Two different patterns. One concise. One overkill, emotional. Two different killers, maybe?"

"I believe so, Detective. But I'm just the lowly medical examiner. You're the big shot detective. You tell me."

"I will after you extract those bullets and confirm what you just hypothesized."

"Well, as soon as I get these bodies on my table, I'll have answers for you."

"Sounds good, Chris," I said and shook the AME's hand. "Thanks."

"Don't mention it, Mitch. I'm a public servant."

I left Chris Diggs and walked to the back of the house, to the bathroom. Crime scene technicians were all over it. I'd seen the bathroom before they arrived and something about what I'd seen intrigued me. Someone had gone there and thrown up all over the place. Was it the killer, or at least one of them? Or was it a witness to the murders? Someone who couldn't stomach the sight of blood and carnage. Was it the person who had called in the shooting? I made a mental note to check with dispatch and see if the caller's identity was known.

"Bobby, I'm gonna need a sample of that vomit. We can get DNA off an object that's been underwater for years."

Bobby replied. "What's the story here, you think?"

"Too early to tell, but I'm thinking someone killed the female first and then the male. Then possibly came in here and threw up. Not sure though. I wanna expedite things a little, Bobby. Call in a favor and press Jenifer Lumpkin to process a sample of that vomit a little quicker than usual. Wanna see if the DNA matches either of our victims. It's a shot in the dark, but it's possible."

Bobby Patrician pulled a separate, clear glassine baggie and put a swab smeared with vomit into it. Then he sealed the baggie and passed it to me. "Good luck then. Hope it helps solve the case."

"Don't believe in luck, Bobby. I believe in good ole fashion police work."

I walked through the house surveying everything. The house was big. It was beautifully built. Its decor, affluent. "All the bells and whistles," as Meshawn would say. Upstairs, I wandered into one of the bedrooms. There were three. It had to be the master bedroom. There were pictures on the dresser. The female victim in every one of them. A hijab on her head at all times. She was Muslim. Just like the male victim downstairs. A Holy Quran was the one book on the dresser. It was open. I paused to inspect it. Surch two, ayat 255 was highlighted. I read the ayat.

He is Allah, there is no God but he, the living, the self-sufficient, the eternal. No slumber can seize him nor sleep. His are all things in the heaven and the earth. Who is there that can intercedeth with him, except with his permission?

He knows what preceded them in this life and the next. And they will never encompass aught of his knowledge, except as he willeth. His throne extends over the heavens and the earth, and he feels no fatigue in guarding and preserving them. He is the most high. The supreme in glory ...

After reading the ayat, I went through the drawers, but found nothing of interest. There was a purse near the bed. A Birkin bag made by Hermes. Expensive. I picked up the purse and rifled through it. There was a valid D.C. driver's license in there. It belonged to the female victim downstairs, the woman in all the photos. Detective Jericho Vargas walked into the room. He was tall, half Latino and spent all of his spare time training for CrossFit competitions.

"This house comes back to ..." Jericho said.

"Naimah El-Amin," I replied.

Jericho nodded. "The two luxury vehicles in the garage are also in her name. A Porsche SUV and a Maserati sedan. Seems to be loaded. May have been a home invasion of some kind."

I pointed to the dresser. "She's in all the photos. Always posing with people who appear to be professional. There's a building pass here in her purse that says Whitman-Walker Clinic on it. Address for Northwest, Washington, D.C. Good place to start asking questions about her. We should be able to find a next of kin by then."

"I'm on it, Mitch."

"Did anybody ID the male vic downstairs?"

"Yeah. He had his ID on him. In a pocket under the dress thing ..."

"In 2015, political correctness is a must, Jericho. That dress thing is Islamic attire that men wear. It's called a jalibeeyah or a thobe," I corrected.

"My bad. Didn't know it was Muslim thing."

"Don't apologize, just do better."

"I will. Still learning. That's all."

"It's cool. Did you get a name on him from the ID?" I asked.

Jericho glanced at his notepad. "Sure did. His ID says Samir Nadir. Date of birth 9-16-1968. Address on the ID is 1320 Dubois Place in Southeast, D.C. Davis ran the plates on the new modeled Lexus parked out front and it's his. Registered to him at the same address as the one on the license. I took the liberty of running his info through the system. He's been arrested a few times in the District of Columbia. A couple times for narcotics trafficking and possession. Once for attempted murder. And once for felony murder. Did a stretch at Lorton Correctional. Came home about ten years ago. Works at a place called Berrico Missions, LLC. Place in

Bowie, Maryland. You think this could be domestic? Both of 'em Muslims ..."

"What's the angle, Jericho? He kills her, then over kills himself in grief?"

"Forget I said that. I'm entitled to a dumb moment every now and again. Like I said earlier, I'm still learning. Maybe they're related."

"Could be. Why don't you earn your keep and find out? Then let me know."

"If I didn't know better and wasn't a good Christian, I'd think that was a little dismissive."

"You're really perceptive, Jericho. You made detective for a reason. You figure it out."

"Are the two victims downstairs related? Let me go and find out. Later, Mitch."

"And be sure to let me know, Jericho. Thanks."

I went back to the photos on the dresser. In a majority of the photos, there was a little girl present. A beautiful, exotic-looking kid. I left the master bedroom and walked into the two smaller ones. One was surely a guest bedroom. It wasn't adorned a lot. It was basically basic. The other was different. It was filled with stuffed animals, toys, a video console, the newest Sony PlayStation and hundreds of games. The drawers were filled with little girl things. The closet full of sneakers, clothes and more toys.

The bed was a single, adorned in Dora the Explorer sheets, the blanket plush. The bed was unmade and appeared to be recently slept in. I felt it. It was still warm. My mind went into overdrive as the questions piled up. Was the little girl here when the shootings happened? Had she witnessed them? Was that vomit in the bathroom hers? How was she related to the female victim? Where is the little girl now?

Leaving the room, I walked back downstairs. At the entrance to the house, a throng of uniformed cops congregated. Xavier Devonshire looked at me as I approached. "Hey X, do you know who called this in?"

He looked at his notepad. "Dispatch didn't get a name, Mitch. Said the caller just called in a shooting, gave the address and then hung up."

"I need a few of you guys to canvas this neighborhood. Knock on some doors and see if anyone heard anything, saw anything. Ask them about a little girl that lives here. She's about eight or nine years old. See if anybody knows who she is. Then call dispatch and see if the caller was a child."

"Got ya, Mitch," Xavier Devonshire replied.

"Thanks, buddy."

My cell phone vibrated again suddenly. The caller was Meshawn. I answered the phone this time. "What, Meshawn?"

"Don't fuckin' what me, nigga. When are you coming home?" Meshawn spat. I smiled. Meshawn Tate was a firebrand. Five foot four inches tall and a body like Serena Williams. Her sex drive was Janet Jacme. I thought about her on the other end of my phone. Her dark burgundy dyed hair was shaved on one side, the other side flat ironed straight and long.

She had tattoos all over her arms, legs, ass and stomach. Straight out of a *Black Ink Magazine*. Her manicured nails were long and shaped like claws. Her toes always painted to match her fingers. I could see her oiled body and pretty face in my head. The expression on her face, sinister. I couldn't get enough of her feisty ass. "I'll be there in like forty minutes. I'm investigating a double in Clinton."

"I'ma investigate the double between your legs after I kick you in 'em. All them muthafuckin' detectives they got on the force in P.G., why you gotta always be investigating shit?"

"Because I'm one of the best, maybe." I replied.

"You need to get your 'best' ass here before I get mad and leave," Meshawn said and hung up.

I laughed at Meshawn's threat to leave. It was an empty threat. The woman loved three things more than the air she breathed. The money I provided for her, my dick and her daughter. She'd be there when I got home, no matter what time it was. I put away my phone and walked around the house again. As Meshawn left my mind, the little girl entered it. Where was she?

Chapter 4

Angel

All the lights were out in the house on Benedict Court. But that didn't mean Honesty wasn't inside with my daughter. There were two cars parked in the driveway. The same two cars had been parked there before. The Lexus Tony used to drive, and the burgundy Mercedes truck Tina Brown had been driving the night I killed her. It was easy to see neither car had moved in months. They both had leaves gathered on the windshields. The scene looked just as it did the last time I'd been here. I remembered glancing at the driveway as I exited the house after the shootout with Honesty.

I was headed to the van I'd gotten from Cheeks, when I made a double take. My mind's eye flashed back to that night almost a year ago, and I noticed something different between that night and now. There was a vehicle missing. A black Cadillac Escalade. It was parked directly behind the Lexus that night. I remember thinking it was Tony's Caddy truck. Honesty must have driven it home, I remembered thinking.

Then all of a sudden, another thought hit me. The night me and Najee was leaving my store in Southeast, there was a black Cadillac truck parked across the street. The gunshots that rang out seconds later had undoubtedly come from the Caddy truck. I was the only person injured that night. Shot once through the shoulder. I never made the connection between that Caddy truck and Honesty. Najee had convinced me that the people inside the Caddy truck were associates of Carlos's, and the bullet I'd caught was meant for him.

That night he made the decision to go directly at Carlos. I never even thought about Honesty. I had completely forgotten all about her. Thinking about it all now, all I could do was shake my head. My silly ass had been getting fucked so good that all I thought about was Najee and his dick. How could I have been so blind? Thoughts of Honesty brought on thoughts of Aniyah. I wondered where my baby was and what Honesty was doing to her. Tears flooded my eyes and fell. The reality of what I'd done to my uncle also hit me.

I blamed him for my mother's death, but in all reality, all of the blame was mine. I was never supposed to have run away to Newark. I knew better than to leave a stone like Honesty unturned. I should have made it a priority to kill her. To not stop trying until I had. It was my responsibility. My job to handle and I hadn't. "Oh, Allah, please forgive me for killing my uncle! Uncle Samir, if you can hear me, I'm sorry!"

What my uncle had said earlier was right. Everything that had happened was my fault. I was the one that had grandiose desires and champagne dreams. It was my ambition and greed that made me trick Tony and kill him almost thirteen years ago. That was the event that put everything into play. After killing Tony, I hooked up with Carlos, Tony's plug and started copping thousands of bricks that I distributed to dudes in the city as if I was a point guard. Along the way, my sister Adirah was killed, Fatima betrayed me and was poisoned by Carlos's people. Then came Honesty, as a fourteen-year-old, blazing her gun.

As disturbed as I was about her having my daughter, I couldn't front. I had to respect the young woman's gangster. I had to admit our similarities were so close, it was surreal. She had the same unquenchable thirst for vengeance I had. Her willingness to kill no matter who or what, was my exact character trait. Honesty's ability to wait, plan and strategize mirrored my own as well.

I laid my head back and closed my eyes. A question came to mind. How had Honesty found my mother? The answer to that question spoke next. "The same way you found hers. On the internet." Shaking my head again, I told myself it was foolish of me to never think Honesty would go at my mother, just as I had done hers. I never thought she had that in her. I was wrong.

I had tried to kill the woman one time. Her attempts on my life numbered three. If only I could find her and end this cat and mouse game once and for all, there'd be no fourth attempt. I needed to find Honesty to get Aniyah back and to kill her. I thought about calling Najee to tell him about my mother's death and Honesty's connection to it. About the bullets that evening being fired from the Caddy truck coming from Honesty's gun and not Carlos's. But then I quickly dismissed that thought because according to the news, things between Najee and Carlos had already gone too far. There was no reverse course. Still, I yearned to hear his voice. To feel Najee's touch. My body shivered.

Then the car became claustrophobic. I exited the BMW and walked across the street. I walked into the yard and crept along the side of the house. I tried the door at the rear of the house. It was locked. I peered inside a back window but couldn't see a thing. Not knowing what else to do, I knocked on the door. Nothing. I came to the conclusion no one was inside the house. Honesty wasn't stupid enough to be there. Walking back to the car, the day my mother called me to tell me my sister was gone came to mind. I remember the terror I heard in her voice that day.

Now, I was the mother in search of her daughter. Déjà vu. I thought about the cruel twist of fate life had dealt my sister, Adiah, and prayed that didn't happen to Aniyah. I could never live without my daughter. Never.

Anthony Fields

Chapter 5

Gunz

All I could smell was dirt. Cold earth. My face was covered on one side by dirt as I lay on the ground. A blindfold had been placed over my eyes. I knew death was imminent and although I thought I was always ready to die, I realized I wasn't. I couldn't hear any voices, although I knew there were people close somewhere. My hands were cuffed behind my back where they'd been for the last hour or so. My shoulders ached with pain. If not for the pain in my shoulders that rippled throughout my body, and the fear of dying I felt, I might've noticed the cold air that threatened to freeze me. I laid on the ground and thought about how I'd come to be where I was …

The pretty light skinned policewoman who locked me in the holding cage came back and unlocked the cages. "Minnis, your ride is here."

"My ride? What ride?" I asked, totally confused.

"A U.S. Marshal is here to get you," pretty cop replied.

"U.S. Marshal?"

"That's what I said. C'mon."

Pretty cop led me through a labyrinth of cubicles until I reached a side door. Sitting at a desk filling out paperwork was a white woman with thick, blonde hair. She was clad in dark blue cargo pants, tan boots and a dark blue shirt. She wore a navy blue, fluffy coat with the words U.S. Marshal emblazoned across its back. She reminded me of Heather Locklear, the actress. Pretty Cop took her cuffs off me, and the Heather Locklear clone put a set of her own on my wrists. She led me out the side door to a waiting vehicle.

Once I was in the back seat, seatbelt secured by her, we took off. I hadn't been in D.C. long, but I'd been there long enough to know once we crossed the 14th Street bridge, we were leaving D.C. "Marshal, where are we going?" I shouted at the glass position that separated us, but I received no reply. As we took Exit 6C to Interstate 66 West, the city got further and further behind us. Alarms went off in my head. I knew then I was in deep trouble. An hour into the drive, I saw the lady marshal pull out a cell phone and speak into it softly. I tried but couldn't make out a word she was saying. Minutes later, the Crown Victoria I was riding in, turned off of the highway, down onto a dark, dirt road. Then it stopped abruptly.

"Ayo, Marshal? What the fuck is going on? Where the fuck am I?" I bellowed.

The lady marshal never replied. As I watched in curiosity, she got out of the car and leaned on the hood, cell phone still at her ear. Ten minutes or so later, two vehicles pulled off of the dirt road and parked near the Crown Vic. One of the vehicles was a new model Lexus Sedan, the other a Mercedes Benz Maybach. I watched as men got out of both vehicles. My blood ran cold, and my heart stopped momentarily. At first glance, none of the men looked particularly menacing. They all wore suits and expensive looking coats.

What made my heart pause was the nationality of all the men. Each one was Hispanic. And over the last seventy-two hours, I had killed dozens of Hispanics. The men approached the Crown Vic. Then the back door was snatched open, and I was forcibly removed from it. A handsome, well-dressed Hispanic, stepped to the front of the Crown and said, "Gerald Minnis, I presume, or should I call you by your street name, Gunz?"

I never replied, but I didn't have to. The man knew exactly who I was. I had a good guess of who he was. Seconds later, he confirmed what I already knew.

"Allow me to introduce myself. My name is Carlos. Carlos Trinidad." I was in the middle of nowhere, cold and alone. Completely surrounded by men who were my enemies. I was a dead man for certain.

"Dorothy, come here," Carlos Trinidad said. The blonde lady marshal appeared by his side in seconds. They embraced. Then kissed. Carlos finally broke the kiss. "Thank you for everything. I appreciate it."

"Anything for you, Carlos. You know that," Lady Marshal answered.

"I'm glad you feel that way. Now, I need you to go back to D.C. and find Angel for me, since Benito can't. Call Susan and see if anything has turned up on Najee as well. Call me later with whatever you learn."

Lady Marshal nodded, then kissed Carlos Trinidad again. Afterwards, she got into the Crown Victoria and peeled off. "Enrique, put Mr. Gunz here somewhere safe until the others arrive." That's when I was blindfolded and tossed to the ground like an unwanted rag doll.

***

I heard a car's engine as a vehicle approached. Then suddenly, the engine died, and car doors opened and closed. Men spoke in rapid Spanish.

"Remove his blindfold and the handcuffs," a voice said in English. I recognized it as belonging to the man who'd spoken to me about an hour ago.

"Turn over, Gerald, and sit up," Carlos Trinidad ordered. I complied with the command.

"I don't think I like Gerald too much. I like Gunz better, so I'll call you Gunz. Is that okay with you?"

"Call me whatever you want," I replied with false bravado.

"Yeah, I think I'll use Gunz since there's no need for formalities. After all, you and your friends knew a lot about me, my businesses and associates, so we're practically friends already. I want to introduce you to a few other friends of mine. I'll do that in a minute, but first, let me tell you I really respect you, Najee and your other friends. No one has ever killed as many people in my organization as you have. No one.

"With that said, you're probably wondering why you're out here in the middle of nowhere. There are no landmarks, signs, or mile markers. You either have to know how to get here or you don't. It's a hundred or so acres here, that I own. And nobody knows about the land, but all the people present, the woman who just left and somebody else I want you to meet." Carlos turned to a man near him. "Bring Brett and his wife to me."

My eyes followed the man to a third vehicle. What I had thought to be a car turned out to be a dark-colored Chevy Tahoe. The man opened the back door and led a man and woman out of the SUV. Both were blindfolded, gagged and bound at the wrists. I could see both were white people. The man was short, with graying hair that surrounded a large bald spot. The woman was taller, with long flowing black hair. The man and woman were dressed in nightwear, pajamas and a nightgown, their feet bare. They appeared to be recently rousted from bed. They were made to stand just feet away from where I sat.

"This gentleman, Gunz, is Brett. Brett Tousdale. And this is his lovely wife, Amanda. Brett works for me. He's my accountant and realtor. Brett here is the only person outside of the people I named earlier who knows where this place is. He's the only person who knows all of the businesses I own. He knows all the properties I hold, all the land I own. Since Brett purchased this parcel of land and all its surrounding acres for me, I thought it only fitting that he gets buried here. He's betrayed me, Gunz and by doing that, he's sentenced himself and his wife to death." Carlos Trinidad pulled a large caliber revolver from his back. He walked over to Brett and shot him in the head. Brain matter and blood erupted from the man's skull. His body dropped with a thud. Next, Carlos shot Amanda in the head. Her end was the same as her husband's.

"Now, bring me the others, please," Carlos said calmly.

I watched as several men went to the Chevy Tahoe and came back with three more people. As they approached, I could see the newcomers were black people. A light-complexioned man and two brown-skinned women. Their clothes were different, regular clothes. I could see that the man had been beaten. His clothes were bloody.

"These three people are not friends of mine, Gunz, but one of them is important to the narrative I'm about to explain to you. In fact, this man, you know. Remove his blind fold."

The blindfold was removed and without meaning to, I gasped. The man standing before me badly beaten was none other than George Foreman. George had helped us get the info on Carlos's businesses. The day Najee introduced me to George quickly came to mind ...

"*George, this is my man, Gunz. We call him Gunz because this nigga been busting his guns since we were kids. And this right here is Youngboy Tye.*"

"*What's up with y'all?*" *George said. "This move you making is a big move. Nobody has ever went at this dude and...*"

"*Gee, don't tell me you came here for nothing, son,*" *Najee said. "I could've heard the untouchable stories over the phone.*"

"*Hold on for a minute moe,*" *George replied. "Always let a man finish what he's saying before you speak. I gathered the info you need. I just wanted to let you know what type of challenges you face. I never said Trinidad was untouchable. Nobody's untouchable. History has shown us that. What I was tryna say is that this nigga is rarely seen in the streets. He wields power from afar. What you are gonna have to do is, draw him out. Hit him where it hurts. His pockets. You create enough terror in his organization, he'll surface and then you can kill him.*"

"You already know George Foreman, right, Gunz?" Carlos asked me. I didn't respond.

"You don't have to say anything. I already know you know who George is. How? Because George already admitted he knows you. He admits to knowing Najee, too, but won't tell me who else is with you and Najee. But it's okay, because before this night is over, I'll know everything I need to know. Let me fill you in on a few other things I know, too. Brett, may he rest in peace, picked up a drug habit over the years since he'd been working for me. Fate brought Brett and George together. Supplier and customer. They did a lot of business together. For years.

"As Brett spirals deeper and deeper into addiction, he gets heavily in debt to George. When you and Najee come to town with all your stolen drugs...don't look surprised, I know all the cocaine y'all sold was stolen in New Jersey and from whom. Najee gets in his head that he needs to go to war with me. Najee then goes to George for help. He needs info on me and my organization. George goes to Brett, who by the way, had told George that he worked for me. Since Brett is heavily in debt to George, George agreed to squash the debt if Brett provides him with the info Najee needs.

"Brett agrees and gives Najee the info you and your friends used to kill my friends and associates. Several innocent people as well." Carlos walked down the line of people, stopping in front of one of the women. "Speaking of innocent people, Gunz, the two women with George are definitely innocent in this. This woman here is his daughter's mother, Brianna. And the woman next to her is their nineteen-year-old daughter, Bianca. Bianca …"

Carlos upped the revolver quickly and shot George's daughter in the side of the head. Her brains and blood, coating her mother next to her. George's eyes grew large, and he threw himself in Carlos Trinidad's direction. But he was grabbed by the men standing nearby. His bestial cries were muffled by the gag in his mouth. His eyes filled with tears as he crumpled but was made to stand by the hands that gripped him. Carlos then moved inches until he stood in front of George's baby mother. He shot her, too. Her body dropped and laid next to her dead daughter. All George could do was watch his family be killed as he whimpered like a sick child. George closed his eyes as Carlos made his way to him. He was resigned to his fate. Carlos's last two bullets from the revolver were fired first into George's chest, then his head.

"As I tell you this, Gunz, men are on the way to Morgantown, West Virginia. Brett has a twenty-year-old son who attends West Virginia University. In twenty-four hours, he'll be dead. Brett's parents, Matilda and Brett Sr., live in a quiet little house on Lumberton Road in Scarborough, Maine. Men are on their way there as well. Both will be dead in twenty-four hours." Carlos put the now empty gun back into his waist and pulled out a cell phone. He dialed a number. "It's me. Put one of them on the phone." Carlos walked over to me and put the phone to my ear. "Say hello, Gunz."

Fear gripped me and squeezed my chest. "Hello?"

"Gerald?" a familiar voice said.

"Grandma?" I replied, tears forming in my eyes.

The phone was removed from my ear. I looked into Carlos Trinidad's face and shook my head. "No! Please ... don't!"

"My men are already in Newark, Gunz, as you just heard. Your family's death won't take twenty-four hours. Just minutes. If I give the word, they die. Do I give that word, Gunz, or do you call Najee for me? Decide now, Gunz! Quickly. Are you gonna call Najee for me, or does your family die?"

With tears streaming down my face, I made my decision.

Anthony Fields

Chapter 6

Najee

"Naj, what the fuck is going on with you down there?" Salimah blew into the phone as soon as I answered her call. "And why the fuck you don't be answering your phone when I call? I been calling your ass for hours."

"Not right now, Limah. I'm not in the mood for your bullshit. Gunz is missing ..."

"Missing? See, that's what the fuck I'm talkin' about. That bitch got you down there slipping, pussy whipped and shit. That's why I been calling your ass for the last ten hours. Have somebody check the local lock-up, because he probably in the bing. Bitches been blowing up my phone since yesterday talking about y'all. About how you, Gunz and that bitch Angel been all the news crazy. Mike Jones' sister Kelly and Jayla's cousin Crissy go to Howard University, and Choppa from Spruce Street, his girlfriend lives in D.C. They been calling me nonstop about y'all. You ain't been in D.C. but nine or ten months, fuck y'all done did down there?"

I smacked my forehead and ran my free hand down my face. I had completely forgotten about the call I'd gotten from George earlier, telling me about us being on TV.

"Najee, y'all hot, Slim."

"What the fuck you talkin' about, son? Who hot?"

"Naw, Slim, not that kinda hot. Hot as in them people on y'all line."

"What people, son? They on whose line?"

"Turn on the TV, Slim, and you'll see what people I'm talkin' about."

"What channel?"

"Fox News. Channel five."

I was so preoccupied with finding Gunz, I had totally let that important bit of news slip my mind. I thought about all the bodies me, Gunz and Tye had sent to the local morgue. If the police was looking for us in connection to those murders, we had fucked up somewhere and left a loose end. But how had they gotten onto us so fast? And why would they be looking for Angel? She wasn't connected to anything we had done.

"Maybe it wasn't the bodies? Maybe it was the drugs? Some type of conspiracy to distribute drugs. But I had to quickly dismiss that thought, because there was no way that Gunz could be connected to any drug selling. He wasn't even here for that. Gunz had only been in D.C. for a matter of days. Him and Tye.

"I ain't done shit down here, so I don't know what the cops looking for us for. Best believe though, before I get judged by twelve, you gon be putting a size-twelve in my feet for a janazah prayer."

"Please miss me with all that gangsta rap shit, big brother. That talk ain't for you and me. I don't need you dead. I need you alive. Ya got everything that you need, Naj. You got the record company putting out hits. You got houses, cars, property and a whole lotta money. Why throw it all away after you done built an empire? And for what? Your rep in the streets? Fuck that shit, Naj. You gotta live, big brother. We've come a long way from the Brick Towers days. Eating greasy ass turkey burgers from halal spots. You need ... hold on for a minute, Naj. Bitch, don't you see me on the phone? Move around."

"Who the fuck was that?"

"Some bitch that's about to get her feelings and her body hurt."

"Where you at, yo? I hear loud music and shit."

"I'm at a club in A.C., but like I was saying, you need to come home to Jersey. That's what you need to do. So, I can keep an eye on your ass. You can relocate everything and bring it up here."

"Is that right? I need to come home to Jersey, huh?"

"Yeah, that's right. And make sure you leave that conniving ass bitch Angel right there in the Nation's Capital where she belongs."

"What did I tell you about that 'bitch' shit when you speaking about shorty, Limah? Angel's wifey," I said with a conviction I no longer knew was true. I couldn't bring myself to admit to Salimah that all the wild shit she'd said about Angel was on point.

"Wifey? Nigga, you trippin,'" Salimah replied.

"Naw, Limah, you trippin." You gotta respect my choice. Like I do yours. Do I call you and stress you about them lame ass niggas you be fuckin' with? That nigga Que from Prince Street is a bitch. Cold blooded. You might as well strap up and fuck him."

"I did ... naw, I'm just kidding. Que was cool. He was good to me, but I got rid of him months ago. If you called me a little more, you would know that. He was never my new man. He was 'rebound guy' after Mu got killed. Que was the appetizer. My new dude is the whole meal. He might be hubby ..."

"Your new dude? Who's he?"

"You don't know him."

"Says who?" I asked.

"Says me. He's from North Ward. Grafton Avenue," Salimah said.

"Grafton Avenue is a 'Blood' hood now. All them niggas gang bangin' and shit. That's what you on now? Gangbangers?"

"Look, don't judge me. My dude is the 'Big homie' over there. He passed the gang bangin' shit. He's a boss. All I fuck with is 'boss' niggas. You already know."

"Does this boss nigga know you're my sister?"

"How could he not? The whole Brick City knows I'm your sister."

"And therein lies the problem. I gotta lotta enemies, Limah. You know that."

"Yeah, I know that, but—"

"But nothing, you a grown woman and I can't govern your box. Just make sure your boss nigga knows that if anything happens to you on his watch, I'ma body his whole fuckin' bloodline. Literally."

"I'm not telling him that," Salimah replied sassily.

"It don't matter. Tell him or don't tell him. It's still law. Facts. I'ma hit you back later, sis. I gotta find out what's up with Gunz. Love you."

"Love you, too. Call me later and tell me what's up with Gunz."

"I will. Peace." I disconnected the call and glanced to my right. Tye was in the passenger seat of the Maxima with his eyes closed.

I climbed out of the Maxima and entered the fish spot called Horace & Dickies. It was almost three in the morning and the greasy spoon spot was still open and packed. I spotted an older, dark-skinned woman sitting down behind the counter. Her apron was filthy, and she looked exhausted. Getting her attention, I motioned for her to come to me.

"I'm on my break, baby, but how can I help you?" the woman said when she reached the counter.

I pulled out my cell phone and pulled up a picture of me and Gunz. I zoomed in on Gunz's face and showed it to the woman. "The last time I saw my brother, he told me he was coming here. That was hours ago, and I'm concerned about him. I need to know if you saw him in—"

"Ayo, Naj!" Tye called out.

I turned around to face him. "What's good, Tye?"

"The truck Gunz was driving is parked outside. He ain't in it, but it's definitely in the parking lot, parked about three cars away from where we're parked. When you pulled in, there was a van there, so we couldn't see it. A few minutes ago, it pulled out and I spotted it."

"You sure it's the one Gunz was driving?"

"Positive, burgundy Expedition. Paper tags from VA. It's the one."

"Let me go ..."

The woman behind the counter cut me off. "I do remember seeing your brother. He came in and ordered the special. No, wait ... two specials. Six-piece whiting on wheat with mac & cheese and greens. Also, the ten-piece wings with fries. He tipped me good. Gave me twenty dollars. I don't know what he did out there in the parking lot, but he got arrested."

"Are you sure he got arrested?"

"These eyes ain't good as they used to be, but they're still pretty good. I'm sure of what I saw. Saw them put him in the squad car and everything. I'm sure of it. Your brother went to jail."

I pulled out some money and gave the woman a big-face hundred. "Thank you for that info."

The woman's smile lit up the room as she accepted the money. "No, baby, thank you."

I followed Tye to the parking lot, where he pointed at the Expedition. Sure enough, it was the one I'd purchased days ago in Arlington. I checked the passenger door. It was unlocked. I opened the door. There were bags sitting in the passenger seat. I checked them. It was the food Gunz had ordered. The driver's side door opened, and Tye's face came into view.

His eyes dropped to the floor. He reached down and picked up something. "Here go the keys to the truck, son. Gunz must've dropped them before getting bagged." He moved the seat and peered into the back. "And you ain't gon believe this, but the choppa is on the floor in the back. Check it out."

I did just that and Tye was right. The Calico machine gun was on the floor behind the driver's seat. I was completely befuddled. "The cops didn't search the truck. They just arrested son. That tells me they couldn't be looking for us about no bodies. If they did, after seeing Gunz near the truck, they would've towed it and searched it with a fine-tooth comb. They didn't do that."

"Makes sense to me. But now that we know Gunz got bagged, now what?" Tye asked.

"Ain't nothing we can do until we talk to Gunz. You got the keys. Move the truck. Follow me to the spot and park it. I'll call Mark …" My cell phone vibrated. I pulled it out and saw a 202 number I didn't recognize. I answered the call. "Hello?"

"Baby boy, it's me."

"Gunz?"

"Yeah, son, it's me. I need you to listen to me. Shit wild, you heard?"

"I hear you, son. I hear you. What's good?"

"I got bagged out the fish spot by the D.C. cops. They turned me over to the U.S. Marshals…"

"U.S. Marshals?" I repeated, confused.

"You heard me, right, son. U.S. Marshals. Do you remember what you told me Angel said about the nigga Carlos Trinidad?"

"Huh? Naw…yeah, she said a lot of shit about son. Fuck that gotta do with anything though, yo? Where are you, big boy?"

"Let me finish, yo. What she said got a lot to do with what I'm about to say. Angel told you that son had mad powerful friends, judges, prosecutors and cops. She said son was a powerful nigga … Well, it turns out Angel was right. I'm in a fuckin' dirt field in the middle of nowhere, and son is right here. The U.S. Marshals gave me to him."

"Wait, I'm lost, yo. You in a dirt field with who?"

"Carlos Trinidad. The U.S. Marshals gave me to him."

"Get the fuck outta here. Are you serious right now?"

There was a pause on the other end of the phone. Then a new voice, a deeper voice said, "Everything Gunz just said to you is true. How are you, Najee? Nice to finally put a voice with the face."

"Ayo, son, by Allah, if you kill Gunz …"

Laughter erupted on the other end of the phone. "Gunz should be the least of your worries, Najee. Your grandmother in Newark and your sister Salimah should be your primary concern."

Hearing my sister's name in Carlos Trinidad's mouth made my heart stop.

"Still there, Najee?"

"I'm here," I told the man.

"We need to talk. You and me. The Italians call it a 'sit down.'"

"We ain't got shit to talk about, yo."

"Oh, I disagree. I think we have a lot to discuss."

"Like what?"

"You'll have to wait and see. I'll be at the Live! Casino in Arundel Mills in two hours. I suggest you join me. If you want to see the people you love again after tonight, I insist you be there."

The line went dead and so did my hopes of his whole ordeal having a happy ending.

Chapter 7

Carlos Trinidad

"Still there, Najee?" I asked.

"I'm here," Najee replied.

"We need to talk. You and me. The Italian call it a 'sitdown.'"

"We ain't got shit to talk about, yo."

"Oh, I disagree. I think we have a lot to discuss."

"Like what?"

I smiled to myself. "You'll have to wait and see. I'll be at the Live! Casino in Arundel Mills in two hours. I suggest that you join me. If you ever want to see the people you love again after tonight, I insist that you be there." Before Najee could say another word, I ended the call. The sound of Najee's voice rattled me inside. His voice sounded just like mine did at his age. After so many years of not knowing where my son was or what he looked like, it felt good to talk to Najee. I looked forward to seeing him in person and seeing his face when I broke the news to him.

"I did what you asked. Call your man off my family," Gunz said.

"Nobody's going to hurt your family until I tell them to. If I tell them to."

"Don't hurt them, yo. Please!"

"Their safety depends on you. You and Najee." I told Gunz and walked away. I walked up to Pedro Herrera. "Get the shovels out and bury these bodies. Nobody leaves here until those bodies are in the ground. Understood?"

"Understood, boss," Pedro replied and got to work. Benito Alverez met me at the Maybach. "Ya held cards close to your chest, mi amigo. Why is that?"

"What cards are speaking about, Benito?"

"You never told me you discovered it was Brett who betrayed us. You never told me our men are in Newark, at Gunz's mother's home. You didn't tell me you have a line on Najee's moth ... grandmother and sister. And most importantly, you haven't said why you need to talk to Najee or even that you wanted to talk to him. Everything I've just said, I've just learned in the last hour. Am I not your best friend still, and your closest advisor?"

"Benito, you never have to question your position with me. The shadow of Benito Alverez looms large still. Don't ever forget that. I never told you about Brett because I knew you'd try to make excuses for him."

"I always liked Brett."

"That I know, comrade. I didn't need my judgment clouded. As for the men in Newark, Marcus, Juan Carrales and Pablo Estrada have been in Newark since I learned Muhamad Farid Shahid wanted to come to D.C. to find Najee. I sent them there in case I needed to send a message to Shahid. Since they were already there, I put them on Gunz's family. Najee's family ... his sister and grandmother have been harder to find. When I just told Najee that his family's lives depended on him meeting me, I lied, old friend. But hopefully soon, I'll know exactly where they are. Lastly, my meeting with Najee has been long overdue ..."

"Long overdue?" Benito repeated.

I nodded. "Just be patient with me, comrade. In time you'll understand everything. After tonight, things will be a little clearer and you'll have all the answers to the questions in your mind. Trust me."

"I trust you, mi amigo. I trust you. Can I kill this piece of shit over there, now? Seeing you do so much killing has whet my appetite. I'm feeling left out."

"No, Benito. I still need Gunz. I need Najee in front of me and Gunz has to be there to make sure that meeting takes place. After that, maybe you can kill him."

"Maybe? Maybe I can kill him? I'm confused."

"Patience, comrade. Patience. Come on." I led Benito back to where Gunz sat on the ground. "Gunz, what role does Angel play in all of this?"

A confused look crossed Gunz's face. "Angel? Who, Najee's bitch?"

I nodded my head.

"None, as far as I know. She helped Najee move all the coke he brought to D.C. They met in Newark and became a couple. They moved to Virginia ... Alexandria. Once Najee started moving all the work, Angel got paranoid. She warned Najee that you'd find out he was moving coke in the city. She stressed to him that you ran the whole town and that you'd notice there was competition around. But Naj wasn't hearing that shit. He stubborn like that. Then the dude's Doodie and Faceman got killed and Angel told Najee their deaths were because of them buying their coke from him. Still, Najee paid that extra shit no mind. It was business as usual until somebody tried to body Najee, but hit Angel ..."

"What do you mean, tried to body Najee but hit Angel?" I asked.

"Najee and Angel were inside a store that she owns in Southeast, one evening. As they left the store, someone let off some shots in their direction. Angel got hit. The bullet went in and out of her shoulder. After that, Najee went ham."

Suddenly, it all made sense. "Najee thought that the person responsible for firing those shots was me, right? That's what set all of this in motion?"

Gunz nodded. "Him and Angel both thought it was you. That's when Najee called us ... I mean me. I jumped on the road and heeded his call."

"So, you're telling me Angel has absolutely nothing to do with this war Najee has waged against me?"

"Nothing at all. In fact, after she got shot, although she believes it was you, once Najee made his intentions clear to her about going to war, Angel begged him not to do it. She told Najee that you were too powerful an adversary to war against. She pleaded with Najee to leave town. Even offered to leave with him. But he refused. He called you a bully and Najee hates bullies. Trust me, I know. He's killed all the bullies that we grew up with in Brick City. Even if he wanted to leave town, once he made up his mind to fight, he'd never change it, that's how son is built. He fell out with Angel that night and left her. According to him, he hasn't seen or spoken to Angel since that night, maybe a week ago."

"So, you're telling me that Mamacitas, Salazar's, the pool hall … the drive-by's, that was just you and Najee?"

Gunz nodded his head.

Chapter 8

Salimah Bashir

Club Starlight

Atlantic City, NJ

"…Make no error/we getting money like the Reagan era/06' summer, I prayed to Guerrere/top down, facing the weather (speeding)/I'm zigzagging through the traffic, see the Jakes in The mirror/and the wings got the spoiler kit/but fame got me 'noid a bit/the more cases and shit, the more the lawyer get/I guess his new friends wanted him dead/and his old friend's wanted the bread/dipset/like I'm rollin' with Richie/I guess murder is a business (true steel)/and I hope that God grant serenity (pray for me)/we cop the cars with all the amenities (balling)/like the Ferrari out in Italy/drop tops with all The scanners in 'em/(what else/top drops with the hammers in 'em (loaded)/fuck with the book price/we getting money, it's the crook life …"

"Soo-woo! He called the bet, so I shook the dice …" Drama rapped along with the song.

Ten minutes later, a man with braids and a red Vamp Life bandana approached our table. I recognized him instantly. He was accompanied by several other men whom I didn't recognize. The men each embraced Drama who stood to greet them. I watched as they exchanged gang handshakes.

"Jim, how you, fam? So, what's good, blood?" Drama said.

"I'm good, blood. It's always a pleasure to see a real one, ya' heard?" Rap superstar Jim Jones said.

"What's bracking, blood?" the tall, slender man said next.

"Muthafuckin' 'O.G.' S.I. Murder, glad to see you out of the belly. Heard you was home from the feds, son. You good?"

"Always, blood, always. What's poppin with you?"

"Whatever you need it to be, as long as it's us and never them. Get with me later and we'll figure it out. I'ma lace you, blood. It's only proper that I do. Feel me?"

"Definitely. Jim got your number, right?" S.I. asked.

"Jim knows how to reach me, son. Just holla whenever." Drama said and embraced the man again. "Jim, get at me, fam. Asap."

"Sure thing," Jim Jones said, embraced Drama and then turned to leave, his entire entourage with him.

The VIP section suddenly felt less crowded as all the women present followed the group of men around the club.

"You never told me you know Jim Jones, boo," I whispered in Drama's ear as soon as he sat down.

He looked at me and smiled. "I know a lot of niggas, ma. All types of niggas. Rap niggas, basketball and football niggas, street niggas ... there's a lot about me you don't know, but you gon learn, though."

"Is that right?"

"Yeah, that's right. But on some real shit, Jimmy's Blood. He's Nine Trey as was the dude with him, S.I. Jimmy just an entertainer, though. The nigga S.I. is official. He's like the godfather or some shit for the Nine Trey set. I was on the Island with son many years ago. Him and some other niggas started the 'Blood' shit on the 'Island.' A lot of these rap niggas out here bangin' blood, but them niggas ain't real. Them niggas who just left is real."

"That's really interesting and all, but I think it's time for me to turn in. I'm tired. I've had enough fun for one night. Met enough gangsters and gang bangers. Let's get out of here."

"Your wish is my command."

***

Newark, NJ

When Drama's Porsche Panamera turned onto Cypress Lane, I saw a Buick Lacrosse parked behind a GMC SUV. They were both parked near the new house I'd been in since last November. The house was a gift from Najee. I had seen the two vehicles when we'd left the house and wondered who could've been driving them. I dismissed the thought as we left, but as Drama pulled into my driveway, I eyed the two vehicles again. I had never seen either of them on the block before. Maybe it was just me being paranoid.

"What's on your mind?" Drama asked as he killed the car's engine.

"Nothing too much. Just checking out a few cars I've never seen on the block before," I told him while retrieving the house keys from my purse.

"Gotta be somebody here seeing your neighbors."

"Maybe. Maybe not. It's all good. I get this paranoid shit from my brother. Living in Brick City will do that to muthafuckas."

"True dat. And your brother is a real live animal out here, so I get the extra precaution and paranoia. Son gotta be on point always. From what I hear, he been peter rollin' shit in these streets for a mad long time. He's all we heard about when I was at Rahway back in the day doing my bid."

"Yeah, my brother is somewhat of a legend out here. Come on. I need some dick and sleep. In that order. That Grey Goose got my pussy juicy as shit."

"Gotcha, ma. I'ma drink every bit of it."

Anthony Fields

Chapter 9

Aziz Navid

The woman was beautiful. Her allegiance to the culture of the streets, undeniable. Tattoos were strategically placed on her body, as to draw attention to her every asset. Dark, curly hair fell over her shoulder and hung close to her breasts. Her skin was the color of creamy soy milk. My eyes did the math and I put the woman at five foot three or four, give or take an inch. Her feet were small, her heels expensive. The large LV logo could be seen from across the room. Her dress fell in a heap at her feet. Her nakedness revealed large perky breasts with dark nipples that reminded me of Hershey Kisses.

Light from either the moon or a lamp somewhere came through the balcony's glass in the bedroom. The muscular man with the long dreads was hungry for her. He stood in front of her as she undressed him. Afterwards, she attacked him with feral ferocity. She wrapped her arms around his neck while standing on her tiptoes and kissed his mouth. Then her lips found his chest and headed south. The man caressed her head as her tongue lapped at his ab muscles. Side to side she moved, head darting around like a cobra snake preparing to strike. Suddenly, the woman fell to her knees and faced his erection head-on. Without using either hand, she licked him slowly, base to tip.

The woman was extremely beautiful. I could easily see why Muqtar Kareem was cheating on his wife with her. The woman's hair covered her face as she let her tongue say what her body couldn't. With varying speeds, she sucked him methodically, meticulously. Loud moans escaped his mouth and died at the ceiling. Then her loud slurping sounds overpowered his moans. I watched as the man's hand gripped the woman's curly hair and guided her face onto his erection deeper, closer.

"Damn Limah, baby! You a beast, ma!!" the man exclaimed. The beautiful woman responded by gurgling and gagging, then deep throating the man. She was a porn star appearing in her own private movie. His breathing labored and his body convulsed as he climaxed. Seconds later, he pulled himself from her mouth. He lifted the woman off her feet and carried her to the king-sized bed not far from where they'd just stood. He laid her down and dove between her legs headfirst. It was the woman's turn to moan in ecstasy. Her toes curled and her leg bent at the knee. The other leg wrapped itself around the man's head. I watched the woman's breasts rise and fall rhythmically. Both of her hands clawed at the comforter beneath her.

The man's arms appeared powerful. They were covered in crude ink. Jailhouse tattoos. Those arms locked the woman into his embrace as he stepped up his oral assault on her middle. The woman tried to wiggle out of the man's grasp, but her efforts were futile. Her moans turned to soft cries then got more intense as the minutes passed. The letter "O" formed on the woman's lips as she finally surrendered. Shortly thereafter, her body shook violently in purposeful orgasm.

"Oh, my … fuckin' gawd … nigga …!" the woman shouted.

"You ain't the only one around here with a mean head game," the man replied.

When he lifted up, he was hard again. He crawled up the length of the woman and grabbed her feet. One in each hand. He put both feet on his shoulders.

"Drama, no!" the woman protested. "It hurts when you do it like that."

"I'ma be gentle this time, I promise," the man replied, before leaning down until his body rested completely on top of her. He reached beneath him and slid himself into the woman.

"Wait … wait … hold on! Drama, stop! Put … my … feet … down!"

The man ignored her pleas.

"It's … it's … too … too … deep … in … me! Drama! Stop, it hurts!"

Pound and ground. Grind and pound. Repeat.

"Drama … stop … baby … let … me … ride … it!"

The man with the dreads pounded a few more times and relented. He released the woman's feet from his shoulders then lifted himself up and out of her.

The woman rolled gingerly out from under the man. She positioned herself to strike the man hard across the face with an open palm. "The next time I tell your ass to stop, stop!"

The man laughed a deep, throaty laugh. "You got that, ma. Straight up."

The woman stood up and climbed on top of the man, then squatted over his hard on. She placed him inside her and sat down slowly. Her head fell back, and her palms fell to his chest.

"Damn, Limah ... ride that dick, ma! Ride that dick for big Drama!"

"Damn, this dick feels good! I love this dick!"

"You love it?"

"Yes! I love your big dick."

"On what you love this dick, ma?" Drama asked.

"You already know on what," Salimah replied.

"Say it. Tell me what it is."

"On blood. On Brim. I love this dick."

"That's what I'm talkin' bout, baby. Put that shit on the set, then. Say that shit! Say that shit!"

Salimah Bashir went wild then. She rode Drama with energy and passion. "On Grafton. On Blood. On Brim. I love this dick! I love it!"

I decided then I'd seen and heard enough. My dick was bulging inside my pants, and I felt ashamed I had witnessed so much. I felt like a voyeur, a pervert. Stepping from the closet with the ten-millimeter Smith and Wesson in hand, I shot the woman first. The bullet entered the back of her head and exited the front. Her blood and brains coating the man beneath her before she fell forward, lifeless.

"What the fuck?" the man exclaimed.

I moved around the bed with alacrity. A shocked expression crossed the man's face as his eyes met mine. I fired the gun again, the bullet hitting the man in the neck. The hole appeared, blood trickled out and the sounds he made became gurgling sounds. My next bullet stopped his suffering. A perfectly placed bullet to the head ended his life. I stared down at the scene I'd left. It would have been better to talk to Najee's sister to find out exactly where he was, or to at least use her to get to Najee. But my instructions had been clear. Kill. I thought about the conversation I'd had earlier with Muhammad Farid Shahid …

"From what I'm hearing, Trinidad and his organization are having a hard time finding and killing Najee Bashir. I think we can do a better job. In order to bring Najee back to Newark, you have to kill the people closest to him, those that he loves. His parents were killed in an accident on the Hudson River when he was twelve, his sister, ten. Najee's mother's mother was raised in Newark. Her name is Miranda Santiago. She is still there. Have you found her yet?" Muhammad asked.

"I have. I'm going there after I leave the sister," I replied.

"So, you have finally found Najee's sister?"

"I'm sitting near her house now. She's within my grasp."

"Good, Aziz. Kill Najee's family. Bring him back to Newark. Then finish him."

"As you wish."

"Assalamu Alaikum."

"Walaikum Assalam."

I pulled at my cell phone and dialed a number.

"Assalamu Alaikum," a man's voice said.

"Walaikum Assalam. Bring him into the house."

"We're on our way." The line went dead.

***

I let the man's eyes take in the bloody mess on the bed before speaking. "I couldn't have found Salimah without you, Yasir."

Khitab Abdullah and Amir Ibn Musa held up the big man as his knees threatened to buckle. Tears formed in the man's eyes and fell. He tried to speak, but he could not because of the tape that covered his mouth. His wrists were bound behind him with tape as well.

"Remove the tape from his mouth. He wants to talk," I ordered.

Khitab pulled the duct tape completely off the man's face, taking hair with it.

"You fucked up, son! Word to my mother, you just fucked up! You didn't have to kill her! "You said you just wanted to talk to her!"

"I did talk to her. I just didn't use words. I used bullets."

"Do you know who her fuckin' brother is? Do you know who the dude with her is?"

I smiled a wicked smile. "Her brother's name is Najee and the man's name is Drama. He's a Blood gang member from Grafton Avenue. So, what?"

"The entire city is about to be looking for you. You don't have a clue what you did!"

"I know exactly what I just did. You know what I just did. But how is anybody else, besides the people in this room, gonna know what I just did?"

"They'll know. The universe has a way of righting all wrongs."

"The universe, huh?" I laughed as I upped the ten millimeter and shot Yasir in the head. When his body slumped, Khitab and Amir let him go. The dead man fell to the floor. "Take the tape off his wrists." I walked over and put the gun I held into Yasir's hand.

***

Getting into the house on Ridgeway Avenue was simple work for my man. The locks on the doors were antiquated.

"Search the house," I ordered.

I walked through the house that smelled of cooking spices and fruit, and it made me nostalgic for my days as a youth in Newburgh, NY. Sitting down on the couch, the bones in my left knee popped. Years of constant exercise had worn out the cartilage in my knee and caused the bones at the joint to rub together, thus creating the popping sound from time to time. Standing for so long in the closet at Najee's sister's home had stiffened my knees. I rubbed my left knee as I thought about what my wife Nadia had said to me over the phone when I told her about Muhammad Shahid's orders …

"Killing Najee's family is collateral damage, Aziz. But collateral damage is always necessary at times of war. When Najee killed Muqtar almost ten months ago, he unknowingly started a war. Instilling fear in your enemy is imperative, husband. It's been that way since and before the time of the Rasoolalah, Sallalalu Alaihi Wasalaam. Stay the course and do as Muhammad says. You have been trying to find and kill this man for months. Killing his loved ones will expedite Najee's pilgrimage back to Newark. Watch and see. Then you can kill him."

"There are three bedrooms upstairs," Khitab said, breaking my reverie. "Only one is occupied. The old woman is alone in bed. Asleep."

In response, I screwed a silencer attachment onto my weapon. Then, I rose from the couch and went to commit another senseless murder.

***

Outside the red brick house, I stood with my men around me.

"Khitab, you and Amir go to the house on Hazelwood Avenue. You have the address, right?"

Khitab nodded.

"Go there and do what needs to be done. By any means necessary but be cautious and be safe." I turned to Farouq Salaudin. "Go to the apartment in Weequahic on Lyons Avenue …"

"Apartment 12A. Building 3203," Farouq answered.

I nodded my head. "Go. Keep in touch with Khitab and let him know when everything is done. Take RuKan with you." Farouq turned and left. "Khitab, get in touch with Basil and Kareem. Send them to 9th Avenue and Market Street. Leave no one alive."

Khitab Abdullah nodded his head. "And what about you, Aziz? Where are you going? Who will drive you?"

"Don't concern yourself with my safety, Ocki. I'm good, Insha'Allah. I need to clear my head. I will walk home."

"You're kidding, night?" Amir asked.

"Does it look like I'm kidding, Amir?" I replied.

The two men left with me, looked at me, then turned and left me alone. They got into the car and pulled off. I pulled my collar up to ward off the night chill, then I began to walk.

Chapter 10

Najee

Live! Casino

Arundel Mills, MD

"Why did you decide to come here, yo?" Tye asked.

I exhaled and ran my hand through my hair. "Fuck I was gon do? Leave my nigga Gunz at the mercy of that nigga? Say fuck my man Gunz? My sister, too?"

"Ayo, fam, you saying that shit like Gunz ain't my family, too. I was just asking, yo, to see where your head at. You ain't said two words all the way here."

"Just been thinking, yo. About all this shit. Mu and the coke, the record label, Angel, the two niggas I did business with that Trinidad nem killed. FACE and Doodie, Gunz getting grabbed by the cops and ending up with Trinidad and this nigga threatening my sister. A lot of wild shit done happened in the last year."

"You spoke to Limah, though and she was good. Wasn't nobody strange around ..."

"She was at a club, she said, how can you say nobody was around?"

"I'm telling you, yo. I think that nigga bluffing about Limah," Tye said.

"Bluffing? Stupid ass nigga, how the fuck does Carlos Trinidad, a fucking drug lord in D.C., even know that I gotta a sister named Salimah in Newark? Huh? He can't be bluffing. That nigga got Gunz from the fuckin' cops, yo! The cops and a U.S. marshal. That's some whole other, next level, big boy shit. Niggas with that type of juice don't bluff."

Capitulating, Tye nodded his head. He fingered the guns in his lap. "True dat, true dat. Aight, so now what? How the fuck we gon get Gunz back and make sure nothing happens to Limah?"

I had to gather my thoughts before responding. I had spent the last hour or so asking myself the exact same things. "I think if Trinidad wanted to kill Gunz, he'd be dead already. He doesn't need Gunz to get to me. He could've done that with just the threat of hurting my sister. So, Gunz is alive for a reason. What that reason is … I don't know. He wants to meet with me, to talk, he says. Why? I have no fuckin' clue. What do he and I have to discuss? A truce? I seriously doubt that.

"But that's why I'm here … you're here, we're here. The one thing I have on my side is you. Trinidad hasn't mentioned you. And I'm sure Gunz didn't either. So, you're the ace in the hole. The X factor. You won't be with me, but you stay nearby the entire time. The only people who'll know about you, is me and Gunz. It's a super public place. Too public to commit a murder. Even for a well-connected nigga like him. He knows a casino is a bad place to kill people and yet he chose it. A place that has cameras everywhere. There's a method to his madness, yo, I just don't know what it is. So, I guess we'll just have to wait and see. If things go bad, you know exactly what to do."

"Kill him and everybody with him," Tye said with conviction. "You already know how I get down. I got you, fam. Wallahi."

"I already know, yo. I already know." I pulled out my phone and called the number back that Gunz had called me from.

The other end was answered by the man I assumed was Carlos Trinidad. "Hello?"

"I'm here, yo."

"Good. I'll call you back with further instructions in minutes."

The line went dead. I put the phone up and laid back in my seat. I was tired, but anxiety and trepidation kept me alert. No more words exchanged between me and Tye. It was do or die. We both knew that. All of a sudden, Angel invaded my thoughts again. I couldn't deny the fact the woman had permeated my being. Made me feel a way about a woman I had never felt before. She was the living, breathing manifestation of me. If there was really such a thing as a soulmate, then Angel was mine. We were different in some ways, but still too much alike.

I had never met a woman like Kareemah El-Amin. Angel was a woman who was a struggling Muslimah. And I am a struggling Muslim man. She was street in every sense of the word. A former queen-pin who had controlled the drug flow into one half of Washington, D.C. A woman who had killed her enemies. She was a woman who had a lot of money, was smart and beautiful. My soulmate. I glanced around at the casino's parking lot, then up at the bright lights everywhere. Mi vida loca. My crazy life.

I wondered if I'd survive the day. Comfortable in the fact that whatever happened, it was the decree of Allah. Preordained. I wondered if Angel would miss me if I died. If Carlos Trinidad and his men killed me. I wondered if she'd avenge my death. Then I could hear her words in my head. Words she'd said to me the last night I'd seen her.

"Pick your opponents wisely ... Najee, this is a fight you can't win!"

"Thanks for the vote of confidence, ma. That's your opinion and everybody is entitled to one."

"Najee, I wasn't totally honest with you. When we first met... well, when we first talked about our lives together, I never lied to you. I just purposely left things out. They never seemed important to me then. I was worried about the way you'd view me. But now I feel like you should know everything. Remember when I told you about the dude named Tony Bills?"

"Yeah."

"Well, what I didn't tell you was that Tony was hooked up with Carlos. I learned about Carlos Trinidad from Tony. I had met Carlos on a couple of occasions, but that was it. I saw how he operated. How he manipulated people, situations and events. When Tony got killed, Carlos was at the funeral. I talked to him. Remember when I told you I hooked up with some people and started getting bricks? These people were Carlos and his organization.

"I dealt with him directly most of the time. Then we became friends. I told you I went to jail for some murders, and I beat the case because the witness... my friend Fatima, never showed up in court. What I didn't tell you was that she never showed up because

Carlos had her killed. He had her killed while under armed guard in the 'Witness Protection' program. That showed me just how powerful Carlos Trinidad really was ..."

I could hear Angel's raw emotion as she had said those words. Had tried to warn me. Then I remembered my own words moments ago to Tye ...

"That nigga got Gunz from the fuckin' cops, yo. The cops and a U.S. marshal. That's some whole other, next level, big boy shit ..."

Angel's words came back again ...

"Carlos has the advantage over you, Najee. He has cops, politicians, judges and all kinds of people in his pockets. He dictates to the city council here, not the other way around. That's why I say you can't win. I know Carlos, Najee, and I know how powerful he is. The deck is stacked against you..."

Emotion is a muthafucka. I had been so caught up in my feelings when Angel had told me I couldn't win a war with Carlos Trinidad, that I had failed to grasp the true meaning behind her words. Until now. My pride, conceit and overconfidence had formed a shield inside me that her words couldn't penetrate. What I had thought was betrayal and deceit, had really been the exact opposite. Love and concern. I was finding out now just how truly powerful Carlos Trinidad was, and all Angel had done was try to tell me that weeks ago.

I owed her an apology. I pulled out my phone and quickly dialed Angel's number. Even though it was almost five in the morning, I still needed to hear her voice. To apologize and tell her that I understood now. That I had finally gotten exactly what she had been trying to convey to me the night I'd left her. I needed to tell her I was wrong, and she had been right. The line on the other end of the phone just rang and rang. Then the voicemail came on. I felt like the wind had been knocked out of me. I hung up and called again, getting the same result.

Damn! Angel, answer the phone.

Chapter 11

Angel

Unable to rest my mind and feeling no fatigue, I didn't go home. I couldn't go home, knowing my daughter was in the hands of my enemy. After leaving Honesty's house in Kettering, I ended up at the Glen Willow apartment complex in Seat Pleasant, Maryland. I sat in the car in front of the building, where I had shared an apartment with Tony Bills, Honesty's father. It was where this whole story had begun. I could see the balcony door I had jimmied to appear broken into, so my "intruders had killed Tony" story would be more believable. I thought about the two years I'd spent with Tony before pulling a .40 caliber handgun from under the bed and blowing his brains out.

I left there and drove to the house I was raised in, on 46th Street Southeast. The house looked exactly as it did when we'd last lived there about ten years ago. So many memories, good and bad, flooded my brain. I didn't know whether to laugh or cry. I thought about the traumatic events of my past. The childhood sexual abuse I suffered at the hands of my father. The man who was supposed to protect me had hurt me more than anyone ever had in my entire life. He'd become my monster under the bed. The boogeyman in my closet. Thoughts of him, took me next to Anacostia Park.

It was dark and deserted at this time of night. I parked the car and got out, walking to the spot where I had stabbed my father to death over twenty years ago. Him being the very first person I had ever killed. Deep down inside that day, I'd known he wouldn't be my last. I got back into the BMW and drove to Queens Chapel Road in Northeast, D.C. The Beauty and Barber Palace Salon was still there. The sign over the entrance was different, a new one Philicia had installed, but everything else was the same. I sat and stared at the salon and remembered the two men I killed on the premises, before its construction was complete. Dearaye James and Thomas "Tommy Gunz" Murphy had both lost their lives on Queens Chapel Road for their roles in the kidnapping, rape and murder of my younger sister, Adirah. I tried not to cry but my eyes betrayed me. My traitorous eyes. Wiping my eyes, I pulled away from the salon before the past overwhelmed me emotionally.

I needed to let the past handle itself while I focused on the present and my current conundrum. As I drove towards Bladensburg Road, two things happened. My cell phone vibrated loudly, and I picked it up to see who the caller was. It was Najee, but before I could answer the phone, I realized I had just run a red light on New York Avenue. My eyes scanned the area and saw the police car parked across the street. I prayed that my inadvertent blunder had gone unnoticed by the cops. But my prayers weren't answered.

The police car beelined for my direction and fell in directly behind me. It activated its lights. I dropped the phone beside my seat and pulled the car over. My driver's license and registration were in my purse. I fished around inside the purse and noticed the gun. The Glock .40 was still warm with murderous afterglow. I knew my credentials were good, so I wasn't too worried about a search. After all, it was only a traffic violation. Two police officers approached the car. One on either side. I let the window down and smiled at the cop at my driver's side window. "What's the problem, Officer?"

"Ma'am, you ran the red light back there at Bladensburg and New York. Didn't you see the light was red?" the cop asked. He was brown-skinned and young looking. His hair was cut low in a taper and there were braces on his teeth. Ma'am?"

"Uh ... no, I didn't see it. I had looked down ..." I replied.

"Have you been drinking tonight, ma'am? I notice your eyes are red."

I shook my head. "I haven't been drinking at all. I've been cryin. I just lost my mother, and I was driving around trying to clear my head. I couldn't sleep."

"Sorry to hear that, ma'am, but I'm gonna need to see your license and registration, please. Is this your vehicle, ma'am?"

"Yes, it's mine," I replied as I passed the cop my license and registration.

"Well, just sit tight while I run your info. If everything comes back okay, I'll just issue you a citation and let you be on your way. Okay?"

"Okay."

I watched through the rearview mirror as both cops walked back to the squad car and got inside. Minutes later, they were both coming back to my car.

"Ma'am," the cop with the braces on his teeth said, "I'm gonna need you to step out of the vehicle."

"Step out of the vehicle?" I repeated, confused. "Step out for what?"

"You heard my partner, ma'am." This from the cop at my passenger side. "You need to keep your hands where we can see them and step out of the car, now!"

"Shit!" I mumbled under my breath and complied with the cops' command.

"Turn around, ma'am and please put your hands on the car. There's an all-points bulletin that's been broadcasted with your name on it. Something about being wanted for questioning. We're gonna have to take you in to the station."

As the handcuffs were placed on my wrists, I saw the other cop open the passenger side door of the car and began to search it. I closed my eyes and cursed under my breath. A few minutes later, the other cop stood up with something in his hand. He showed his find to the cop behind me. Without looking at it, I already knew what it was.

"Does this gun belong to you, ma'am?" the cop on the other side of the car asked.

"You can ask that question to my lawyer," I responded.

"You're absolutely right, ma'am," the cop behind me said. "You are under arrest for the handgun. You have a right to remain silent. Anything you say can and will be used against you in a court of law …"

Anthony Fields

Chapter 12

Carlos

The Lexus Sedan carrying Gunz parked beside my Maybach in the parking garage below the casino. Beside me, Benito stirred and awoke.

He opened his eyes, looked out the window and then back at me. "So, what's the plan, mi amigo?"

"Take Gunz and go to the Maggiano's restaurant on the first level of the casino. The restaurant is closed at this hour, but the owner, Giovanni, is inside waiting for you. Knock once and he'll let y'all in. Find a table in the rear of the restaurant, so that you'll be hidden from prying eyes."

"And what about you, Carlos? You speak as if you won't be there."

"I'll be there, old friend. Moments after you've all been seated."

Benito snorted. "What if there's some type of trap set? Are you prepared for that?"

The snort and condescending tone of Benito's voice vexed me. "Am I not always prepared? There are always safeguards in place. Even ones you cannot see. I am the same man, Benito, that I have always been. I know what I'm doing."

"You say you are the same man you have always been. Sometimes, I am not so sure, comrade."

"How so? Whatever is on your heart, old friend, please get it off," I encouraged.

"I do not understand why we are here. Unless it is really to catch Najee and kill him. If that's not the plan, then I am lost. The old you would have killed this Gunz guy and hunted Najee until he was found, then killed him, too. This decision to meet with the man responsible for the murder of so many of our friends and associates, befuddles me. Annoys me. The old you would be in the streets killing whole families to avenge the lives of our people that were needlessly taken. And I would be at your side. A gun smoking in both hands, just as I have always been. The action of these men ... Najee and Gunz, have beetle blood flowing in the streets, not conversations. What in the Virgin Mary's name could there possibly be to discuss with them?"

To be a leader of men, you must know every whim and emotion of the people under you. Having known Benito all my life and hearing the raw emotion in his words, I knew that I had to word my response carefully. I had to assuage his anger. "Benito, there are things at play here that you know nothing about. But soon, you will know everything, and you'll be able to understand my actions. Now, please do what I have asked you to do. I'll be at the restaurant shortly."

Benito exited the vehicle without another word or a backward glance. But his words remained inside the car as if he were still there.

"The old you would be in the streets killing whole families to avenge the lives of our people that were needlessly taken. And I would be at your side. A smoking gun in each hand, just as I have always been ..."

The old me. The old me would be covered in blood to avenge my people. The old me. I closed my eyes and remembered every word Benito had just said. Words that penetrated me like a knife to the heart. I couldn't help but to think about the decisions I was now making and why. But in order to understand the new me, I had to go back and visualize the old me...

****

Carlos Trinidad

The Beginning

April 1978

Bodies were everywhere. I walked through the house and stared wide eyed at all the men I had known and grown to love. As

I walked into the house's front door, there was Gordo. The heavy-set man was my uncle's best friend growing up. He told me the fun-niest jokes I'd ever heard over the years. He was a natural born co-median who had missed his calling. Looking at him now, I knew the world would never get to know about his genius and humor. The bloodstained shirt plastered to his chest didn't tell the story of his demise the way the bullet hole in his forehead did. Gordo's eyes were open. They stared lifelessly at something unknown.

If the eyes were truly the window to the soul like my uncle had often said, I didn't want Gordo's soul to witness the carnage and death that surrounded him. I knelt down beside his massive frame and closed his eyes. A few feet away from Gordo's body was his constant companion. Sitting up on the wall was Flacco. The fat man and skinny man as they were called, were never far away from my uncle Julio's side. Flacco was the tallest man I had ever seen. At six feet, five inches, he was affable, but spoke very little. His ever-pre-sent shoulder holster was always visible, along with one of the larg-est revolver handguns ever made.

Flacco's blood stained the wall as if he'd been shot while stand-ing and had slid down the wall. The hole in his forehead resembled a third eye. One hand rested in his lap, the other beside him on the floor. The large handgun he always carried in his hand. I walked on, until I reached the next body, which sat at the foot of the stairs. I recognized the man immediately. Pablo Estrada was one of the old-est men in my uncle's organization. He was in his middle to late sixties. Pablo was Colombian and had helped to raise Uncle Julio. He always had a cigar trapped between his lips. It was still there now. I could smell the sweetness of the cigar, mixed with the smell of death. The bullet holes in his neck, chest and cheek were easy to spot. I made the sign of the cross and climbed the stairs. At the top, I encountered two more bodies immediately.

Lying not far from one another were twin brothers, Victor and Viccaro Arrellones. The irony of their story wasn't lost on me. They had been born together and killed together. The twins, as they were called by everyone in my uncle's organization, were of average height, with dark skin and black curly hair. My uncle had told me the twins were of Cuban descent. They were killers who had been hired to kill Fidel Castro and had failed. They were being hunted by the Castro regime until friends of my uncle smuggled them off the island of Cuba. They'd left Cuba on a small dinghy with nothing in their possession but two handguns, two assault rifles and one hand grenade. I stood in my spot and remembered the twins in life, then moved on.

Down the hallway, there were bodies sprawled along the way. Juan Castillo, Eddie Cruz, Vasily Ochoa nicknamed the "Russian," Emilio Vasquez and Jose "Gato" Guerrera were all dead. As I approached my uncle's study, a sense of foreboding gripped me. The feeling inside my stomach told me what I'd find. I could hear a woman's cries. They were low, but unmistakable. I pulled open the big, wooden door and saw my aunt Rosalie with my uncle's head cradled in her lap beside his desk. Aunt Rosalie looked up as I walked in. The mask on her face was one of pure pain and anguish. She laid Uncle Julio's head down softly, then rose to her feet.

"You shouldn't be seeing this, Carlos," Aunt Rosalie said. "You shouldn't be here."

"I live here," I replied. "Where else would I go?"

In response, she grabbed my shoulders and ushered me out of the study. In the hallway, surrounded by dead men, Aunt Rosalie said, "You must forget about what you've seen here today, Carlos."

"How can I do that, Auntie? Everybody is dead. Look. Gordo, Pablo, Flacco, the twins, the Russian, Emilio ... uncle Julie," I broke down crying then. "They're all dead. How can I forget that?"

"You must forget it. Other men are on the way here to clean this place and remove all the bodies ... even Julio's. You can never speak of what you've seen here today. Not to anyone. Ever."

"But my uncle—"

"Julio Trinidad was not your uncle, Carlos. At least not your blood uncle. I am your only living blood relative—"

"That can't be! Uncle Julio said—" I protested but was cut off.

"Listen to me and listen to me good, Carlos. You are only thirteen years old, but it's time you learn the truth about who you are. You were born in Managua, the capital of Nicaragua in 1965. In the year of your birth, Nicaragua was controlled by an oppressive regime, led by a man named Ruben Chemmora. Your parents Carlos and Marilin Venegas, along with tens of thousands of Nicaraguans, who craved a more democratic political system, rebelled in the streets. The military arm of the Sandinista government quelled the uprisings quickly. When all was said and done, your parents, along with 350 other people were killed.

"The rebellion left thousands injured, illegally detained, tortured and missing. Others were forced into exile. I was a young girl at the time. Your father was a powerful man in Minocqua and was loved by many. His friends helped you and I get here to America. A man named Tomas Trojulo met us in Florida, then sent us here to this house in D.C. Men who worked for him, including Julio Trinidad, welcomed us to this house, to this city. Julio was only a teenager like me then. He raised you like his own and I became his lover. Do you know what drugs are, Carlos?"

Continuing to wipe tears out of my eyes, I nodded.

"Tomas Trujillo deals in cocaine. He is a very powerful man who works for other very powerful men. Julio worked for him still, under him but, a boss in his own right. Recently, Julio's man made a move against a man named Armand Rueles Sr. I don't know all the details, but men on Rueles's side were killedd by the Cuban twins. The killings you've just witnessed are retaliation for those murders. I called Tomas Trujillo."

This man named Armand Rueles had Julie killed?" I asked.
Aunt Rosalie nodded. "He might as well had killed him himself because the men who came here today worked for Armand Rueles."

"How do you know for sure that they were Armand Rueles's men?"

My aunt looked at me. Her eyes bore into mine, "I can see your father in you. I never noticed it before, but you have your father's eyes. He killed many Sandinistas. I witnessed him do it on several moccasions. There was always this distinctive look in his eyes before he killed. After seeing that look, it's not something that you can easily forget, When your father was angry, his demeanor would become calm. Sometimes, he'd smile, but he always had that look in his eyes. I cannot beliueve what I am seeing. But you have that same look in your eyes, Carlos. I see it clearly."

"How do you know for sure that Rueles's men killed Uncle Julie?"!

Aunt Rosalie's face went blank and she looked away from me. "Because I was here when the men came, Carlos. I witnesses the killings. Heard all the gunshots. Julio was betrayed by one of his men. A man he trustyed."

"Who was it? Who betrayed my uncle?' I asked attentively.

"It was Hecxtor Santiago. He let the men into the house. He unlocked the doors in the basement. The men who killed here today … like butchers, they were trained. They were swift, precise. Unrelenting. Hector he close to him. Made me watch the executions. He laughed the entire time. I can still hear his laughter in my head. There was a man with him; the leader of the killers. He had a tattoo on his face. He's the one who shot Julio. I don't know why I was allowed to live. Maybe because I am a woman. Whatever the reason, I was left to tell the story. I watched the killers leave. Hector Santiago left with those men. He told me why the killings and Rueles'were taking place. That's how I know the killers were Armand Rueles' men."

"One day I am going to kill Armand Rueles and all of his men."

Without uttering another word, I turned and went to my room. I packed two bags, then left the house. Ten minutes later, I reached my destination. Benito Alvarez was my best friend. I knocked on his door and minutes later, he answered.

"Carlos? Are you okay?" he asked.

"No, I'm not, Benito. My uncle is dead. I need a place to stay."

Chapter 13

Two years later ...

"Happy birthday, nephew," Aunt Rosalie sang.

"Happy birthday, Carlos." Raphael Pena, Rosalie's boyfriend said.

"Happy birthday, mi amigo," Benito chimed in.

"Blow out the candles, Carlos." This from Maria Santiago.

I closed my eyes and blew out the fifteen candles on the birthday cake. It was the second birthday I had without the one man I loved wholeheartedly. I missed my uncle Julio with everything inside of me.

"What did you wish for, Carlos?" Horace "Cheo" Santiago asked.

"He can't tell you that," Aunt Rosalie said as she cut the cake. "Or his wish won't come true."

"Which wish were you asking about, Cheo? I made two of 'em," I informed him.

"You only get to make one wish per birthday, Carlos." Maria scolded.

"Well, I'll be sure to apologize to the 'wish' police if they ever come to arrest me."

Everybody at the table laughed.

***

An hour later ...

"Cheo, every time I go to your house, your father is never home. What does he do for a living?" I asked as Benito put the adapter on the back of the TV, to connect the Atari video game console.

"Cheo's father is a powerful man. Ain't that right, Cheo?" Benito asked.

"My father is a good businessman. He sells insurance."

Benito and I burst out laughing.

"Insurance? He sells insurance?" I asked.

With a confused look on his face, Cheo Santiago said, "What's so funny about that? My father is a traveling insurance salesman."

Again, Benito and I laughed uncontrollably.

"I hope to be a good businessman one day, too. And sell insurance just like your father, Cheo."

"You'll need to be, Carlos Venegas. Taking care of my sister will take lots of money." Benito eyed Cheo suspiciously. "Why would Carlos need money to take care of your sister?" Cheo smiled a sly grin.

"Because Maria is in love with Carlos. She has been ever since she was a little girl. She promises everyone that she will marry the great Carlos Venegas one day."

"Is that so?" I asked, trying not to blush.

"It is so," Cheo said and laughed. "Everybody in the neighborhood knows this, but you."

"How old is Maria?"

"A year younger than you, Carlos. Fourteen."

"Well, I don't know if I will ever marry Maria Santiago, but one thing you just said will definitely come true one day."

"And what part is that?" Benito asked.

"I will be a great man one day. Feared and respected by all."

***

"Are you really going to kill Cheo's father, Hector?" Benito asked me.

I nodded my head. "I promised myself I would kill him, and I plan to keep that promise. At the party the other day, I made two wishes before blowing out the candles."

"I remember you said you did. What were the two wishes?"

"I wished for the courage to kill and the instruments I'd need to bring about Hector Santiago's death."

"And?"

"Both of my wishes came true. C'mon, let me show you."

***

"Where did you get these guns from?" Benito asked as he fingered the chrome revolver in his hand. "This is a beautiful weapon. It says here engraved on the metal, Taurus .357."

"When we moved into this house two years ago, after the deaths of my uncle and his men, I noticed these boxes down here in the basement. They had my uncle's name on them, but I never bothered them. For some reason, after I made those wishes the other day. I decided to come down here and look inside the boxes. I opened them all. Several of the boxes were filled with clothes, shoes and papers. But one box..." I pointed out the small box. "Had guns in it. All kinds of guns and the bullets for them." Benito grabbed the small box off the pile and opened it. "Look at all these guns."

"I already saw them, Benito."

"There are some beautiful guns here," Benito said, but turned the one in his hand over and over. "But I prefer this one. The .357."

"Well, keep it, then, Benito. It's yours. The bullets for it are inside the box."

Benito extracted a small box of bullets from the box.

I moved quickly, took the revolver from Benito and the box of bullets. "Let me show you how to load the gun, Benito. I don't need you to kill yourself before I kill Hector Santiago."

"How do you know so much about guns all of a sudden, mi amigo?"

I pushed the button back on the large revolver until the cylinder opened on it. Then I methodically loaded six bullets into the cylinder's chambers. Once that was done, I closed the cylinder with a smack of my hand. I spun the cylinder and passed the gun back to Benito. His eyes were glued to the loaded weapon of death.

"For the last two days, I've been practicing with every gun in the box. I have been up at night for hours, learning about each weapon. I think I know how to use each one, but I like the nine-millimeter handguns. It's what I'll use on Hector Santiago. I made two wishes, Benito, and they were answered. But I made a third wish. The day after my birthday. I wished that you would become my partner, Benito. My partner in crime. "What do you say, comrade? Did my third wish come true? Will you be my partner in crime?"

"We've been friends since I can remember, Carlos. We're already partners. In crime and everything else."

I smiled. "That's exactly what I needed to hear. But I have one more question for you."

"Ask it," Benito said.

"Do you have the courage to kill, Benito?"

"Whenever Hector Santiago is around, there are men with him. When you kill Hector, someone will have to kill his men. I guess we'll have to see, won't we, mi amigo?

***

The dark-colored Buick Sedan pulled alongside the curb in front of the house on Spring Road. It was dark outside, but the streetlights illuminated the block of row houses. There were two men in the front seat of the Buick, a man and woman in the backseat. I looked across the street at Benito who was hidden behind a large conversion van. His face came into view and our eyes locked. I nodded my head. He reacted as planned. Benito ran out from behind the van into the street. He stopped at the driver's side of the Buick and opened fire on the man behind the wheel. I moved with the quickness of a cat and reached the passenger side of the Buick in seconds. The man in the passenger seat up front looked at me. I smiled and fired the gun I was holding.

A mist of blood erupted from his face. Then gunshots came from inside the car. Glass shattered, and bullets whizzed by me. I dived for cover. The back passenger side door opened, and Hector Santiago spilled out of the car. I got to my feet quickly and prepared to shoot it out, but no bullets came. Then I saw why. Hector Santiago had run out of bullets. He tossed the revolver in his hand and reached into his coat. I closed the space in seconds and fired my gun. The bullet hit Hector Santiago in the stomach. His hand went to the wound as if it could stop the bleeding.

I walked closer to the doomed man. "You helped Armand Rueles kill my uncle Julio. Now, it's your turn to die."

Before I could pull the trigger again, I heard a female voice scream my name.

"Carlos! Noooo!"

I looked into the backseat of the Buick and saw my aunt Rosalie. Confusion etched across my face.

"Carlos … wait! I have to tell you something! You must listen to me!" Rosalie said loudly.

My confused look turned into an angry scowl. My thirst for revenge growing by the second as the realization of what I was seeing set in. I looked down into the face of Hector Santiago and to my surprise, he was smiling. I aimed my gun at his face and fired repeatedly until he was unrecognizable. Movement to my left caused me to swing the gun around. It was Benito joining me on the sidewalk. Aunt Rosalie exited the Buick through the open back door. She had to step over Hector Santiago's dead body.

Her eyes were filled with tears. "Carlos, you have no idea what you did. But it was my fault. Hector's blood is on my hands."

"It was you," I muttered, then spoke louder. "It was you the whole time. You betrayed Uncle Julio and let the men in the house. That's why you were spared that day. You were the enemy the whole time and Uncle Julio never saw your deceit, your betrayal coming. All these years, you've been parading Raphael around as your boyfriend, that was a lie. It was Hector Santiago you've been with. Why? Why Aunt Rosalie? Why did you do that to Uncle Julio?"

"I did it for reasons you'd never understand, Carlos. You're too young."

"Tell me! Why?"

"I did it for love, nephew. For love. It was Hector that I loved. It was always Hector. But he was married, and I couldn't have him to myself. Plus, there was Julio, standing in the way of our love. He was never going to let me go. With Julio gone, I thought Hector could then leave Miranda and be with me. But that wasn't the case and Hector told me that the day of the killings. That's why I was crying when you walked into the study that day. Not for Julio. My tears were for Hector. In my pain and anger, I told you Hector was the traitor. But he wasn't, Carlos. The traitor was me.

"I knew you'd try to kill Hector. I was banking on it. I wanted you to do it. But I never thought you'd wait two years to do it. In those two years, things changed. Hector made plans to leave his wife. They are… were getting divorced. Miranda was moving back to New Jersey in weeks. We were to be together. But now that can't be. You've ruined it all, Carlos. Ruined it all." Aunt Rosalie broke down crying.

Unmoved by her tears, I said, "it's not ruined, Auntie. You can still be with Hector."

"How can that be, Carlos? He's dead. You killed him!" Rosalie screamed.

I upped my gun and pointed it at her. "You both can be together in hell for an eternity." I fired the gun repeatedly, hitting my father's sister in her face with each bullet. The gun's pin hitting on an empty chamber snapped me out of my zone.

"She's dead, Carlos. Let's go. The police are coming."

Benito and I turned and ran off into the night.

Chapter 14

"Cheo and H.J. have been running their mouths to everyone who'll listen, about how they are going to kill whoever was responsible for killing their father," Benito told me two days after the murders on Spring Road.

I kept loading clothes into the washer in the basement of my house.

"Their father was a killer for two different organizations, mi amigo. Masquerading as an insurance salesman. I'm sure he had guns inside his home. Guns both of his sons have access to." When I didn't speak, Benito continued, "How long do you think it will be before someone who lives on that block and knows we're the killers, runs their mouths? Not to the cops, but to other people who'll then tell Cheo and H.J.?"

Closing the lid after adding detergent, I looked at Benito. "Do you really believe Hector Jr. or Cheo will really kill somebody?"

"Do you want to end up on the opposite end of their guns and find out?"

I thought about what Benito was saying and quickly decided my answer was, "No."

***

Saint Mary's Catholic church was packed with mourners for the funeral service of Hector Santiago, Sr. The service inside the church was somber and long. But it didn't matter to me, I'd wait. Dressed in loose fitting black slacks, a black shirt, covered by a black hoodie, black Nike Cortez tennis shoes and a black hat pulled down on my head. I stood across the street from the church and read a program from the church service. Benito leaned against the gate of a house adjacent to the church. His clothes matched mine. In his hand, too, was a program.

The double doors of the church opened suddenly, and people spilled out. Pallbearers with Hector Santiago Sr.'s casket in tow came next. I could see both of Hector's sons as they carried their father's casket. Four other men I didn't recognize, brought the total of pallbearers to six. I could see Hector Santiago's wife, Miranda, holding the hand of her only daughter, Maria. The sight of Maria in pain tugged at my heartstrings but didn't break my resolve. I glanced at Benito, who nodded and lifted the hood of his sweatshirt over his head. Then I did the same.

Hector Jr. was the lead pallbearer on the left side. His brother Cheo, the lead pallbearer on the right side. Hands on my gun, I crossed the street. I could see Benito marching towards the casket as well. Adrenaline took over as I jogged the final steps. I pulled the nine-millimeter and opened fire on Hector Jr. I watched his body drop and the casket fall as Cheo was hit by Benito. The casket hit the ground and turned on its side as people scattered and ran in every direction.

I took off running and became one with the wind.

***

Two weeks later, I walked past a row of houses on Newton Street and saw movers taking boxes to a U-Haul moving truck. The house belonged to the Santiago's. Outside on the porch sat Maria Santiago. I bypassed two of the movers and walked up to Maria.

"Hey, Maria, I'm really sorry to hear about what happened to your father and your brothers," I said and sat down on the step.

"People say the drug cartel killed my father and my brothers. They say my father killed someone important or stole money."

"Do you think that's true? The cartels being involved?"

"The newspapers have linked my father to a Colombian man named Tomas Trujillo. Him and other criminal organizations. They say my father was a hired killer. That my brothers were killed to end the bloodline at them. No more Santiago men. I have been taking care of my mother around the clock. I haven't had time to decide what I believe."

"Who's moving? You?" I asked.

"Not me. My mother is. I mean, we're ... she's moving out of this house. Well, so am I, but my mother is leaving D.C., running back to Newark."

"Newark? Where's Newark?"

"You really should go to school more, Carlos. Newark is a city in New Jersey. My mother is from Newark. She came here to attend school and stayed after meeting my father. But now that he's gone ... and my brothers are gone, there's nothing here for her but bad memories. She thinks leaving here will help her heal and not think about them as much. I never told you this, but I'm sorry about your aunt Rosalie, too. I don't know why she was with my father and his friends that night, but she didn't deserve to die like that."

Oh, yes, she did. "I know and thank you for saying that. It's been hard for me, living alone, but I'm learning how to deal with hurt, with death. I'll be aight. I can manage on my own. The house is paid for. I have a little money. I'm good. So, if your mother is moving to Newark, why aren't you?"

A defiant look set in Maria's face. "Because I'm from Washington, D.C. I don't know anything about Newark, New Jersey. My friends are here. My father's family is here. I'm staying here to finish school. My aunt Jasmine is letting me stay with her on W Street. Besides all that, how can I leave here when you are here?"

"Me? What do I have to do with anything?"

"What does this have to do with you?" Maria repeated. "It has everything to do with you."

"How?" I asked, confused.

"Because one day soon, you are going to be my boyfriend. Then my husband."

***

The coin pay laundromat on Sixteenth Street was filled with women doing laundry. Benito and I sat on two milk crates out front. I watched all the people come and go from the Tropical Sun lounge and convenience store across the street. Several men congregated on the side of the lounge.

"How do you know Armand Rueles owns the lounge, mi amigo?"

My eyes never left the man standing beside the lounge. "In one of the boxes in the basement, there were records of properties owned by Rueles and Tomas Trujillo. There were personal notes that Uncle Julio made about his competitors and associates. How he obtained all his info is beyond me, but it's there. The Tropical Sun belongs to Armand Rueles. So does Amarillo's Cafe on Decatur Street and the bicycle repair shop on Kenyon Street, near Georgia Avenue. He also has several strongholds ..."

"Strongholds?" Benito asked.

"Yeah ... strongholds. Places where his people sell the majority of his drugs. Places like 7th and T Street, 9th and S down to Rhode Island Avenue, 14th and W, Clifton Street on both sides of 14th Street, Kennedy Street, Morton, Euclid, Upshur, Allison Street, the Walter Reed area ..."

"Whoa ... that's a lot of fuckin' strongholds. Do you plan to wage your own personal war against all of those places?"

"Of course not," I smirked at Benito. "Do you think I'm crazy?"

Benito smiled but kept quiet.

"There are a few people left that I need to kill, Benito. Armand Rueles, if I can find him. The man with tattoo on his face and as many as Rueles's men as I can. Then and only then have I honored my promise I made to my uncle."

"As many of Armand Rueles's men that you can find?"

I nodded my head. "Starting with all those men over there."

***

Later that evening ...

Benito and I entered the Tropical Sun minutes before it was scheduled to close for the evening.

"Hurry up and make your purchases guys, you'll be the last customers of the day," the man behind the counter said.

"Okay, sir," I replied before pulling the hood over my head of my sweatshirt. I headed towards the rear of the lounge. Benito had separated from me and walked down a different aisle. Both destinations, the same. A TV roared loudly. A soccer game was on the TV. I could see the same four men who'd been outside the lounge earlier, huddled around the TV.

I eased out the Israeli Uzi submachine gun and envisioned Benito doing the same thing in the next aisle. The element of surprise was key to our success. The four men huddled around the TV never knew what hit them. Benito and I met up in the open space at the rear of the lounge and mowed down the men. They fell like bowling pins hit by a bowling ball. Calmly, I walked back up the aisle and looked over the counter. The man who'd spoken to us when we entered the Tropical Sun, cowered behind the counter with his arms over his head.

"If you want to live, tell me the names of the man with the tattoo on his face," I barked. "And tell me where I can find Armand Rueles?"

The frightened man behind the counter looked at me and said, "He'll kill me if I give you his name. I'll die if I tell you anything."

"Nobody will know that it was you who told me, Padre!"

"They'll know. I'm sure of it."

"Take the info to your grave then," I hissed before obliterating the man's face with the Uzi.

***

Emboldened by my ability to kill and get away, I talked Benito into making the thirty-minute trek to Decatur Street with me. We walked into the Amarillo Cafe and replicated the savage butchery that we put down on 16th Street at the Tropical Sun. After killing seven people, we walked out the cafe and headed home.

***

Days later …

"Can I have two tickets for *Rocky*, please?" I asked, pushing cash through the window.

The lady behind the glass at the Odyssey Movie Theater accepted the cash and in exchange, pushed two tickets through the window. Maria and I walked hand in hand into the movie theater.

"What's this *Rocky* movie about, Carlos?"

"Do you know who Sylvester Stallone is? I asked.

"Of course, I do. He's the man who played Rambo." Maria replied.

"*Rocky* is his new movie. About a boxer or something."

"A boxer? We might as well go and see *Godfather 2*."

"*Godfather 2*? I don't need to see that movie to see gangsters. D.C.'s full of gangsters."

"D.C. is also full of boxers," Maria said.

"You're right, but this one is supposed to be a love story, too."

Maria's face brightened. "A love story, huh?"

I nodded my head. Then smiled.

"Rocky, it is then," Maria said, faced me, then kissed me.

***

For my sixteenth birthday, instead of blowing out candles, I found more of Armand Rueles's men and blew their brains out. I was one year removed from wishing for a gun, then getting several to never putting them down. I had at least twenty murders under my belt and vowed to keep killing, until I either found Armand Rueles himself, or the man with the tattoo on his face. Between the money Aunt Rosalie had stashed and money Uncle Julio had left, I was well off. I lived in the big house on Monroe Street by myself, but I was never alone. Maria spent every minute she could with me at the house. I learned what love was through her eyes. The lens in which Maria viewed the world was totally different than mine. And that's what I needed. Her estrogen balanced out my testosterone. Whenever life threatened to turn me into an animal, Maria Santiago softened my heart and reminded me that I was still human.

***

The sun sat in the sky like a petulant child and gave off so much heat that the temperatures in the city reached over a hundred. Little kids played in the water coming out of the fire hydrant on Thirteenth Street. I sat on a wall and laughed while admiring the childish simplicity of it all, remembering my days as a kid. Benito and Manny Perez walked up and broke my reverie.

"Carlos, do you see that silver car over there by the curb?" Benito asked without pointing. "Near the corner store on Otis."

I looked up the street to Otis Place and saw a silver Lincoln Mark 8. "I see it."

"Well, it's been following us all day. Ever since we left the rec center," Manny added.

"Think it's someone from Armand Rueles's crew?" I asked Benito.

"Armand Rueles?" Manny replied. "Who the fuck is Armand Rueles?"

Benito ignored Manny. "Could be, but are you really trying to stick around and find out?"

"I'm not strapped. Are you?"

"Nope."

"Aight, cool. This is what we're gonna do. We need to split up. Manny you go with Benito. Y'all take off running down Thirteenth. Hit the corner on Spring Road and run behind Raymond Elementary. Hit some cuts and disappear. I'ma hit the alley behind me and run towards Fourteenth Street. Once I hit Newton Street, I'm ghost. Y'all got that?"

Benito and Manny nodded.

"Aight, go! Now! Run!" I shouted and took off.

I ran through the alley and saw Fourteenth Street ahead. As soon as I get to the mouth of the alley, I was blindsided by something hard. My body flew into the air and landed in the grass a few feet away. I tried to sit up, but I couldn't. I tried to look up, but my head was spinning. Seconds later, I blacked out.

***

I felt cold water hit my face and opened my eyes. My body ached, but the pain was bearable. I was on my knees and my hands were behind me bound at the wrist. I lifted up slowly. The room I was in was well lit. A man sat in a chair in front of me. I glanced to my right and saw two figures kneeling in the same position as me, arms behind them, hands bound at the wrists, their heads covered with hoods. Fear gripped as the pain in my body worsened. Without being told, I knew the two figures beside me were Benito and Manny.

I turned to face the man in the chair. His body was rotund, his suit was ill fitting, but appeared custom made. His shoes looked expensive, his socks, a light tan color that matched the suit. The man's skin was the color of caramel. His hair was dark and curly with streaks of gray. His hands sat on his lap. Each of his pinky fingers wore a large ring. His gold watch sparkled in the light.

"It's good to finally meet you, Carlos Venegas," the man said.

I was too frightened to speak.

"No words for me, ey? Maybe if you knew who I was, you'd speak to me. My name is Tomas Trujillo. Ever heard of me?"

I nodded my head. "Everyone has heard of you."

"So, you can speak. Good. For a minute there, I thought all you could do was kill. Sorry to have to get you here like this, but precautions are everything. Especially since you've proved to be a really efficient killer. I couldn't chance you trying to kill my men before we had the chance to speak." Tomas Trujillo called out to someone in Spanish. Seconds later, another well-dressed man appeared. They spoke in rapid Spanish. I understood every word. The man left the room and returned shortly with scissors and a bag. He handed the bag to Tomas, then used the scissors to cut the restraints from my wrists and the wrists of my friends.

I watched as Tomas Trujillo pulled my Israeli Uzi out of the bag.

"This is the Uzi you've been using to bring about so much death, ey? I remember it well. I gave it to your uncle Julio five years ago. He killed a man named Rios Sanchez for me on Harvard Street. Rio Sanchez had robbed a friend of mine. Your uncle killed him as a favor to me. A favor I repay today. I could kill you, Carlos Venegas, as a favor to Armand Rueles, but why should I do that, ey? I could use Armand Rueles and his soldiers to strengthen my position here and in Maryland. But no, I will not do that. I attended the funeral for Julio Trinidad. I saw what those butchers did to him beforehand. I saw you at his funeral, Carlos. Saw the grief that lived on your face, in your heart. But I had no clue such a young man would grow to be so vicious, so dangerous, so skilled at murder …"

"Someone had to make them pay," I said, anger replacing fear. Tomas Trujillo put the Uzi back into the bag.

"You have to be more careful where you hide these things, young Carlos. You don't want weapons like this to fall into the hands of your enemy, ey? As you say, someone had to make them pay. You're correct. And make them pay, you have. You and your friend here, the elusive Benito Alvarez. Son of Beneficio Alvarez and Anibel Dominiquez." Tomas rose from his seat and approached the figure next to me. He removed the hood to reveal Manny Perez. "And who might ya be, ey?"

"He doesn't have anything to do with this," I said immediately.

"I'll be the judge of that. Who are you?" Tomas asked again.

"Manuel Perez," Manny replied.

"Never heard of you." Tomas put the hood back on Manny's head. He moved to the next kneeling figure and removed the hood. It was Benito. "Ahh! Benito Alvarez. Good to finally meet you as well."

"Likewise," Benito answered, eyes shooting daggers at Tomas. Tomas Trujillo went back to his seat and sat down.

"Enough with the small talk. Let's get down to business, ey? I know who you both are and now you know who I am. Since you've successfully killed so many of Armand Rueles's men, you already know he sent the hit squad to kill your uncle and his men. Your uncle was a hothead. All brawn, but with little brains. He wanted to control Ledroit Park, Garfield Terrace, Morton Street and CHV. But those places were always Rueles's territories.

"He sent men at Rueles. Rueles retaliated by sending a hit squad. Your uncle worked for me and as upset as I was about his untimely demise, I understood the nature of the business. His move wasn't personal, it was business. Strictly business. So, I ordered no retaliation against Rueles. Then you came along. As incognito as you might think ya are, I learned you and Benito Alvarez killed Hector Santiago and his men. You also killed Rosalie, your aunt. She was Santiago's mistress. Her betrayal angered you. How can I not respect a man who'd kill his own family to right a wrong? When Rueles's lounge got hit, then his cafe the same day, I knew it was you. Weeks later, you hit his bicycle shop, then several of his dope houses. But herein lies the problem, Carlos Venegas, just as I know all these things, Rueles knows them, too. So, I have a proposition for you. Care to hear it, ey?"

I nodded. "I want to hear it."

"You've been killing Armand Rueles's men because you don't know where to find him. It's the man himself you seek, ey? The head of the snake. You want to cut off the head of the snake, correct? The man that sent the execution squad to your uncle?"

Again, I nodded.

"Good. I can help you with that, plus I have something else for you. I can help you avenge your uncle by giving you the man who actually pulled that trigger. His name is Omar Vasquez ..."

"The man with the tattoo on his face."

Tomas nodded. "The man with the tiger tattooed to his face."

"Your proposition. What is it?" I asked, knowing whatever it was, I'd agree to it.

"A simple one. You and Alvarez come to work for me. No more lone wolves or cowboy stuff. You kill for me, when I say kill and only when I say kill."

I glanced at Benito, who looked my way at the same time. He nodded his head.

"What if I refuse? Then what?"

Tomas Trujillo shrugged. "Then I let you go back into the streets and tell Armand Rueles where to find you. It won't be long before they find you and Alvarez and kill you both. Nothing lost and nothing gained. For me, at least. Is that your answer?"

"And turn down the opportunity to get Armand Rueles and Omar Vasquez? Never. My answer is yes. And Benito agrees with me."

"So, we have a deal, then, ey? You work for me?"

I nodded my head. "But I have a question for you, Mr. Trujillo."

"Please, call me Tomas. Ask your question."

"When I was running in the alley, what was I hit with that knocked me out?"

Smiling, Tomas Trujillo answered, "you were hit lightly with a car, Carlos."

"If I am gonna be working for you, I have to kill the man who hit me with the car."

"You're kidding, ey?"

The deadly look in my eyes answered that question.

Chapter 15

"The house is mucho grande. There are four levels. Terraces and balconies on every level. On the main level, there is an office inside the house. Inside that office are two guards with two Cane Corsos. The dogs are more deadly than the men who control them. The two guards with the dogs make rounds inside the gates every thirty minutes. One then checks the entire grounds from front to back, while the other checks the inside of the house from first level to the roof. Outside the gate is a security booth. It sits off of the main street as not to be seen by passersby. There are two guards inside that booth at all times. Their job is to monitor the streets surrounding the entire property and to open gates wherever and whenever needed.

"There's a vehicle ... a Ford Bronco, that patrols the perimeter of the gate twenty-four hours a day. There's always two guards in it. Both armed. All of the guards on the outside ... in the booth and the SUV can be neutralized easily. It's the two guards inside the gates that cause concern. The two with the dogs. Because once you've gotten onto the property, you need time to disable the alarm. At the rear of the property, inside the gates is a pool. Directly in front of the pool, attached to the house is a small metal box. You have to get to the box unseen, then jimmy the lock that's attached to the box. Inside that metal box are wires, different color wires. The wires are connected to the alarm.

"Every week these wires are changed, so no one can know which wires disable the alarm. Thereby, making your job of getting into the house a lot easier. If you cut the wrong wire, the security company gets a ping to their system, they alert the guards inside the house and the authorities nearby. If that happens, you'll be able to hear the alarm and thus make a hasty retreat and escape. But then your chances of getting to Armand Rueles decrease by a hundred. They will find the immobilized guards and the family will flee. Giving you no second chance. Comprende?"

Benito and I both nodded.

"But, let's say your prayer is answered and you disable the alarm, you could gain access to the house by door or window without it being heard. Somewhere near the garage would make perfect sense. Because of its proximity to the office where the guards hang out with the dogs. Kill the guards … and the dogs and you're home free. Armand Rueles's bedroom is on the top floor. He shares a bed with his wife, Griselda. At the top of the stairs to the left is one bedroom. Armand Rueles's twelve-year-old daughter sleeps there. In a room next to the others is the nine-year-old boy, his youngest child. Rueles's bedroom is on the other end of the hall to the right.

"It is up to you as to the fate of the children, but Armand Rueles and his wife both must die. If you decide to kill the children, there is but one remaining child left. Armand Rueles, Jr. he will not be in the house. He is currently living abroad. He's twenty years old and he will one day seek revenge for his family, should you be able to kill them. If you successfully complete your mission, then you get Omar Vasquez. Our associates can provide you with silencer attachments for your guns."

"Sounds good, Alejandro, but we will need a few more things from you," I told Tomas Trujillo's right-hand man.

"You are family now, Carlos, you can get whatever you need."

***

Three weeks later

Ruxton, MD

I decided to focus on the Ford Bronco with the two guards in it first. The good thing about the property surrounding Armand Rueles's palatial estate was that it was covered with trees. Trees made for good cover. Taking Alejandro up on his offer of silencer attachments was also pivotal. Benito stumbled out of the woods in front of the Bronco, pretending to be lost and drunk. The Bronco stopped on the path near the perimeter gate. The two men … guards got out. I appeared like an apparition, and we killed them both … quietly.

The security booth was next. One of the guards exited the booth. It was all the offensive we needed.

Splitting up, I caught the guard still inside the booth literally snoozing and killed him. Benito finished off the first guard. After dragging both guards out into the woods nearby, we scaled the gate. It didn't take long to find a spot to hide. Once in position, we waited until the guards with the dogs made their rounds. Immediately after they went back into the house, Benito and I made our way to the small metal box. Men in Tomas Trujillo's organization had spent weeks teaching Benito how to pick locks. He was inside the metal box in seconds.

"There are three wires here, mi amigo. One yellow, one green and one red. Which one should I cut?" Benito asked and smiled.

I closed my eyes and said a prayer to a heavenly being I didn't believe in.

"Say something, Carlos. We don't have much time. Which wire?"

"What if we just say fuck it and cut all three?"

"I'm not the sharpest knife in the drawer, but I was paying attention when Alejandro said that if we cut the wrong wire, the security company gets notified and so do the guards in the house. Stop playing around, mi amigo and say which one."

I peered into the box with a pen light. "I'm thinking the green one."

Benito chuckled. "And I'm thinking the yellow one."

"Cut the green ... no, the red one, Benito."

"Are you sure, Carlos?" Benito said, prepared to cut the red wire.

"Alejandro said to say a prayer, well earlier I said one. Cut the red wire."

Benito looked at me, shrugged, and then cut the red wire. We braced for an alarm to sound or guards to come running with dogs, but nothing happened for the next ten minutes we waited. Nothing.

"That was divine intervention, comrade."

"You don't even believe in God, Carlos. What do we do now?"

"Find somewhere to hide. Then let the guards do their thing. After they go back into the house, we'll break in. Close the box back and put the lock back on."

**

Alejandro's advice about the garage was accurate. We broke into the house there and minutes later, we were inside.

"The dogs are the danger, Carlos. Remember that. Kill the dogs first," Benito reminded as we crept through the house in search of the office where the security guards were.

Hearing noises alerted us to the office's location.

"Let's let them come out, Benito. The element of surprise is on our side," I told Benito, before crouching near a table and sofa.

When the guards appeared, before they could separate, we gunned them down. The dogs met the same fate. Armand Rueles and his family had no idea how close to death they were. Benito and I climbed the stairs. Quietly.

At the top level, Benito said, "Carlos, I'm not killing no kids, mi amigo."

"Nobody asked you to," I replied.

Following Alejandro's instructions to the letter, I found the twelve-year-old girl's bedroom first.

"Stay here." I whispered to Benito.

I entered the room. The bed was large. Too large for a twelve-year-old girl. The room was filled with stuffed animals. I approached the bed and saw the girl. Sleeping on her side, blankets pulled up to her chin. Her hair was pulled back into a ponytail. Held there with a light-colored ribbon. I pulled my gun and shot her twice in the head.

"What did you do, Carlos?" Benito asked as I exited the room and closed the door with a gloved hand.

"What needed to be done. The boy is next. I'll be right back." I walked into the bedroom next to the one I'd just left and did the same thing I'd done to the girl. I killed the boy. As I exited that bedroom, I realized I had no compunction killing anyone. Man, woman, child, elder … no one. Anybody could get it. There was no remorse in me, no empathy, no compassion. I led the way to the master bedroom.

"Do you kill the woman who birthed the children, Benito?"

Without a reply, he walked into the bedroom. I could see Armand Rueles was on one side of the bed and his wife on the other. I looked at Benito. He walked around the bed and stood over the wife. He pulled his gun and shot her in the head. I was now inches away from the man I'd dreamed of killing since I was thirteen years old. I gently tapped the elongated silencer on Armand Rueles's head.

"Wake up, Armand!" I said.

Armand Rueles awoke suddenly. His eyes squinted to focus. The light coming into the room from the balcony was all the light he had. It was enough. "Who are you? And what do you want?"

"What do I want?" I repeated. "I want your life, Armand."

"Who are you?"

"Look to your left, Armand. Your wife is dead."

Armand Rueles looked and saw the blood under his wife's head on the pillow. He looked up at Benito, tears formed in his eyes. "I know who you are. You look so young. You've been lied to, Carlos Trinidad. But that's of no consequence now. You've killed my wife …"

"And your children, Armand. Little Alex and Samantha are dead, too. You had my uncle killed and I am avenging his death. Do you need a moment to pray, Armand? I'll give you what the man with the tattoo on his face didn't give my uncle."

Armand Rueles smirked. "Omar Vasquez didn't kill your uncle. Nor did I send anyone. You have killed my family unjustly. I will be avenged, too, Carlos Trinidad. Do what you come here to do."

I did exactly that. I emptied the clip into Armand Rueles's face.

"Did you notice he repeatedly called you Carlos Trinidad?" Benito asked as we descended the stairs.

"I heard him, Benito. And like the way that name sounds. So, from this day forward, that will be my name. Carlos Trinidad."

***

"Do you know why there is a gate around most cemeteries, Carlos?" Tomas Trujillo said to me one day. When I didn't reply, he said, "Because too many people are dying to get in." Then he laughed hysterically.

I thought about what Tomas Trujillo had said as I threw my bag over the black cast iron gate, then threw the shovel over. Once that was done, I scaled the gate. Grabbing the bag and the shovel, I made my way to my uncle's gravesite. I knew where it was by heart, I'd been there so many times. The moon was full and high in the sky. My thoughts went to werewolves and whether or not they really existed. When I reached the spot where my uncle's tombstone was, I dropped the bag and started to dig a hole. In minutes, my arms started to ache, but I kept digging. The hole didn't have to be that deep. Once I was satisfied with the hole I'd dug, I dropped the shovel, then fell to my knees.

"Uncle Julio, I did it. I kept my promise. Everybody involved in your death is now dead. Aunt Rosalie, Hector Santiago, Armand Rueles and Omar Vasquez. I killed the man with the tiger tattoo on his face today. I killed his three children. I killed his wife as she left work at Providence Hospital. I killed his mother and father in their house on Shepherd Street. I love you, Uncle. I will always remember you. I brought a gift for you, too, Uncle."

I stood up and grabbed the bag. I reached into it and pulled out the severed head of Omar Vasquez. "I am going to bury his head here, Uncle, so that his eyes can see you for eternity and know that he fucked up when he took your life. Rest well, uncle. Your nephew forever. Carlos Trinidad. Goodbye, Uncle." I dropped the head into the hole and covered it with dirt.

***

"I don't know what it is, but there's something different about you, Carlos. Can't quite put my finger on it, but I can feel it. You're different in a way."

"I'm the same person, Maria. What do you mean?" I asked.

Maria held my hand as we walked through Rock Creek Park one evening. "Maybe it's me. I don't know. You just seem less stressed, less occupied mentally."

I played coy, but I know what Maria was talking about. After finally killing all the men who'd been responsible for killing my uncle, I felt better. I smiled more. Laughed longer and louder. It was as if the weight of it all had been lifted from my shoulders. "I guess I am less stressed. I just don't let things get to me anymore. I feel light."

"You feel light? Maria giggled. "I guess that's a good way to put it. Living with my aunt is cool and being close to finishing school makes me less stressed. Due to my grades in school, I get to graduate a year early. I'm motivated by my father and brother's deaths to be something great in life. Something they never accomplished. So, I guess I feel light, too. I feel stronger. I feel more mature. I feel like I wanna become a woman, Carlos." Maria stopped walking. She turned to face me. "I'm sixteen now. And I've loved you my whole life. I think it's time you made me a woman, Carlos. A complete woman."

Maria's tears started then. I wiped them away. I didn't say a word. I simply nodded my head.

***

"Be gentle with me, Carlos, please!" Maria said, naked beneath me.

"I will, Maria. I will," I assured her.

Slowly, methodically, I did to Maria what I had been taught by elder women who each had made me a man. I kissed Maria's lips as if they were candy coated. I sucked on her tongue, her neck, her breasts, her nipples. Maria moaned and squirmed beneath me. When I finally entered her, we became intertwined in mind, body, and spirit. I felt like we had become one. Two hearts beat in sync. I was in love like I had never known before.

After that night, Maria left her aunt's house and moved in with me. Life became a rollercoaster ride, with more ups than downs.

Chapter 16

Columbia Hospital for Women

June 1984

"It's still kinda early in your pregnancy, Ms. Santiago, but," the black nurse spread the clear gel all over Maria's stomach. She pulled out an odd-looking instrument from a cabinet, attached it to a computer of some kind and proceeded to rub the instrument around on Maria's belly. "We can still determine the baby's gender. Would you like to know whether it's a boy or girl?"

Maria looked up at me and smiled. I nodded and smiled back as I held her hand. "Yes, please tell us."

"The baby's heartbeat is strong. Can you hear it? Listen…" The nurse moved the instrument around as the images on the computer monitor changed.

I could hear the baby's heartbeat. The realization set in then, I had created a life. My seed had done the job to bring a little person into the world. I was excited. I was nervous. I was proud.

"I can hear the baby's heartbeat. I can hear it," Maria exclaimed.

"Beautiful, huh? Uh … Let me see here, have to find the right angle. Okay, there it is … let's see … you are going to be the parents of a baby … boy!"

"A boy? Carlos, do you hear that? You're about to have a son."

I leaned down and kissed Maria. "No, we're about to have a son. Do you think I'll make a good father?"

"I think you'll be the best dad in the world."

***

"I can't stop thinking about this shit, Benito. I'm about to be a father. I don't know shit about being no father."

"You didn't know shit about killing people either, but that didn't stop you from doing it, did it?"

"You got a point there. I'm just saying, though … my father was never around because he was killed when I was a baby. I had Uncle Julio, but that's not the same. I'm also concerned about the baby's life. Look at who we are, comrade. You and I are professional killers. Look at all the people we've killed. The fathers who couldn't protect their children. Children that I have killed. The faces of Armand Rueles's children and Omar Vasquez's children, they never leave my head. How can I feel good about bringing a child into this world, who may one day be killed because of something I did or might do?"

"Have you voiced these concerns to Maria?"

"How could I, Benito? Maria doesn't know anything about the life I live. It's as if I'm two different people. 'Carlos the boyfriend, about to be father' and 'Carlos Trinidad the killer.'"

"You should have thought about all of this, mi amigo, before you started making love to Maria with no condoms. Eight ball in the side pocket," Benito called out, before hitting the cue ball with the pool stick. The cue ball ricocheted off the three ball, hit the eight ball, which shot into the side pocket.

"Good shot, but you didn't say 'off the three ball,'" I replied, reached into the side pocket, retrieved the eight ball and put it back on the pool table. Right in the center. "Eight ball, corner pocket," I called out. The cue ball smacked the eight ball from an angle that sent it flying into the corner pocket. "You gotta call your shots when there's money on the line, comrade. And you gotta use English on your shots, that way you wouldn't need the three ball to put the eight into the side pocket. Pay me!"

Benito laughed. Then pulled out a wad of money and peeled off two twenty-dollar bills. He threw the money onto the pool table. "All techs in effect, I see. You win again. But speaking of English, our friend Manny Perez speaks mostly English these days and he's speaking it too much."

I pocketed the bills. "What do you mean, Benito?"

Coming around the table to where I stood, Benito leaned on the table right next to me. "It's been almost three years since Tomas Trujillo's men kidnapped the three of us. But for some reason,

Manny cannot seem to forget it. Can't forget what he heard in that room. He's been telling people that you and I are hired killers for Tomas Trujillo. That we've killed a hundred people …"

"A hundred?"

Benito nodded. "His number changes every time he tells the stories, but it's a hundred or better every time. He's also naming names, mi amigo. He's telling people that you and I killed Hector Santiago."

"How come I've never heard these things before?"

"Because, when you are not on a job, you are home with Maria, Carlos. You are not in the streets the way I am. I hear everything. Things you do not, cannot hear. It is my job to listen to the streets. It is the language of our survival."

"Stupid muthafucka!" I hissed. "Who has he been telling these things to?"

"That's the wrong question to ask, Carlos. Your question should be, who has he not told these things to?"

I turned to Benito with fire in my eyes. "How long have you known about this?"

Benito took his time answering. He pulled an apple out of his jacket pocket. He bit it, chewed, then said, "For months now. I tried to tell you on at least two occasions before tonight, but the only thing that has been on your mind is Maria and the baby."

"Is there something you need to get off your chest with me?"

"I'm doing it now, mi amigo."

"Am I not supposed to be concerned about my woman and child?" I asked.

"Of course, you do. That's not the point. The point is that in our line of business, your head must always be in the game. To use basketball terms, in this game, mi amigo, if we foul out, we die. Simple as that. I understand your concerns, Carlos, they are warranted. We've made a lot of enemies in the streets. You cannot let your personal life consume you so much. You have to stay focused on what we've done in the streets. Before it gets us both killed."

Benito was right. Everything he's said was on point. I had to stay focused or all I'd gained would be lost. "Okay, comrade. Point received. I'll remember what you just said. But back to Manny. I really don't need his words to get back to Maria. What do you suggest we do about Manny?"

"I think you already know the answer to that question."

***

"Do you remember the time we smoked that angel dust, stripped naked and ran up and down Park Road?" a drunken Manny Perez asked.

"I do remember that," I told Manny as Benito and I held him up, walking through Meridian Hill Park. "We were about eleven or twelve."

"Eleven," Manny insisted. "I'm sure of it. I had just turned eleven."

Benito looked over at me, his eyes saying things that his mouth didn't.

I nodded. The liquor we'd drunk was demanding to be released from my bladder. "Let's stop right here for a minute. I gotta take a leak."

Letting my arms go from around Manny's shoulders, I slid into the woods to relieve myself. As I finished urinating and zipped my pants, I heard the loud cough of Benito's gun. I thought I had no feeling, no remorse, but it seemed I did. Manny Perez was a childhood friend. Just like H.J. and Cheo Santiago had been. I hadn't felt no kind of way for them because of the hate I had for their father. But knowing Manny was dead brought a tear to my eye. He was more like family. Before leaving the woods, I wiped away my tears. Then moved on with my life.

***

When I entered my house, the lights were out. I figured Maria had just gone to bed earlier than usual. There were flowers in my hands and takeout food from the Ben's Chili Bowl. When I hit the light switch in the living room, the scene I saw gave me pause. I dropped the flowers and food and reached for the gun in my waist. "Leave your gun where it is, Carlos Trinidad, or you will die. Then in twenty-four hours, everyone you know and love, will be dead. Think about your unborn child."

I couldn't believe what I was seeing. Men had come into my home and shattered my wall of security and feeble sense of invincibility. My eyes scanned the room. Just as I had laid in wait in the homes of my victims, others had now done the same thing to me. My eyes found Maria and settled on her. She appeared small and waif-like seated on the couch, sandwiched between two burly Hispanic men in suits. Her hands were together and rested in her lap. Her cotton night gown covered her body completely and fuzzy slippers covered her feet. Maria was not bound or gagged and that gave me hope.

There were two other men standing on both sides of the living room, with guns in their hands. My eyes then settled on the man who'd just spoken. He looked young with the absence of facial hair. He was dressed in a dark suit and a crisp white shirt. His shoes were suede loafers, dark with a gold link chain across the middle of them. His hair was cut short and was as black as night. His skin was like vanilla. No jewelry adorned his wrists, neck or fingers. He sat alone on the loveseat in front of me. The silence in the room was palpable, intense. I was reminded of the night I met Tomas Trujillo.

"My name is Pedro Escobaro, Carlos. I am the head of the Medellin Cartel, based in Medellin, Colombia. I rarely make this trip to the states, but it's necessary in this case. An associate of mine was killed by you, and I want to know why."

"Associate?" I asked. "What associate might that be?"

"Two and a half years ago, Armand Rueles was killed in his home. His wife and children were killed in their beds as they slept. I was supposed to come here years ago, but I was in the middle of some more important things around the world. Forgive me for the delay, but better late than never, right? I've known about you and your companion Benito Alvarez killing Armand, but as I said before, I couldn't make the trip until now.

"I need an answer to my question, Carlos Trinidad. The one I asked moments ago. But before you answer it, please choose your words wisely. If I don't like your answer, the world will never know your unborn child ever existed. You and Benito Alvarez will simply disappear. Why did you kill Armand Rueles?"

"Because he ordered the death of my uncle. He sent men to his home to kill him. My uncle and all of his men were killed that day. Every one of them family to me. I killed Armand Rueles and his family to avenge my own. It was my duty to do it. And I don't regret it at all. That's my answer. If that is not a good enough reason for you, then take my life. It is yours to take. But, please cause no harm to Maria and the baby. They are innocent in this."

"By your uncle, you mean, Julio Trinidad, correct?"

I nodded my head.

"You have been deceived, Carlos Trinidad. You have been lied to and now I understand why that happened. Julio Trinidad was not killed by men sent by Armand Rueles. The man you call your uncle was killed by one of the greatest assassins Nicaragua ever produced. This assassin killed the Sandinista regime leader, Ruben Chemmera, when no one else could. This assassin came to the United States and killed with reckless abandon. This assassin killed for money, for power, for prestige. This assassin killed your uncle."

"Where is this assassin? Tell me so I can kill him."

Pedro Escobaro laughed. "Him? That assassin was not a him, Carlos Trinidad, and she is already dead. You killed her almost four years ago."

The realization of Pedro's words cut through me like a sword. "No, that can't be!"

Pedro Escobaro nodded. "It's true. I can be ... Carlos Trinidad. Or should I call you by your birth name, Carlos Venegas?"

"How do you know—"

"Your birth name? Simple. There's not a lot I don't know. My father, Javier Luiz Escobaro, knew your parents. Your father killed for my family. It's where you get it from, Carlos. Your ability to kill with no regard, it was a trait passed from your father to you ..."

"His sister, too. It's where Aunt Rosalie inherited—"

"Your father, Carlos Venegas, Sr. had no sister, Carlos. Rosalie Zampero was not your father's sister. She was your father and your mother's killer. She was paid to kill the entire family, you included. But for some reason, she didn't kill you. Instead, she brought you with her to the states after killing Ruben Chemmara. You were raised in a house by men employed by Tomas Trujillo. Tomas was the man who paid for Rosalie's and your escape to the U.S. He loved Rosalie. Somewhere along the way, Julio Trinidad, the man you call your uncle discovered Rosalie's secrets. He confronted her. That's why she killed him and all of his men."

"Aunt Rosalie, she told me…Tomas Trujillo told me—"

"They both lied to you, Carlos. Tomas Trujillo used you to kill Armand. You killing Armand, removed Armand from his path to become the main supplier of drugs to D.C. and the region surrounding it."

My thoughts raced a mile a minute. I thought back to Armand Rueles's last words.

"I know who you are. You look so young. You've been lied to, Carlos Trinidad. But that's of no consequence now. You've killed my wife ..."

"And your children, Armand. Little Alex and Samantha is dead, too. You had my uncle killed and I'm avenging his death. Do you need a moment to pray, Armand? I'll give you what the man with the tattoo on his face didn't give my uncle."

"Omar Vasquez didn't kill your uncle. Nor did I send anyone. You were lied to. You have killed my family unjustly ..."

"They capitalized off of your grief and your ignorance. And your age. Tomas played you like a fiddle. He became your puppeteer. Honed you into a finely tuned killing machine. Just like your father was. Just like the woman who betrayed him."

"Rosalie?"

Pedro Escobaro nodded. "Now, your vision is getting clearer. And mines as well. Ya were a pawn in a chess game, Carlos, and now I see, so was I. What is the least important piece on the chess board, Carlos?"

"The pawn."

"Correct. That's been you, the pawn. "What is the most important piece on the board?"

"The queen."

"That was Rosalie Zampero and you removed her. No queen can be truly powerful without what?"

"Her king," I answered, knowing where the conversation was going.

"Right, again, Carlos. That king is the most important piece left on the chessboard and it needs to be removed. Do you understand?"

"I do. Tomas Trujillo is the king."

"You are a very smart man, Carlos Trinidad. Remove Tomas Trujillo from the board and you win the game. You will by default become the most important piece. You will take over the territories both Armand and Tomas controlled. You will become our man here in the states. You will report directly to me. And grow very rich in the process. How does that sound to you, Carlos Trinidad?"

"Like music to my ears."

***

Late that same night …

Maria sat in a chair near our bed in the bedroom. Her hands covered her face.

Her soft cries filled the silence in the room. I stood in the doorway and let her have her moment. Suddenly, her hands fell, and her eyes found mine.

"I don't even know who you are," Maria said and wiped out her eyes.

"You've always known who I was, Maria. I haven't changed. Maria, please calm down," I chided. "I know you're upset by what you heard, but please let me explain."

Maria laughed hysterically. "Let you explain. Let you explain. I don't even know who you are."

"I'm the man you love. The man you've loved ever since you were a little girl. I'm the same man."

"Lies! All you do is lie. Saying you are the man I always loved is a lie. Who are you, Carlos? I mean, really … who … are … you?"

"I am the same—"

"Carlos Trinidad. Is that who you are now? The notorious killer called Carlos Trinidad?"

"Maria, you have to listen to me. You don't know everything—"

"I know enough. I know you lie to me. I know you keep secrets from me. I know that. And I never wanted to believe the things I'd heard. At the beauty salon, people talked. At the laundromat, I heard the whispers, at the bodegas, corner stores and at the grocery stores. I heard people speak of this man Carlos Trinidad and his friend, Benito. I tricked myself into believing there was another man named Benito, friend to a different man named Carlos. And tonight, I found out everything I've heard is true. You are the Carlos Trinidad people talk about. The feared killer.

"How could this be? How could you be the man I love and still be the man who's killed so many? The Carlos I know is Carlos Venegas. The kind, sweet, intelligent, gentle man that I love could not have killed a man and his entire family as they slept. The Carlos I know could never kill his aunt … wait, Rosalie was not your aunt. But still, you killed her when thought she was. I don't know you, Carlos … I don't know who you are!"

"Maria, stop this. Stop these histrionics. I am the man you know. The gentle, kind, peaceful man. I am the sweet, intelligent man you love. I am the man that will be your husband. I am the father of your unborn child."

"Husband? Father?" Maria hissed, then laughed again. "Are you insane, too? You are a hired killer, Carlos. A hired killer. A man that takes life, not protects it. I could never marry you! Never! I could never let you raise my child. You just agreed to kill someone else, Carlos. The man named Tomas. You agreed to kill him. Or should I say, 'remove him from the board?' And for what, to become a drug dealer? Take over territories? The man I loved would never do that. Never agree to kill to be a drug kingpin. I don't know who you are, but you are not ... Wait, if it's true that you killed Rosalie, then you also killed my father!"

"Maria, that's not true!" I protested.

"Whoever killed my father and his men also killed Rosalie. The police told my mother that. Before she left D.C., she told me. Their killer was the same person. And that person was you. I ... can't ... believe ... it!"

"I did not kill your father! You're traumatized. You're not thinking straight. Please! Don't think like that!"

"Carlos, please ... leave me alone. If you really love me, you'll leave. Leave for the night. Let me think these things through. I need to figure things out on my own. Give me some time alone. Give me a day or two. We'll talk then."

"Maria, please ..."

"Carlos, leave! Get out! Leave or I will!"

"I'ma leave, Maria, but I'll be back soon. Today is Friday. You can have the weekend to get your thoughts together. I'll be back Monday. We can sit down and talk, then. Okay?"

"Okay, Carlos. Just leave."

I moved in to kiss Maria, embrace her, but she wasn't having it. She backed away from me as if I had the smallpox virus. I was hurt. I was dejected. But I did as she asked. I turned and left.

***

"The entire time I was being used, lied to," I said, finally finishing my story as I paced back and forth in Benito's mother's living room.

Benito's arms were locked behind his head as he lay on the couch. For minutes, he remained quiet, but then he spoke. "So, let me make sure I understand what you're saying. Ya already know Julio wasn't your blood uncle, because Rosalie told you that the day he was killed. And today, you just found out not only wasn't Rosalie your father's sister, she's actually the person who killed not only your father, but your mother, too?"

I stopped pacing long enough to face Benito and nod my head.

"She was supposed to kill you, but she didn't. You ended up here being raised by her and Julio, while you thought they were a couple. Julio gets killed, him and his men and Rosalie tell you his killers were men sent by Armand Rueles, namely the tattoo face dude. You grew up thinking what she said was true. You and I kill a rack of people until we catch the attention of Tomas Trujillo. He gives up the info on Rueles and the tattoo face dude and the whole time, he knows we were killing innocent men—"

"And their families," I interjected. "Tomas Trujillo was the master manipulator the whole time. Here's what he did … I just figured this out. Pedro Escobaro said Tomas Trujillo paid for Rosalie and me to come here to the U.S. He put us up at the house where Julio and his men lived. They worked for Tomas. I'm assuming Rosalie started out messing with Uncle Julio, but then according to her, she fell for Hector Santiago. Somehow, both Tomas and Uncle Julio had to have been spurned by Rosalie.

"I think Tomas told Uncle Julio about Rosalie's true identity, knowing Uncle Julio would confront her about it, and Rosalie would kill him to protect her secret. By doing that, Tomas removed Uncle Julio from the chessboard. Rosalie lies to me and tells me the men who killed Uncle Julio was sent by Armand Rueles. And that Hector Santiago was a part of it …"

"But if Rosalie loved Hector like she said the night you killed her, why would she lie to you and include Hector? Especially if she knew that one day, you'd avenge Julio?"

"Good question. I don't have an answer for it, though. Maybe Rosalie and Tomas both were in cahoots … sending me on a dummy mission …"

"Well, it wasn't a dummy mission. You said Tomas wanted Armand Rueles out the way so he could step in and be the main connection to the Medellin Cartel, right?"

"Right. In short, it was all a game, every move orchestrated by Tomas Trujillo. Armand Rueles was innocent and so was Omar Vasquez."

Benito stood up and stretched. "And we killed them and their families. Plus, a whole lot of innocent men along the way."

I nodded my head. "Tomas Trujillo deserves the same fate, comrade. His family, his men. Are you with me?"

"Are you with me? Says the man who's about to be king. I was with you from the beginning, I'll be with you at the end. Let's do it, mi amigo."

***

"Welcome to the Dupont Circle pawn store," the old black man behind the counter said as we approached. "How can I help you boys?"

I looked around the display cases for what I wanted. I found it. "I'm looking for a good hunting knife," I told the man.

"Yeah, something like the one *Rambo* had in the movie," Benito added.

"Oh … you mean the one from the Sylvester Stallone movie. I caught that film. I have a few right there that you're looking at in the case. I got a few more in the back. Ain't much to hunt around here in the city. What're you boys gonna hunt?"

"Deer," I said.

"Bear," Benito said at the same time.

The man behind the counter looked confused.

"Bear and deer, sir. If we can find some. We're going out to the woods near the Shenandoah Valley. Heard there's plenty of animals to hunt out there."

"Okay, whatever you say, buddy. Let me get those knives out the back for y'all."

Chapter 17

Adams Morgan is an upscale enclave inside of Northwest, Washington, D.C. Tomas Trujillo owned and operated a Peruvian restaurant there called Eva's Patrone. On most nights the restaurant was open to the public and filled to capacity. But on Sunday and Monday, it was closed and used as the base for its owner's illegal operations. I walked up to the restaurant's entrance door and knocked. Johan Ramirez peeked at the door and then unlocked it.

He opened the door. "Que pasa, amigo?"

"Que pasa, Johan," I replied and walked past him into the restaurant. I immediately noticed there were Trujillo soldiers loitering around the dining area. Quickly, I did a mental count in my head. One, two, three, four, five. Johan made six. I'd been to the restaurant on hundreds of occasions over the years and all the people in Trujillo's organization know who I was. I walked straight to the rear of the restaurant where Tomas's office was. I knocked on the door and walked into the office to find Tomas behind his desk with the telephone at his ear. Alejandro Ochoa sat behind him by the back wall. Tomas motioned for me to sit while he finished his call. I gave Alejandro a head nod and grabbed a chair off the side wall. I sat down for about five minutes.

Suddenly, I grabbed at my stomach, feigning sickness.

"Are you okay, Carlos?" Tomas pulled the phone from his ear and asked.

"Yeah, my stomach, just a little bubbly. Must've been something I ate," I replied.

"The bathroom is down the hall, hombre. Straight back to the right," Alejandro told me.

"Gracias," I responded as I stood up and headed for the shitter.

I found the bathroom easy. I ducked inside and closed the door. Seconds later, I flushed the toilet for effect. After my second flush, I went to the window and unlatched it. Then I used all my strength to open it. It seemed to not have been opened in years. As soon as the window was up, I looked out and saw Benito. "C' mon, jump,"

I told Benito. Benito leapt the short distance and grabbed the window ledge. He pulled himself up and into the window. I flushed the toilet again. "In the dining area is six men. Paco, Juan, Toro, Gypsy, Rico and Johan. You gotta take them all out. I'll be in the office with Tomas and Alejandro. I'll handle Alejandro. You ready?"

Benito smiled. "Of course, I am." He pulled a mini assault rifle from under his sweathood. He pulled its clip out of his waist and slammed it home into the rifle.

"Good. Wait here for about five minutes and then slip out. Go straight to work. Once I hear the first shot, I'll kill Alejandro. Got it?"

Benito nodded. "Got it."

I washed my hands in the sink, then headed back to Tomas's office. When I entered, Tomas was off the phone.

"Carlos, my friend, what brings you to Eva's today?" Tomas asked. Scooting my chair up to a position in front of Tomas's desk, I eased my gun out and put it in my lap.

"I gotta problem, Tomas. It's with my woman. She's thinking about going to a city called Newark ..."

"In New Jersey. I'm familiar with it," Tomas said.

"She wants to go there to raise our baby. Her family is there. If she leaves, I'm gonna have to go with her. I know I have—"

"An agreement with me. I'm sure you are aware that as men, we must be men of honor, honor our word and all agreements?"

"I know that, but—"

"No buts, Carlos Trinidad, you are an important piece of the puzzle here in D.C. I need you here, not in New Jersey. Your skills at eliminating people ..."

I glanced down at my watch. When I looked up, the first burst from the Carbine M-15 mini that Benito had rung out.

"What the ...?" Alejandro shot up out his seat.

I stood with him, gun in hand. I surprised him when I gunned him down. My gun swung instantly in Tomas Trujillo's direction. A wide smile crossed my face.

"Carlos, what are you doing?" Tomas shouted. In the background, we both heard the unmistakable spits from the mini assault rifle.

"You speak of honor, Tomas, but you have none." I told the doomed man. "You're a hypocrite. A toad. A liar. A plain piece of shit."

"Carlos, I have no idea what you're talking about ..."

Benito appeared in the doorway of the office. "Johan was a good man, Tomas. He died valiantly. Juan, Paco, Toro and Gypsy died without knowing what hit them. Rico Sanchez thought he could fly. He was wrong."

Tomas's eyes darted from Benito back to me. You could see the fear in his eyes.

"You should've killed me when you had the chance, Tomas," I said.

"But why would I ever want to do that, Carlos? You're like a son to me."

I laughed at that. "A son, huh?"

"Yes, Carlos. It was I who provided you with shelter as a toddler when you first arrived here from Nicaragua."

"Julio Trinidad provided me with shelter, not you."

"But it was I who provided Julio with shelter and a means to feed ya. He could not have done that without me. If I wanted you dead, you would have been dead a long time ago. You must believe me. I never wanted you dead. Then or now."

"Well, maybe I misspoke. But you have used me, Tomas. Lied to me. Do you deny that as well?"

"What have I lied to you about, Carlos?' Tomas asked, visibly afraid.

"As my friend Benito so eloquently said it a couple days ago, you're asking the wrong question. Your question should be, what haven't you lied about?"

"I've told you no lies, Carlos Trinidad. I swear it on my mother's grave." I shook my head.

"Tsk. Tsk. Tsk. lying on your mother's grave. Have you no shame, Tomas? The night your man kidnapped me and my friends,

Anthony Fields

you told me Julio wanted to control Rueles's territories. You said
Julio sent men at Rueles, and Rueles sent a hit squad to Julio's
home. You called Rosalie Zampero my aunt and Julio Trinidad my
uncle. Then you sent me after Rueles and Omar Vasquez."

"You wanted to go after them. I didn't send you. I simply provided you with the information you needed to get revenge—"

"Tomas, please ... stop it! You lied about everything. You
knew Rosalie wasn't my aunt. You knew Julio Trinidad wasn't my
blood uncle. You knew Rosalie Zampero killed both of my parents
in Nicaragua in 1966. You helped her to escape Nicaragua after she
killed Ruben Chemmera. You loved her, wanted her. But for whatever reason, she wanted other men. Julio, Hector Santiago ... you
knew Armand Rueles had nothing to do with Julio's death. You
knew it was Rosalie who had killed him and his men, not a hit squad
like you said. Not Omar Vsquez. You knew I would be killing innocent men, yet you furthered the lie I had been told by Rosalie.
You did that to remove a threat ..."

"Armand Rueles and Omar Vasquez were never a threat to me."

"Maybe. Maybe not, but I knew you wanted Armand Rueles out
of the way so you could insert yourself into his position with Javier
and Pedro Escobaro, the family that heads the Medellin Cartel. Having Rueles gone would give you complete control of D.C., Maryland and its surrounding areas ..."

The look on Tomas Trujillo's face was priceless. "Who have
you been talking to?"

"Pedro Escobaro paid me a visit recently. He's decided a
change of power is required in your organization." I walked around
Tomas's desk and stood directly behind his chair. I put the gun into
my waistband. Then pulled out the Rambo-esque knife I'd purchased from the pawn shop. "It was you who orchestrated everything, Tomas. You and Rosalie both knew who my father was. The
skilled killer he was. You knew his blood was in me. Ya told Rosalie to feed me the lies about Armand Rueles. About the man with
the tattoo on his face. You pulled her strings and she pulled mine."
I leaned down and whispered into Tomas Trujillo's ear.

134

"The truth always comes to the light, Tomas. When you get to hell, give Rosalie my regards." I plunged the knife into the fleshy jowls of Tomas's neck. Then I cut and sawed until I held his completely severed head.

"I'm starting to think you enjoy doing that shit, mi amigo. Shall I start to call you Carlos the Butcher?" Benito asked. "C'mon, let's get out of here."

I laughed out loud, then sat the severed head on the desk. "Call me whatever you want, comrade, but soon you'll be calling me, boss."

"Whatever. Come on, let's go, before your head gets any bigger."

"Okay, but first let me cut his heart out. I'm taking them both with me."

***

For the second time in two years, I went to Uncle Julio's grave and dug a hole. I put Tomas Trujillo's head and heart in the hole.

"Uncle Julio, I put Tomas Trujillo's head in your hole so you can keep an eye on him better this time. It's over now. The people included in your death are all dead. Rest well."

***

When I got to the house on Monday morning, Maria was gone. From the way the bedroom looked I could tell she hadn't taken much with her. The bed was made and unslept in. It looked the way it had before I left on Friday. I searched the whole house for any sign of her or any clue as to where she had gone. I found none. I called her aunt Jasmine and all of her friends. No one had talked to Maria. The one person in life I loved more than myself was gone. And there was nothing I could do about it. As days turned to weeks and weeks into months, the pain in my heart never subsided. All I could do was pick up the pieces and move on.

Shipments of cocaine, marijuana and heroin poured in from Colombia. Me and Benito built our organization from the ground up. All the while hoping that one day, I'd find Maria. One day, I'd find my son.

Without Maria and the baby to remind me of my humanity, I became ruthless, barbaric and even more animalistic. I was a different Carlos Trinidad. That was the old me.

The Present ...

2015

The phone in my hand vibrated. The caller was Benito. "I'm coming in a minute. I'm calling Najee now." I ended that call and made another. "Najee?"

"Yo," he replied.

"On the first level of the casino is a restaurant. Maggiano's. Go there now. Men are there as we speak, waiting for you. I'll be there momentarily."

"Is Gunz with you, son?" Najee asked.

"He's already at the restaurant. See you in a minute."

I disconnected that call and then patted my pocket where the envelope was. The contents of it were needed to make the meeting go more smoothly. My thoughts were suddenly flooded with thoughts of Maria Santiago. The woman I loved. The woman whom I grew to hate for leaving like a thief in the night and taking my unborn son with her. Maria Santiago. The woman whose death I had ordered.

Chapter 18

Najee

There were two Hispanic men in suits standing at the entrance to Maggiano's. They both eyed me with hate in their eyes. If looks could kill ... They allowed me to walk right into the restaurant. The first face I saw looking at me was Gunz. I smiled, but before I could head his way, a hand reached out and gripped my shoulder, stopping my forward progression. I turned around slowly to free myself from the man whose hand was on me. "You gon fuck around and lose that hand, yo," I hissed.

The man was obviously Hispanic. He was my height, stocky and dark. His dark, curly hair was peppered with gray and tempered on the sides. His suit was expensive looking, his shirt was gray, his tie the same color. He reminded me of the dude who played the role of Santana in the movie, *American Me*. A wicked smile was plastered to his face. "Blowing up Salazar's in Georgetown was creative, but that doesn't make you a savage. Killing innocent people in a cafe, even a fifteen-year-old boy doesn't make ya a gangsta. Drive-by shootings are for gang bangers who are afraid to get up on their targets and kill them. I've killed more people than you can ever imagine, so excuse me if I don't appear afraid or impressed by you. Nor do I believe that you are man enough to take my hand. After you've had your talk with Carlos, we'll see if you can or not."

"I'm looking forward to it, son. Believe that," I said through clenched teeth.

"Turn around, tough guy. I forgot to frisk you. No weapons allowed at this meeting."

I snatched away from the man. "Says who, son? I never agreed to that."

"Says me," a voice says from behind me. A voice I recognized immediately. It was the voice from the phone. I turned to see a man standing there. In the flesh, the man, the myth. "Carlos Trinidad?"

"Benito, go and have a seat at the table over there," the man said and pointed. "Let me try and persuade my friend Najee to give me his gun." After the stocky dude left, the man who I assumed was Trinidad, smiled and said, "Give me your gun."

"Are you Carlos Trinidad?" I asked.

"I am. Now that you know that, can I have your gun?" Carlos replied.

"Now that I know who you are, my answer is definitely the same. Not on ya life will I disarm myself. Every man in this room besides Gunz is packing. I'll pass."

Carlos smiled. "Okay, Najee, you can keep your gun. I respect that. In your position, if it was me, I wouldn't willingly give up my gun either. Sit down with me and let's talk."

"Talk about what, yo? You could've tried to talk to me before you tried to end my life."

"That's what we need to talk about. You think the people in that black Cadillac Escalade that fired those shots and hit Angel, was my people. It wasn't. I had nothing …"

"I don't believe that, yo. Real talk."

"Najee, please, sit down and let's talk like men. Hear me out. That's all I ask."

My temper flared. I thought about everything that had happened up until that moment. "Now, you wanna ask? A few hours ago on the phone you were demanding and insisting, threatening my family and shit. I don't even know why I agreed to come …"

Carlos Trinidad stepped closer to me. "I'm trying to be the bigger man, Najee, but you're pushing it. Please don't mistake my kindness for weakness. When my smile turns into a frown, there's no coming back from that. I used the tactics to get you here because I didn't want to spend the next few days finding you. And make no mistake about it, I would have found …"

I looked Carlos right in the eye. "Find me? I wasn't hiding, son. I was the one who came after you, remember?"

"Najee, listen to me carefully. This cannot become a pissing contest between us. That's not why I wanted to see you, to talk to you. You have already crossed lines with me … with my organization that no one has ever crossed. Ever! All the people who have attempted to cross me, are all dead men. If I choose, I could have you killed," Carlos snapped his fingers. "Just like that. But that's not …"

"I'm glad you think that, son. I've been slept on all my life. All the people who've slept on me are all dead men. I can pull this gun." I snapped my fingers. "Just like that and we can all die in this muthafucka. Fuck it!"

Carlos Trinidad laughed, breaking the tension. "Brave, cocky, conceited, impetuous … just like I was at your age. You stare death in the face and thumb your nose at it. You get that from me."

"What? Come again, son?"

"Since you don't want to sit and talk, fine. We'll have the conversation standing up." Carlos called out to his man, Benito and told him to come over to us. "Our friend here doesn't seem to like tables and chairs, so I'll just say what I came here to say standing. Benito, you asked me why I called this meeting and what's here to talk about. Najee here wants to know the same thing. Here's my answer. I called this meeting to talk to Najee because he's my son."

"What?" we both said in unison, me and Benito.

Carlos continued. "It's true. Benito, Najee is Maria's son."

"Maria Santiago?" Benito asked.

Carlos nodded.

"Wait … how do you know my mother?" I asked, confused.

"It can't be," Benito said as he stared at me. "Out of all the people …"

"Look at him, Benito. Najee looks just like I did at his age. Look."

"I can't believe this shit," Benito muttered over and over.

"Hold on … your son? My father? You know my mother … this is bullshit."

"I'm not bullshitting, Najee. If I was, one of us would be dead by now," Carlos said. "Let's all sit down and let me show y'all proof of what I'm saying."

Without another word, I turned and headed for the table where Benito had just been sitting. Once there, the three of us sat down. Me, across from Carlos, Benito closer to him.

"The proof, son. I need to see it," I said, breaking the silence.

"Your mother, Maria was from ..." Carlos started.

"Here in D.C.," I interrupted. "I already knew that."

"That's not what I was about to say. Your mother was originally from El Salvador. Her whole family was from there. Her grandparents came to the States and lived in Newark, New Jersey. Her mother ... your grandmother was raised in Newark. She came to D.C. to attend nursing school at Martha Washington. She met Hector Santiago here. When your grandmother found out she was pregnant with Hector Jr., she moved back to El Salvador. Hector followed her there. Your uncle Horacio, who we called ..."

"Cheo," I said, remembering my mother's stories. "My grandmother nicknamed him Cheo after her father."

Carlos nodded. "When your mother was one years old, the family moved back to the states, here to D.C. Benito and I grew up with your uncles and your mother. In 1980, your grandfather, two of his friends and my aunt Rosalie were gunned down as they exited a car on Spring Road in Northwest. My aunt was allegedly having an affair with your grandfather. Weeks later, at your grandfather's funeral, men ambushed and killed ..."

"Both of my uncles. They were pallbearers for my grandfather."

"Correct. After the deaths of your grandfather and uncle, your grandmother moved back to Newark. But your mother stayed in D.C., moved in with ..."

"My great aunt Jasmine. She died in 1998 of ovarian cancer. She was my grandfather's sister."

"I didn't know that. I'm sorry to hear Jasmine is deceased. I liked her. May she rest in peace," Carlos said. "Your mother was one year younger than me, but we were always friends growing up. When your grandmother left for Newark, Maria often felt I was all that she had left. We became more than friends. At seventeen years old, she became pregnant with you. We were supposed to marry. I was twelve feet deep in the streets, building my legacy and Maria disapproved of my lifestyle. Then people started to spread all sorts of rumors about me. Those rumors reached your mother's ear.

"By then we were living together in a house my aunt Rosalie left behind. I came home one day, and your mother was gone. She was three months pregnant and meant the world to me. I thought that she'd come back after a while, but she never did. I didn't know where she went or who she was with. I looked and searched but couldn't find Maria. I suspected she went to Newark, but I couldn't find her or your grandmother there. A few years later, I received her first letter." Carlos pulled an envelope from inside his suit jacket. He extracted from the envelope a single sheet of paper and passed it to me.

My heart raced as I grabbed the paper and began to read …

Dearest Carlos,

I pray this letter has reached you in good health. I pray you don't hate me, and you can understand my reasons for leaving you. The things I heard that night from the man from Colombia, rattled me more than you will ever know. The guns, them threatening you, me and the baby, that was too much for me. The things he said which confirmed what I'd been hearing about you in the neighborhood, I couldn't get them out of my head.

After hearing you agree to kill someone and to become a drug dealer, I realized you were not the Carlos I fell in love with. You had ceased being Carlos Venegas and had become the infamous Carlos Trinidad. A man I didn't know. Couldn't get to know. I decided right then that I couldn't raise my son ... our son around that man. So, I left. The way I left was wrong. But it was the only way for me to actually go through with it. It was cowardly, I know. What can I say? I'm a coward. I was scared to death of Carlos Trinidad. I still am.

I decided to write you this letter to let you know your son and I are both alive and well. Your son, Carlos Jr. was born healthy. Seven pounds, eight ounces. He's walking and talking like he's been here before. He's the spitting image of you, Carlos. Your eyes, ears, hair, facial expressions, he has them all. One day, when he's old enough to know the truth, I'll tell him my story, my truth.

You were the first man I ever loved, outside of my father and brothers, and that can never change. But I have met a man, Carlos, and I love him. He's a good man and he loves our son as if he were his own. His name is Nadeem and we plan to marry soon. I am thinking about converting to Islam. Nadeem has taught me a lot about the world's second largest religion. I plan to raise CJ, that's what I call Carlos Jr., as a Muslim as well. I'd been wanting to reach out to you, but I was afraid. I finally built up the courage to write this letter. I pray you can find it in your heart to forgive me for hurting you, leaving you. But again, it was for the best. In closing, please don't try to find us, because I've made us hard to find. Trust me, it's better this way. Take Care, Carlos.

Love Always,
Maria S.

Tears filled my eyes and fell. I was overwhelmed with emotion. It was as if I could hear my mother's voice as she wrote the letter. I stared at her loopy cursive handwriting and knew that she had written it. I couldn't believe my eyes. The man sitting across the table from me was my father. My biological father. I looked up at Carlos and it was as if blinders fell out of my eyes. He did look just like me. All of our features were the same. He was me, in twenty years. "I can't believe this."

Carlos removed another sheet of paper and a photo from the envelope. He pushed them across the table towards me. "Your mother sent me that letter and picture almost eighteen years ago when you were ..."

I had picked up the photo and looked at it. I couldn't believe my eyes. "Twelve years old. We were in Wildwood, New Jersey at an amusement park. Salimah and I had just finished eating popcorn and ice cream. It was Salimah's eleventh birthday ..."

Chapter 19

Benito Alvarez

"I remember when we took these pictures. My fath ... Nadeem took us to that amusement park to celebrate Salimah's birthday. We all knew that being Muslim, nobody celebrates their birthday, but Salimah was his only daughter and Nadeem spoiled her. He spoiled both of us. Then two months later, they were gone," Najee said with fresh tears brimming his eyes. "Both killed in a boating accident. Their ferry sunk while crossing the Hudson River. That was the most painful time of my life."

I gazed at Carlos, who never met my gaze. I wondered to myself, how many other secrets my oldest friend had kept from me. Najee called it a boating accident, but he was wrong. Carlos knew that. Especially since I was the person who had planted the bomb in the ferry boat that sunk it. Carlos had never told me Maria Santiago would be on that boat. But he knew it. He had to have known it. And I had never asked who'd be on that ferry. Like a good soldier, I had simply followed orders.

That day, so many years ago, came back to mind. The bomb that I had transported to Newark and placed it on the ferry boat at the bottom near the engine room. There was a timer on the device that I had set for a specific time. An exact time that I had gotten from Carlos. When the bomb exploded, sinking the ferry, it went undetected in the wreckage. Fifty people had lost their lives that day. I'd read about it in the newspaper the next day as I rode the Amtrak train back to D.C. Carlos must have learned that Maria took that ferry daily and at what time. He knew she and her husband would be on it when he sent me to explode it. Jealousy and hate had to have consumed him and guided his head. But he never let me in on his secret. I started to wonder just how well I really knew Carlos. Or if I did at all.

Najee picked up the second piece of paper and began to read. I couldn't stop staring at him. He had to be at least thirty. The more I looked at him, the more I saw a younger Carlos.

"She wanted you to see me. How much I looked like you. She wanted you to see us ... to see me happy. She must have sent you this right before she died," Najee said.

Carlos pretended to wipe his eyes. "I had no idea that your mother was dead. I just thought she never wrote to me again. I loved her, then I hated her, but I never wished death on Maria. May she rest in peace."

I dropped my head and shook it. I couldn't believe what I was seeing, what I was hearing. Carlos was lying through his teeth. He'd known that Maria Santiago was dead. He'd sent me to kill her.

"As long as I remember," Najee continued, "My name has been Najee. I don't ever recall being called Carlos Jr. I do vaguely remember being called 'CJ' but I thought I was buggin' out. And what's really crazy is that I always thought Salimah looked more like our father than me. And I realized as a teenager that I didn't look like my mother. I asked my grandmother one day, who I resembled in the family, and she told me I looked like my father. Back then I thought she meant Nadeem Bashir, but now I understand she meant you." Najee looked at Carlos with a serious look on his face and asked, "So, you knew you had a son out there somewhere and did nothing?"

"Of course, I did something. I looked for you, for your mother, but I couldn't find her. You read what she wrote in the letter. She made y'all hard to find. After a while, I gave up. But I always knew I'd see you before I left this earth. And look what happened?"

"When did you know who I really was?" Najee asked.

"It wasn't until after you initiated your war against me. When I had to put a face with the name of the man who was causing us great harm. Speaking of which, like I tried to tell you earlier, I spoke to Gunz. He told me what happened to make you think it was my organization that made an attempt on your life. He told me about the incident outside of Angel's store. How shots fired from a black Cadillac Escalade hit Angel and you assumed the bullets were for you. From us. The people shooting at you that night wasn't us. You have to believe me."

"If it wasn't you … your people who tried to kill me, then who the hell was it?"

Carlos turned and looked at me. I shook my head and shrugged. "It wasn't us. I put that on my life. I don't know who that could have been. You must have made other enemies in D.C. beside us."

Najee looked between Carlos and me. "Did y'all kill Doodie and Faceman?"

I nodded my head. "We did … Well, I did. I killed Doodie, but it had nothing to do with you. Doodie owed us money. Once he was able to get another source of cocaine, he refused to pay the debt. That's why he was killed. Faceman was different. His death was personal. I adopted Face like he was a part of our organization. When he went broke several years ago, I fronted him a hundred kilos to get back on his feet and waited months until he could satisfy the tab. When he agreed to buy cocaine from you, it was an act of betrayal to me. I killed him personally. Carlos knew nothing about it until after I did it."

"Shit!" Najee exclaimed. "I thought that …"

"We already know what you thought. You thought I wanted you dead. You were wrong," Carlos said.

"You gotta understand why I thought that. Because Angel kept filling my head with all that *48 Laws of Power* shit. Be careful who you offend … pick your opponents wisely … Carlos Trinidad runs the city and he's gonna notice someone is moving major weight in the city. All that shit."

"I can't say that Angel was wrong for trying to warn you, because she was right. I do run shit in the region, and I did notice there was cocaine … large amounts of cocaine being sold in D.C. without my permission. Actually, it was Benito …"

"Oh … shit!" Najee exclaimed suddenly.

"What?" Carlos asked.

"I just thought about something else you don't know. Something that you must know."

"And what's that?"

"I'm not your only child," Najee revealed.

"I sat in silence and listened to the conversation around me and started to feel like I was on the set of a talk show. Like I was on an episode of *Maury Povich*.

"Not my only child?" Carlos repeated. "What do you mean by that?"

"Exactly what I just said. Now that we know I'm your son, I'm not your only child. Angel has a daughter. Beautiful daughter. Beautiful little girl named Aniyah. She's your daughter."

All we were missing was for someone to exit the kitchen and hand Carlos a DNA result. Then Maury Povich saying, "Carlos, you *are* the father!"

"But how could she … it's been almost … what ten years … since …?"

"Listen, Angel told me that she got work from you. That some niggas that she sold that work to got jealous and kidnapped her sister, then raped her and killed her. That made her body some shit. Her best friend Fatima ratted her out to the cops, got her locked up. She told me you pulled some strings and got her friend …"

"If Angel told you all of that, she talks too much," Carlos said.

"I can dig why you might say that, but listen, she told me that you got her friend hit while in the witness protection program. That helped her beat the case. When she got out, she met you at …"

"The Bally's Fitness Center in Prince George's County. I remember."

"Well, you should also remember y'all fucked in the sauna that night and you hit her bareback and busted one in her. Nine months later, she had your baby. A girl named Aniyah, who turned nine a few months ago. Turns out she's my little sister. Ain't that crazy?" Najee said and smiled.

"But she never told me. I wonder why?"

"Angel didn't want to complicate things. Didn't want you to think she was trying to trap you into something because of who you are. Her words, not mine. Verbatim."

"I have a daughter," Carlos said to himself.

"All this shit is crazy for the last month or so, I have considered you as my enemy and now I find out that you're my father. On top of that, I been fucking my little sister's mother. Shit wild, son. Facts."

"I need to talk to Angel. To see this little girl. My daughter. Where is she?"

"Beats me. I haven't talked to her or seen her in days. I was beefing with her. Decided to bury the hatchet. Been calling her all night. Nothing. Her phone's been going to voicemail."

"Give me her number. Let me try. Maybe she doesn't want to talk to you. Here," Carlos said, passing Najee his phone. "Put her number in or dial it. Either one."

Suddenly, I had the desire to leave. Everything that I had heard was a bit much for my brain to decipher. I was confused. I was a little upset. I couldn't believe the latest turn of events. I stood up. "If you two will excuse me, I'ma step outside for a little air."

I walked away from the table. At the entrance to the restaurant, Enrique stopped me.

"I don't know what's going on, Benito, but you gotta let me kill one of them. To avenge Roberto, Javier, Ortega, Little Manuel …"

"Just be patient, Enrique. It may not be tonight, but you'll have your revenge. I promise you that." I glanced back over my shoulder at Carlos and his son, then exited the restaurant.

Chapter 20

Gunz

I was a spectator in the real-life version of the game of life. From my seat in the restaurant, I watched everything that transpired from the time Najee walked into the Maggiano's front door. I couldn't hear what was said, but I saw the heated exchange between Najee and the man named Benito. I saw Carlos Trinidad appear out of nowhere and calm the situation. I saw him and Najee talking, then Carlos calling Benito over. The three of them stood and talked, then they all went to a table and sat. I watched Najee read something that he was given by Carlos Trinidad. Then a long discussion ensued.

A few minutes ago, I saw the man named Benito leave. The expression on his face as he left looked like irritation. Just as I was getting both bored and tired, Najee and Carlos Trinidad headed my way. Najee leading the way. I tried to read his face, but surprisingly, I couldn't. I stood up when Najee was in front of me. "What's the deal, baby boy? What the hook gon be?"

"Ayo, son, you ain't gon believe this shit when I tell you?" Najee replied, shaking his head.

I looked into Carlos Trinidad's face and couldn't read him, either. Then the murders he had committed hours ago came to mind and I wondered would that be my fate as well. "I'm not gon believe what?"

Without saying a word, Najee handed me a folded piece of paper. I unfolded it and saw it was a letter. My eyes searched Najee's for understanding.

"Read it, son." Najee pressed. "Just read it."

I read the letter twice before I spoke. "This can't be real."

"It's real," Carlos Trinidad said.

"That's my mother's handwriting, son, I can spot it anywhere. What's crazy is that as I read it, I could hear her voice speaking. Fucked me up. Made a nigga shed a tear and everything, yo. I feel like I'm caught in an episode of the Twilight Zone, right now. But one thing I know for sure, the letters I just read, including the one in your hand, they official. Here look at this."

Najee passed me a photograph. I recognized it instantly. I'd seen the entire set years ago at Najee's grandmother's house. Smiling adolescent focus of Najee and Salimah lit up the picture. The fact that Najee had the photo now, meant that he'd gotten it from Carlos and that in itself spoke volumes. "Damn, yo!"

"That's what I said minutes ago." Najee said, smiling.

"Small world, huh?" Carlos Trinidad said.

"Small as shit. So, you're really Najee's pops?" I asked.

Najee and Carlos nodded at the same time, looking like twins.

"How long have you known about this?"

"What? About Najee being my son?" Carlos asked.

I nodded my head.

"I asked him the same shit, yo." Najee chimed in.

"I always knew that I had a son, but I didn't know where he was. I never knew that Maria named him Carlos Jr., just like I never knew that eventually she changed his name to Najee. I knew Maria's family was in Newark, but I thought that that would be the last place she'd be, knowing that I knew her mother was there. But evidently, I was wrong. Maria hid from me in plain sight. Somewhere along the way, I stopped thinking about Maria and my son. It's been thirty years, so I gave up hope.

"When Benito came to me and told me that someone was moving major cocaine in the city, I was clueless as to what was going on. Once we began investigating, Angel's name came up. We learned Angel was connected to a man named Najee who was supplying the city with kilos of cocaine. I checked around and found out that a large shipment of cocaine had been stolen from some very important people in New Jersey. But I still had no clue who Najee was. I was told that the Najee who was flooding the city with coke was the same Najee that had taken the shipment of cocaine from the people in New Jersey. Then I was sent a photo of the man named Najee. It was then that I recognized him. I knew immediately that Najee was my son. I could see—"

"Hold on … rewind that back," Najee interjected.

"Rewind what back? What part?" Carlos asked.

"The whole part about the shipment of cocaine being stolen in New Jersey and you being sent a picture."

"When Benito told me about the new supply of cocaine flooding the city, I knew that it had to come from somewhere. It had to have an origin. There are three major drug Cartels in the Southern hemisphere. Only three. The Medellin, Sinaloa and Arellanos-Campos Cartels. The Cartels are warring factions, but they all cooperate in certain situations. Information is gathered and shared in the interests that best benefits the associations. My organization is connected to Don Pedro Escobaro and the Medellin Cartel. I control the distribution of cocaine and heroin to cities and states up and down the Eastern Seaboard.

"But so do other men. Muhammad Farid Shahid is one of those men. His organization is connected to the Sinaloa Cartel. He distributes narcotics to places I do not. I reached out to some people and learned the cocaine that was flooding D.C. had been taken from a man named Muqtar Kareem. And that Kareem worked for Muhammad Farid Shahid."

Najee looked at me and I looked at him, then we both turned back to Carlos.

"According to my source," Carlos continued, "Kareem was killed, then robbed, but his wife Hafizah was spared. She was spared by the men who'd taken the cocaine but not by Shahid's organization. She had been shot and was in the hospital. She was killed in her hospital room days later. But not before she identified the person responsible for killing Muqtar Kareem and taking the cocaine. She identified you, Najee."

"So, this nigga Muhammad Shahid Farid ..."

"Muhammad Farid Shahid."

"Okay ... whatever. He knows I'm the one who took the coke, huh?" Najee asked.

Carlos nodded. "His organization has been looking for you for over nine months. When I sent word about the cocaine and they claimed it as theirs, they found out you were in D.C. They wanted to come here to get you, but I refused them. Territory is respected by all, it's the rule of the Cartels. I was sent photos of you, Najee and you, Gunz ..."

"Me?" I asked, surprised.

"Yeah, you and a man named Hasan Sharif ..."

"They sent you a picture of Ha?" Najee exploded.

Carlos nodded again. "Along with information that he was deceased. Killed after being shot in Atlantic City a little over a year ago."

"Damn, that's crazy, yo!"

"It's crazy to you, Gunz, but not to me. Organizations like ours have resources that you wouldn't believe. We have better intel than the federal government and all their alphabet agencies. Remember how you got here?"

"Of course, how could I forget?"

"Which reminds me, I had people put out the all-points bulletins for you, Najee and Angel. I have to get them pulled. And to answer your question, I've known Najee was my son for about a week or so."

"Damn, Najee thought it was you who had come after him for selling coke in D.C., and it wasn't you."

"And that means the two of you killed my friends and associates unjustly."

"My bad, yo ... real talk," Najee stated. "I sincerely thought ..."

"I know what you thought. We discussed that already. I probably would have thought the same thing in your position. Especially with Angel in your ear." The man named Benito walked back into the restaurant and looked around. His eyes landed on the three of us. "Look, there are people in my organization that want to kill the both of you tonight. But obviously, I'm not going to let that happen. And I need to find a way to settle this beef with Muhammad Shahid before it blows up. I suggest that we call it a day. It's been a long night. We should all get some rest and then talk again in a day or two."

"That sounds good to me. I'm tired as shit," I said.

"That's cool," Najee said. "But I still can't believe you're my father."

"Believe it, Najee. Life is funny that way. It's better than finding out that RuPaul is your father, right?" Carlos said and laughed.
"You got jokes, too, huh? That's what's up. Put all your numbers in my phone." Najee handed Carlos his phone.

***

"Here we are out in the middle of nowhere, when the third and final vehicle arrives. It's an SUV ... a Tahoe. Carlos tells me that he wants me to meet someone. His men walk over with two people. A man and a woman, both white, blindfolded, bound and gagged. Carlos said something about the dude ... his name was Brett, being his accountant and he was the one who gave George the list of his businesses and properties ..." I was saying to Najee and Tye as we made our way around the Capital Beltway in route to D.C.

"He said something about Brett being on drugs and how he owed George money that's why he gave George the information he needed to give to us. That nigga Carlos walked up to the dude, pulled out a big ass chrome revolver and blew the dude's brains out. Then he did the woman the same way. The woman was the dude Brett's wife. After that, his men bring out three more people, bound and gagged and blindfolded. Carlos started talking about George again and how George's family was innocent in everything. George's daughter and his baby's mother. Then in a blink of an eye, he killed both women. Killed them both while George watched. Helpless. My heart broke for the man, yo ..."

"I can't believe that he found out about George like that," Najee interjected. "He killed the homie, didn't he?"

I nodded. "Killed George last. Blew his brains out the same way he did the daughter and baby mother. Shit was sad, son."

Najee shook his head but kept his eyes on the road while driving. "I'm fucked up about that, yo. George Foreman was a real live nigga. He helped us when he didn't have to. Most niggas would have heard Carlos Trinidad's name and got ghost. Son didn't. We got him and his family bodied. I swear by Allah, son, I feel some kinda way about that, father or no father."

Thinking about what Najee had just said about George's family, made me think of my own. I pulled out my cell phone and dialed my mother's house. I dialed both my mother and grandmother's cell phones. Still no answers. I looked at the time on the phone. 6:31 a.m. "They are probably in the house knocked out sleep."

"Who's probably knocked out sleep?" Najee asked.

"My grandmother and mother. Your pops had some niggas in their house last night," I told him.

"Get the fuck outta here, fam. In Newark? Carlos had niggas in the brick at your people's crib?" Tye asked. "Fuck outta here!"

I looked in the backseat at Tye. "Fuck I'ma lie for. Stupid ass nigga! Carlos wanted me to call Najee and arrange a meeting, I refused. Then he pulled out a phone and called some niggas. Whoever he called, put my muthafuckin' grandmother on the phone. I talked to her. And I heard my moms in the background talking. If them niggas wasn't out my mom's spot, how in the fuck did they do that? Merge the call, do a three-way? He had some niggas inside my mother's house, just like I said. Fuck I'ma lie …"

"Yo, y'all niggas chill out. Gunz ain't cappin', son did the same thing to me … well, not like that, but I told you Tye, that son threatened Limah. It was probably niggas somewhere near her. Had to be. I believe that. One thing we know for sure is that son is a powerful nigga. He done showed us that numerous times. It definitely ain't hard to believe that Carlos got niggas on the payroll all over the county. It wouldn't be shit to call up niggas and say go … or even send niggas to Newark. That's easy to a nigga like him."

"Since you put it like that. You right. My bad, didn't mean to doubt your word, big homie. I was just …" Tye said.

"About to get fucked up," I told Tye. Then asked Najee, Have you talked to Limah?"

"Not since last night. I talked to her right before you called. I tried to call her back, but she didn't pick up. I ain't worried, though. Son knows he's my father. He wouldn't hurt my sister and expect us to be cool."

"True dat, yo. True dat. And Limah might go days without answering her phone. You know how she gets."

Najee laughed out loud. "Limah wild as shit, son. She told me she fuckin' with a nigga from Grafton Avenue. Talkin' about she fuckin' with a boss. Said the nigga is the big homie in the hood over there."

"The big homie? From Grafton?" I asked.

Najee nodded his head and laughed.

"Gotta be the nigga Drama, then." Tye offered, "Either him or that kid Brazo. They are the two big homies around there. All them niggas on that blood shit, hard body."

"Nine Trey, G-Shine, Gorilla Stone or Sex, Money Murder?" I asked and laughed. It's too many Blood sets in Newark, yo. Facts."

"You telling me. But naw, they ain't none of them joints you just named. The niggas on Grafton, they reppin' a West Coast set. Brims, I think it is. I was in the feds with both of them niggas. Drama and Brazo cool as fuck."

"Don't you mean, they 'bool'?" Najee asked and laughed.

"Yeah, you right, son," Tye replied. "Them niggas goofy as shit. Takin' all the 'C's out of their language and shit. That shit lame. All that shit is lame to me."

"Tough ass nigga," I told Tye, "bet you ain't say that shit to them niggas when y'all was in the feds. Them 'Blood' niggas would've ate your food, as they say."

Najee and I laughed like hell.

"Fuck you mean, Gunz!" Tye exploded. "Them niggas wouldn't ate shit but the knife I made out the metal on the bunk. Them niggas know what's up with me. They know how Tye Murder get down. I was in the pen, yo … in Hazleton, on my own time. Didn't need no Tri-State car or no gang car to back me! Facts! You better ask niggas about me."

"Sit your super-hyped ass back and chill out. Niggas is just playing with you, son," I said. "We hip to you, gangsta."

"No bullshit though, yo, if Limah is fucking with one of them niggas, I hope they understand that can't nothing ever happen to her, because I'll come for all that shit. I don't give a fuck. Facts! Bloods, Crips, GD … all that shit can get it."

"Trust me, them Blood niggas all over the Brick already know what's good with us. They still ain't got over how we bodied Hashim, Reek and all them Prince Street niggas. Then took over Spruce Street. Ain't nobody gone let nothing happen to Limah. That's the least of my worries. "Damn, yo, I'm hungry as shit!"

"Oh yeah?" Tye said. "That greasy ass fish you got from the fish spot is still in the Expedition. That shit gon taste even better today with a little dust on it."

We all laughed at that.

Chapter 21

Honesty

"My dawg went to court today, they gave him fifteen/bammed my lil nigga, he was seventeen/young nigga, don't even know what all that time mean/pussy ass crackers done shattered my nigga's dreams/they hollerin' mandatory, they want him to do the whole thing/pussy nigga showed up in court on my dawg and did his thing/snitched on my lil nigga, now I gotta bust his brain/if he would've done me, my dawg would do the same/his lady called me crying and I feel her pain/I'm tired of losing all my niggas to the chain gang ..."

The pull-out bed on the couch in Trigger's basement was uncomfortable as hell. I had slept with springs sticking me in the side and I was grumpy as hell. Then waking up to Plies rapping in my ear, ruined my mood even more. I sat up and looked around. Trigger was laid on the bench of the Universal weight set, doing bench presses. Smacking my guns and shaking my head, I got up and walked over to Trigger's phone that was plugged into a USB jack that allowed music from his phone to play out loud on a speaker. I hit the button on the phone to kill the music. Once the music stopped, Trigger stopped lifting weights and his eyes zeroed in on me.

"Fuck you do that for?" he asked. "That's my shit right there."

"Trigger, that shit was too loud. You trying to deliberately wake up that little girl in there?"

"My bad," Trigger replied

"Listen, when the kid does wake up, remember to stick to the story when you talk to me. Her grandmother got sick, and we picked her up to keep her until her mother came to get her. And another thing," I told Trigger, "Call me True around her and I'ma call you Tye. We don't need her telling nobody she was with Honesty and Trigger."

Trigger finished his set of presses, before responding. "Excuse me, Ms. Rocket Scientist slash college grad, with a degree in Socio

Economics, if we're concerned about her saying our names to whoever, shouldn't we change them all together? Instead of True, which
is synonymous for Honesty and Tye, which is short for Tyrone, my
real government name, shouldn't our aliases be different names?"

I thought about what Trigger said and decided he made a good
point. "You're right. But whatever we decide on gotta be easy
enough to remember, so we don't slip up and say our real names."

"What about Sharae and Earl?"

"Sharae is my middle name. It can be connected to me. Call
me Michelle as in Obama."

"Cool, call me Barack then," Trigger said and laughed.

"Ha ... ha... ha... no. That's too obvious. How about Barry?"

"At the end of the day, it don't even matter. Call me Barry,
Michelle."

As if on cue, the bedroom basement door opened and the white
girl, Angel's daughter, walked out into the room where we were.
She rubbed her eyes with both fists and then looked at me and Trigger. "Who are you? And where am I?"

I hadn't had time to get dressed after getting out of bed, clad
only in Trigger's shorts. Afterwards, I walked out within a foot of
the girl and said, "I'ma friend of your grandmother. She got sick
last night and went to the hospital. She tried to call your mom, Angel, but couldn't reach her. So, she called me. I came to the house
last night and got you out of bed, remember?"

"You're the police lady who carried me," the little girl replied,
"I remember."

"That's right. I carried you while you slept. My name is
Michelle, and this is," I pointed at Trigger. "My boyfriend Barry.
We're both police officers. We're off duty, taking the next few days
off to make sure you're okay."

"Okay. I'm Aniyah."

"Hey, Aniyah. Are you hungry?"

Aniyah nodded her head. "But I need to use the bathroom, offer
the wudu and then make salat."

"Offer the who and make the what?" I replied, dumbfounded.

"Offer the wudu and make the Salat." Trigger explained. "She's Muslim. The wudu is ablution or washing up to prepare for prayer. Salat is the prayer that Muslims do five times a day. My man Cat eye KK is Muslim. He taught me that!"

"Oh ... well, I didn't know ..."

"Is my nana okay?" Aniyah asked.

"She's fine," I lied. "Talked to her earlier. Told her you were still asleep. She asked me to tell you that she loves you. And she'll see you soon."

"Okay. Where's the bathroom, Ms. Michelle?"

"It's down that hall right there. The first door to the left," Trigger guided, pointing the way.

"There's an extra toothbrush and toothpaste over the sink for you. There's an assorted array of soaps and body washes in there on the shelf above the toilet. A clean washcloth and towel are folded up on the tub. Make yourself right at home."

"Thank you," Aniyah said and beelined for the bathroom.

After the door closed behind Aniyah, Trigger said, "You need to start figuring out your next course of action, because if you haven't killed Angel in forty-eight hours, that little girl in there goes free. Free to where, I don't know. But she's going free to somewhere. And while she's in the bathroom, you need to decide, do we take her out of the house or not? She can't stay dressed in pajamas for the next two days." Trigger wiped sweat off his face with his shirt. "Figure it out, True and figure it out fast."

My eyes shot daggers at Trigger's back as I watched him climb the stairs and leave.

Chapter 22

Najee

"Najee! Naj, wake up, fam!" Tye said as he shook me.
Stalling and shifting my position on the bed, I answered feebly,
"What's up, yo? I was sleeping good as shit. What's up?
"Wake up, fam! Shit fucked up, yo! Bad!"
"I'm up, Tye, I'm up. What's the deal, son?"
"Shit all bad, yo. It's Limah!"
At the sound of my sister's name, I woke all the way up. "What
about, Limah?"
When Tye couldn't face me, after his head dropped, I knew
something was very wrong. I got up out the bed and looked around
the apartment. Gunz was on his cell phone listening to somebody
talk. He turned to face me. Tears streamed down both of his cheeks.
My stomach flipped instantly. An eerie feeling came over me. I
turned back to Tye for an explanation, but his eyes were filled with
tears as well. "Yo, if one of y'all don't start talking," I grabbed my
gun off the floor beside the bed and chambered a round. "And tell
me what the fuck is going on, by Allah, I'ma start shooting in this
muthafucka! Fuck y'all niggas crying for? And what's up with my
sister?"
Gunz lowered the phone from his face, then turned toward me.
"She's gone, baby boy. Somebody killed her, the nigga she was with
and Yasir ..."
I couldn't decipher anything after hearing the words, "She's
gone, somebody killed her..."
I was still sitting in the same spot an hour later. Tye and Gunz
had left the room, but I wasn't alone. The pain I felt was so great, it
became a manifested being that sat with me and grieved. Tears had
continued to fall despite my efforts to stop them. Because every inch
of my body rocked with pain. It was hard to describe how bad the
hurt was. But it was the same hurt I felt the day I was told my parents
had died on a ferry boat that sunk on the Hudson. I was twelve years

old and completely brokenhearted. I couldn't understand how something like that could happen.

My parents both had taken the ferry across the river thousands of times. Me and Salimah had taken the ferry ride hundreds of times. Being so young, it was hard for me to understand their deaths were the qadir of Allah. His plan. His divine decree. And after thirty years of being on the earth, it didn't get any better or any easier. I still didn't understand life. How could I even begin to wrap my mind around the fact that my sister was gone from this earth? My sister, one year younger than me and nowhere near as sinful as me.

How could a killer's bullets rip her away from her existence and I was still alive and breathing after all the lives I'd taken? How is it even possible that it was decreed for her to die before me when she'd killed no one? I raised my face to the ceiling as if I could see a force that assured me that one day I'd understand. But I saw no one. Nothing but the ceiling. There would be no answers for me today, just like there weren't any for me when I was twelve. I was alone with my manifested pain, destined to forever not understand how life really was or what living really meant. And that realization made me angry from the depths of my soul, an animalistic roar escaped my mouth.

"Aaaarghhhh! I'ma kill allll y'all muthafuckas! Everybody gon diiiiieeee!"

I got up off the bed and threw punches at the air. Wishing, hoping someone would materialize so I could beat them to death. I raged around the room like a madman. I backed up against the wall and finally slid down until I was sitting, hands over my face, tears streaming down. All I saw was my sister's face, her smile. I could hear her laughter. I could hear her voice...

"Miss me with all that gangster rap shit, big brother. That talk ain't for you and fuck that shit, Naj. You gotta live, big brother. We've come a long way from the Brick Tower days ..."

Salimah was everything to me. Everything a sister could be. Yang to my yin, my side kick, my ride or die, my A one from day one. My little sister. Me, her big brother. Her protector. The man who failed to keep her safe. An uncontrollable, insatiable thirst for revenge overtook me. It was stronger than anything I'd ever felt. When my childhood partner, Hasan died after getting shot in Atlantic City, I tore up parts of the city to feed my hunger for retribution. The desire to kill, to punish, to maim was intensified times a thousand now. My desire for blood became so strong that it spoke to me.

"Screaming, crying and throwing pounds at the air ain't gone bring Salimah back. But killing people will ease your pain a little. Go back to Newark and make the ground quake beneath your feet. But before you do that, kill the person who might be responsible. Even if he didn't pull the trigger, he might've made the call. Leave no stone unturned. Start with the man that threatened your family last. Carlos Trinidad." It was like I had an epiphany. I dried the tears from my eyes, got up off the floor and heard my destiny calling me. It was time to answer.

***

I put all the choppas in the duffle bag and loaded extra bullets for each of them. Then I put both arms through the straps and lifted the bag onto my back. I walked into the living room, headed for the door. Gunz and Tye both looked at me like I was crazy.

"Naj, where you going, baby boy?" Gunz asked. "With all them fuckin' guns and shit?"

"I'm going to avenge my sister. Starting with my father. You coming?" I replied, calmly.

Gunz covered the space between us like a cheetah. He stepped in front of the door, blocking my path. "It wasn't Carlos, Naj. Son ain't have nothing to do with Salimah."

My eyes locked onto Gunz's eyes, searching. Mine contained murderous intent. His were pleading eyes. "How can you know that for sure? You was with me here … well, at the casino. Carlos threatened to touch Limah and my grandmother when he talked to me. He threatened you, too …"

"It wasn't them, baby boy," Gunz pleaded. "Trust me, it wasn't."

"Trust you? How the fuck can I do that, and my sister is dead?
I don't trust nobody, yo. I can't even trust myself. Get out the way
and let me do what I gotta do."

"Gunz is right, big bruh," Tye chimed in. "Carlos ain't the one
who pushed the button on this one. I know how you feel …"

'You can't possibly know how I feel! Did somebody just kill
your sister?" I shouted at Tye.

Tye blew right back. "Yeah, they did! When a muthafucka
killed Salimah, they killed my sister! Salimah was a sister to me.
Not by blood, but by actions and love. I loved her with all my heart,
son! So, miss me with that over-aggressive shit like ya the only one
hurting in here. Fam … all of us just lost a loved one. Not just you!
Like I was saying, I know you fucked up … I'm fucked up. Everybody in the Towers is fucked up. But you gotta listen to Gunz … to
me. Carlos Trinidad didn't do it, yo. Listen to Gunz. Hear him out.
After that, you can … we can rip some shit up."

I relented a little and decided to hear Gunz and Tye out. "Talk."

"Shit is all over the news back home. The cops found three people dead in the house. Limah, Damien, McClinton…"

"Damien McClinton? Who the fuck is that?" I asked.

"That's Drama, fam," Tye explained. 'The blood nigga I was
telling y'all about. When you told us about Limah fuckin' with a
big homie from Grafton Avenue, remember I told you that it had to
be either Drama or Brazo. When we was in Hazelton, a nigga from
Trenton came in. He was Blood on the street but got on Tri-State
time in the joint. The homies found out that the nigga had a rack of
wild ass robberies where he was robbing and raping bitches. Nobody in the Tri-State cer wanted to sacrifice and run the nigga in, so
I stepped up. Drama knew the nigga and was fucked up at him for
not getting on Blood time and about the rapes. We caught the nigga
on the rec yard and fucked him around. We was in the box on lock
up together. That's how I know Drama's government name. Damien McClinton is Drama."

"So, what you saying? Some gang bangers killed my sister?"

"Naw, yo … he ain't saying that. The third person they found
was Ya," Gunz said.

"Ya? our Ya?" I asked, befuddled.

Tye and Gunz both nodded their heads. Gunz's tears started anew.

"What the fuck was Ya doing at Limah's house with her and the Blood nigga?"

"I wondered the same thing, baby boy. You remember Aminah from Weequahic Park?" Gunz asked.

"Aminah is Angel's cousin. Aminah introduced Angel to Salimah. I know her. Why?"

"I talked to her a few minutes ago. She got my number from Killa. She called me and told me she got a detective nigga on her line tryna fuck. She said the detective nigga told her the three bodies were found upstairs in the bedroom. That Limah and Damien M ... Drama were naked in bed when they were killed and Ya was fully clothed and shot a few feet away from the bed. He told Aminah that Ya had been bound and gagged, before he was killed."

"When Gunz told me that before you came out the room, I called around the way and found out Ya been missing for about three days. He got snatched outside of a halal spot on Rockland Terrace. People saw him get snatched at gunpoint. They said it was three niggas dressed in kufis and thobes. They put Ya in a black Chrysler 300 and drove off," Tye added.

"Muslims," I muttered. The picture became clearer in my head.

Gunz nodded. "Think about what Carlos told us this morning. Muhammad Farid Shahid and his men been looking for you since Mu was killed and the coke got took. He said that recently, they wanted to come to D.C. to get you, but he told them no. Somehow, they got to Yasir ... wasn't Ya the only person who knew where Limah lived?"

I nodded my head. "As far as I know, he was."

"They snatched Ya. Under pressure, he broke and must've took the dudes to Limah's house. They break in and surprise Drama and Limah. They kill them and then kill Ya. But maybe not in that order. Think about it. It makes perfect sense. Carlos wouldn't have known to grab Ya—"

"Well," Tye interjected, "who did know to grab Ya? Whoever it was, told them Muslim niggas that Ya was the only one with that info. And that had to be somebody from the hood."

I thought about what Tye had just said and thought about a possible traitor in the clique back home. I couldn't discount it. My head was throbbing. I walked over to the couch and dropped the duffle bag from my back. I sat down and rubbed my temples to massage the origin of my headache.

"And besides all that, Carlos has nothing to gain by killing Salimah ... it's a lose-lose for him."

"How so?" I asked.

"Because he loses you. The son he just gained. If he was gon kill Limah, there was no reason to tell you everything he told you and show you the proof. Plus, if he'd done that to Limah, he'd have known to kill you and me because we gon kill about her. And once we were in that restaurant, we weren't hard to kill."

"Tye was outside the restaurant."

"I was out there waiting for them ..." Tye started.

"It don't matter if Tye was there or not. We were sitting ducks. Easy to kill. All three of us done killed niggas in tighter situations. I'm telling you, Naj, Carlos is smart, yo. You don't become the head of your own organization by being no dumb nigga. Not ones connected to international Cartel in Colombia. Carlos is a chess player, son. Everybody else is playing checkers. He wasn't behind the murders. That was the Muslim nigga, Muhammad Farid Shahid. I'd bet my life on that."

"Since you put things in that perspective, I agree. If niggas in thobes and kufis snatched ya, then they are the ones who killed him and my sister. Muslims." My mind was made up. Muhammad Shahid and his men were responsible for Salimah Yasir's deaths. And it was time to retaliate. "I need all the info I can get on Muhammad Shahid. Where he's based at. Where he lives. Where his men live."

"Your pops should be able to get all that. He said their information pipeline is better than the feds," Gunz stated. "Holla at him."

"I will," I replied. "Them niggas don't know who they fuckin' with, but they are about to find out. They touched my family. I'm bout to touch theirs. All of 'em. It's time to go back to Jersey and paint the town red ..."

Tye looked up from his cell phone and said, "It's too late for that, fam. The Bloods done beat you to it. They know about Drama getting bodied. Word in the street is them niggas been killing shit since they heard the news. They been killing Crips from Newark to East Orange."

I snorted in disgust. "They doing drive-bys, yo. And we all know that when niggas do drive-bys, innocent bystanders, bricks and cars are the only ones that got killed. I'ma kill people. Too many people." I stood up and faced Gunz. "Pack up everything, son. We leaving for Newark tonight."

"We gotta lot of shit, baby boy. When you say pack up everything, what exactly do you mean?" Gunz inquired.

I thought about Gunz's question. I did have a lot of shit. I had accomplished a lot while in D.C. I had bags of money everywhere, the house in Potomac, Maryland, and all the acres of land that surrounded it. I thought about the Ferrari and other exclusive whips that sat in the garage made on to the house. The RNR headquarters that took up a quarter block in Ivy City came to mind. That and all the artists signed to the label.

I thought about the hundred or so bricks of cocaine I had left at the spot in Alexandria, Virginia. I thought about all my clothes, expensive shoes and jewelry. I was beyond rich in every sense of the word. But losing my sister made my soul poor. Her death robbed me of the last vestiges of humanity that I had left. And it was humans who treasured those types of riches, not animals, like me.

"When we get home, I'ma need every gun we got. I been neglecting our young wolves since I been eating in D.C. Even though, niggas gon ride about Limah and ya, I wanna feed them some food from my table. Go to the spot, you and Tye, the one in Beacon Hill and pack up three million in cash. Bring it back here. Then we'll leave in separate whips! Y'all take the money and I'll take the guns. I think that's all we gone need. Money and guns."

Gunz nodded. Tye gave me a head nod. Then they left the apartment.

Chapter 23

Carlos

Dorothy's arms were draped around my neck as she sat behind me and rubbed my chest. Her breasts massaged my back. My eyes were closed. I was feeling great after a long night of killing and talking. I opened my eyes and played in Susan's hair as her head bobbed up and down on my dick. Her fists were stacked on top of one another, twisting in different directions as her throat opened to accept my length. She called it the vacuum suction technique. Watching the District Attorney for the District of Columbia eat my dick made me feel important, powerful.

The woman behind me was a United States Marshal and way more freakier than the DA on her knees. As if reading my thoughts, Dorothy Benigan moved from behind me and positioned herself beside me and the bed. She moved her body like a snake and licked my chest and stomach, bumping heads with Susan. That made Susan stop her two-handed assault on my dick. She let my dick fall from her mouth. Dorothy immediately grabbed it and put her mouth where Susan's had just been. I gathered Dorothy's hair into my fist and watched her as she did her thing. It was always amazing to see Dorothy swallow me whole. Then suddenly my mood changed. Tiring of the foreplay, I moved Dorothy's head and stood up.

"Get up on the bed! Both of you!" I ordered. "On all fours. "Side by side."

Both women obeyed my command and got on the bed. They both obediently looked over their shoulders back at me, as if awaiting further instructions. I stood there and smiled as I looked at both Caucasian asses. Although both women were forty plus, their bodies didn't reflect their age. The light sparkled off of the diamond ankle bracelet on Susan's ankle. It was a gift from Susan's husband Grant. I loved to fuck her with it on. Dorothy wagged her ass and feet in anticipation of my entering her. Her pink, pussy lips opened invitingly. The moisture of her arousal dripped from her hole. Stroking my hard on, I entered Dorothy first because of her obvious readiness. Her pussy was snug and hot as an inferno. I smacked her ass as I pounded her. I watched her and Susan share kisses as I stroked. Even that turned me on. The small pill that I had popped before our sex session was doing its job. I didn't feel bad at all about my body's need for Cialis pills. At my age, sexing two women almost daily was exhausting for any man. Abruptly, I stopped fucking Dorothy and entered Susan. Her pussy was equaled to Dorothy's on every scale. I reached down and grabbed both of Susan's ankles. My hands held the anklet as I long stroked Grant's wife. Susan squealed in delight. Letting Susan's ankles go, I reached over and massaged Dorothy's clit and pussy. Her moans and Susan squeals filled the silence in the room.

"Shit! Fuck me, papi!" Susan called out.

"Stop fucking her, Carlos, and fuck me!" Dorothy said next.

Again, I smiled. I alternated fucking both women until finally I couldn't hold back any longer. I pulled out of Dorothy and shot cum all over her ass, then Susan's.

***

The king size bed I laid in was comfortable on every level. After a long, hot shower, I was content and ready to rest. Dorothy laid next to me, rubbing my every body part. Susan Rosenthal walked into the room partially dressed. As she put pins in her hair to hold her bun, she looked at me salaciously.

"I wish that I could stay, but I can't. Grant is expecting me home early. We have to entertain guests at the house tonight. Senator Munchin, the Republican from Iowa, went to college with Grant. They're old friends, so Grant wants to do dinner with Munchin and his wife, Beverly ... Oh, and I just got off the phone with the commander at 5th District, he wanted me to know that they arrested Kareemah El-Amin ..."

Quickly, I sat up. "They arrested Angel when?"

"Earlier today. This morning I believe. A traffic stop, he said. She ran a red light near Bladensburg Road and New York Avenue.

Officers pulled over her BMW, ran her license and saw she was wanted. They searched her vehicle and found a loaded handgun."

"Shit!" I muttered and rolled out of the bed. I grabbed fresh boxer briefs and put them on. "Was there a little girl with her?"

Susan shook her head. "She was alone when they arrested her."

"And you just found this out?"

"Yes. When I was in the guest room talking to Grant, the commander clicked in. He literally just told me about Angel five minutes ago," Susan replied with alarm. "Why, did I do something wrong?"

I walked into my walk-in closet and grabbed a track suit. I slid into the pants and walked back out. "Never said you did anything wrong. I just forgot to tell you last night to cancel the APB. Things have happened that you don't know and her being in jail now complicates things. Can you pull some strings to get her out?"

"At this juncture, no. If it was just the APB for questioning, yeah. But the weapon in her vehicle changed the dynamics. She's probably already at Central Cell block being processed. She's already been charged with carrying a pistol without a license. She'll have to see a judge in the morning."

"Then what?" I asked.

"Depends on what judge she gets. The Attorney General wants all gun cases in the district to be transferred to federal court. It's a process that's out of my hands. The judge can choose to release her on her own personal recognizance or hold her pending the case going over to District Court. It's up to the judge."

"Fuck!" I uttered and went to get my cell phone. I picked it up and dialed a familiar number.

"A man's voice answered on the third ring. "Carlos?"

"Yeah, Jay, it's me. I need you in D.C. by tomorrow morning." I told J. Alexander Williams, the best black defense attorney in the country.

"No can do, Carlos. I got two—" Jay started.

"Jay, this is not a request," I emphasized with brevity in my voice.

There was a brief pause on the other end of the phone. Then Jay said, "Since you put it that way, I guess I'm on the first thing smoking to D.C. tonight. What's going on?"

"Do you remember a woman that you defended for me almost thirteen years ago named Kareemah El-Amin?"

"Angel? Of course, I do. Newspapers called her D.C.'s first queen of cocaine. She was charged with multiple murders. Somebody kidnapped, raped and murdered her fourteen-year-old sister. Charged with about four murders but suspected of being behind the murders of about forty people. How could I ever forget her?"

"She is kind of unforgettable, huh? Well, she's at the Central Cell block right now. In the morning, she'll see a judge. I need you to get down to the Superior Court and get her out of jail for me."

"What's she charged with this time? More murders?" Jay asked.

"No. Nothing that severe. She's charged with a CPWL," I replied.

"Carrying a pistol without a license. That's easy enough. Was Angel ever convicted of a crime in D.C.?"

I turned to Susan. "Was Angel ever convicted of a crime in D.C.? That you know of?"

Susan shook her head. "Not since I been at the U.S. Attorney's office."

"Naw, Jay, I don't think so." I told Jay.

"Good. It's better because she can't be upgraded to carrying a pistol by a convicted felon. That would have made things a lot more difficult in getting her out."

"Jay, my impromptu phone call demanding that you get to D.C. by tomorrow morning tells you how important this is to me, right?"

"It does. I'll do everything in my power to get her out. The Attorney General at justice is pushing vehemently to get all state case firearms ..."

"Sent to federal court. I know that, Jay. Just do what you can. If you gotta call in some markers, do it. I need Angel out of there as soon as possible."

"Say no more, Carlos. I'm on it. I'll call you tomorrow after I know something more definite."

"Thanks, Jay." I disconnected the call. My thoughts were on Angel, but mostly her daughter. My daughter.

Before I could put the phone down, it vibrated. The caller was Najee. I smiled. "Hello?"

"Carlos, it's me, Najee. I need your help. I need those information resources you bragged about."

"Anything you need. Just ask," I told my son.

"I need everything you can find on Muhammad Shahid and anybody in his organization."

"Listen, I been thinking about that situation. I can replace what you took from Shahid. If he's willing to forgive you killing his man …"

"I really appreciate that offer, big guy, but it's kinda past that now. They drew first blood," Najee said.

"What do you mean by that?"

Najee's voice broke. "They killed my sister."

"Salimah? Hell naw! Are you sure … I mean absolutely sure, it was Shahid's people who did it?"

"I'm about as sure as I could possibly be. But honestly, I thought you did it."

"Me? Why would I want to hurt your sister?" I asked, offended.

"You threatened my family last night, remember? Thought you made good on the threat," Najee responded.

"I was bluffing. I never could find out anything on your family. I know about your grandmother from my childhood. Didn't even know if she was still alive. I just threw it out there to see if you'd bite. I tried to locate Salimah and your grandmother, but my sources couldn't. Your friend Gunz, his family was easy to find."

"That's crazy … I told somebody that dudes like you never bluff …"

"Usually, I don't," I assured Najee.

"Whatever. But look, big guy, it seems that Shahid has better resources than you because he succeeded where you failed. And now I'm on his ass. His whole organization is ass. I'ma fuck 'em all. They snatched a friend of mine and forced him to take them to Limah's house. There they killed everybody. So, I need that info I asked for as soon as possible. Any mosque, homes or businesses he's associated with. Anything you can find in Newark or New York."

"Let's meet somewhere face to face to talk about …"

"Can't do that, big guy. I'm already on the road headed home. I'm about an hour or so out. I'm through talkin.' It's time for killing. I guess I got that from you, huh? Gunz told me about what you did to some dude named Brett and his wife, then George and his family."

"The apple doesn't fall far from the tree. That's what they say. I know you feel some kind of way about George Foreman, but I had to do that. Hope you can understand that."

"I can. In the killing field, certain deaths are necessary. George knew the risk. Wish you hadn't done it, but I can't unspill spoiled milk or spilled blood. And besides, I'm focused on the killings I need to do, not ones you already did. I need that info big guy. ASAP."

"Najee … you gotta be careful. Shahid's organization—" I started to say but was cut off.

"Fuck Shahid's organization! I can't worry about him or his men. Just like I couldn't worry about you or yours when I set it off. Them muthafuckas killed my sister. So, I'ma bout to kill a rack of them niggas. If I die in the process, so be it."

"I understand how you feel. I felt the same way about a man once. My uncle Julio. There's nothing I can say to change your mind, so I gotta accept how you feel, what you're about to do. You get your stubbornness from me, too. I was the same way when I was young. Just be careful, son. I just found you, I'm not trying to lose you. So, you gotta let me help you …"

"Naw. I'ma big boy. Can't let it be known that I needed my father to hold my hand in times of war. I'm good. My team is a force to be reckoned with. Trust me."

"Don't remind me," I told Najee. "I gotta respect your call, but if anything happens to you, I'm getting involved anyway. And there's nothing you can say to change my mind on that. I'ma get you that info you need."

"Thank you."

"Don't trip and I found out why Angel hasn't been answering your calls."

"Is that right? Is she okay? Don't tell me ..."

"She's okay. But she's in jail. Traffic stop. Car got searched. Cops found a loaded weapon," I explained.

"Told her ass to stop packing that heat ... can you get her out?"

"I'm already on it. As we speak."

"Aight. Keep me posted, yo. And get me that info."

"I'm on it. Hey ..." The line went dead.

I put the phone down and looked up into two sets of inquisitive eyes.

Dorothy Benigan and Susan Rosenthal had both heard my conversation with Najee.

"It's a long story, but here's the gist of it. Najee Bashir is my son and Angel is the mother of my daughter. And I found out both of those things in the last week or so. "One day, I'll explain everything, but right now I need the both of you to ..."

Chapter 24

Det. Mitchell Bell

I picked up the phone on my desk. "Mitch Bell."

"Hey, Mitch, it's me, Fortune. I gotta call from Jenifer Lumpkin asking me to expeditiously check for DNA in a vomit sample you gave her. I processed everything and extracted the DNA. I ran the DNA through the system and hit a match."

The pen appeared in my hand as if by magic. Getting the DNA from the vomit out the Clinton murder scene and finding a match was great news. "I'm ready. Give me what you got, Fortune."

Okay. Match comes back to a thirty-seven-year-old woman named Kareemah El-Amin. No middle name listed. Birthdate is 6-7-1978 ..."

I wrote down everything Max Fortune told me. "Thanks, Fortune. I appreciate this. Give my regards to everyone in forensics."

"Will do, Mitch. Good night."

After replacing the receiver on the hook, I typed in the name Kareemah El-Amen into two different systems, NCIC and WIAAC. The computer beeped then went crazy. A face appeared on my monitor. The photo was thirteen years old, but the woman's beauty was undeniable. I read all the info on the screen, then ascertained that Kareemah El-Amin was the daughter of my victim, Naimah El-Amin.

"That explains the vomit," I said to myself. "Either she did both killings or she came home and discovered the bodies in the living room. She runs to the bathroom and hurls. But then what? Did she just leave? Is she the one who called the murders in? If she did, why did she leave? Why not stick around and talk to the cops?"

I scrolled and read everything compiled on Kareemah El-Amin. The more I read, the more I understood why she left. My questions I'd just asked myself were being answered. But I needed more. I knew exactly where to get them.

***

Anthony Fields

CNN Headquarters

600 K Street NW

I needed news and newspaper footage to complete the puzzle that was Kareemah El-Amin. The woman was an enigma. But she was possibly a suspect in the murders I investigated.

In the lobby at the night desk, I encountered a woman. She was portly, but cute. Her micro braids put me in the mind of the woman in the car on the movie Friday, that came to see Smokey. Her eyes were on me as I fished out my badge and showed it to her.

The woman's eyes scanned my credentials. She smiled. "How can I help you, Detective?"

"I need to see some old footage, news footage and some old newspapers," I told her. "I know it's kinda late, but it's important to a case I'm working."

"No problem. As you can see, the place is almost empty. Go right in, choose a terminal, then log in using the password taped to the monitor. Once you've done that, just type in what you need. If you need any assistance, just come and get me."

"Thank you, ... uh ...?"

"Keyona. Keyona Winslow."

"Okay. Thank you, Keyona."

"My pleasure, Detective. My pleasure."

***

Fourteen-Year-Old Girl Found Slain
April 2003

Adirah El-Amin, the fourteen-year-old girl who'd been missing for two days, was found today in the Fort Dupont Park. She was discovered in a small ditch, badly beaten, bound at the wrists. Her mouth was covered with duct tape. There has been no mention of a suspect or a motive. Authorities are asking for the public's help in solving this heinous crime. If anyone has any tips, please call Crime Stoppers at 202 727-5800.

The article in the Metro section of *The Washington Post* was a brief one. I typed in the name El-Amin and other articles popped up.

Southeast Woman Arrested and Charged With Murder
July 15, 2003

KAREEMAH EL-AMIN, a woman from southeast in DC was arrested today on Queens Chapel Road in Northeast at a beauty salon she owns. Metropolitan Police acted on information provided by a confidential informant. The southeast woman has been charged with three counts of felony murder.

KAREEMAH EL-AMIN DUBBED THE FEMALE JOHN GOTTI BY LAW ENFORCEMENT
September 2003
Local authorities now call Kareemah El-Amin, the female John Gotti, due to the number of execution-style murders she is suspected of ordering. Metropolitan police believe that Kareemah El-Amin ordered the murders of over twenty men to avenge the death of her younger sister, Adirah El-Amin five months ago in April, Adirah El-Amin was found beaten, raped and strangled inside the Fort Dupont Park.

SOUTHEAST WOMAN CHARGED WITH THREE COUNTS OF MURDER LINKED TO NOTORIOUS DRUG KINGPIN CAR-LOS TRINIDAD
October 2003

KAREEMAH EL-AMIN, the southeast woman jailed at the DC jail as she awaits trial on three counts of felony murder has recently been linked to Carlos Trinidad, the notorious drug kingpin by the DC police. Kareemah El-Amin has allegedly sold hundreds of kilos of cocaine all throughout the city. Carlos Trinidad is alleged to be the source of the drugs.

WOMAN ACCUSED OF THREE COUNTS OF FELONY MURDER, ASSEMBLES A DREAM TEAM OF DEFENSE LAW-YERS.
October 2003

Jailed murder suspect and alleged queen pin, Kareemah El-Amin's defense team is one of the best ever assembled in the District of Columbia according to a source of The Washington Post. Kareemah El-Amin has reportedly hired Rudolph Sabino, Rubin Rabinowits and Jenifer Roberts to represent her in her upcoming murder trial.

I continued to scroll and read newspaper clipping after newspaper clipping. I became completely intrigued by Kareemah El-Amin. I moved down to news video clips. Using the mouse, I clicked on the first file and opened it. The news video clip was from Fox News Channel Five. The date was February 10, 2004.

"Good afternoon, this is Maria Wilson reporting to you live from the Municipal Center, *headquarters for the chief of police, Arthur Ramsey. Fox News has just learned that the key witness in the Kareemah El-Amin murder case is dead. Fatima Ladawn Muhammad was the only witness at the scene of the infamous tourist home where three people, Ernestine Wiseman, Andre Richardson and Mark Murphy were shot to death. Fatima Muhammad also implicated Kareemah El-Amin in three additional murders committed in Prince George's County. The state of Maryland is waiting to try Kareemah El-Amin for the murders of Anthony J. Phillips, Thomas Murphy, no relation to Mark Murphy and Dearaye James. Kareemah El-Amin has also been linked to over thirty other murders in the District of Columbia.*

Fatima Muhammad turned state's evidence over seven months ago and agreed to testify against Kareemah El-Amin. Ms. Muhammad was in the Witness Protection Program, under armed guard when she was killed. Authorities believe, although the investigation is ongoing, that Fatima Muhammad was poisoned. Sources close to the scene have told Fox News five that local and federal investigators are vigorously working to determine how security was breached. I have with me, Deputy District Attorney Susan Rosenthal, Mayor Marvin Barry, and Chief of Police, Arthur Ramsey.

"Mayor Barry, there has been a very public outcry for justice in the Kareemah El-Amin murder case. There has also been strong political pressure. But now it appears that Kareemah El-Amin won't stand trial, in light of the death of Fatima Muhammad. There are over forty families affected by this. All murders attributed to Kareemah El-Amin. How do you feel about the recent turn of events?"

"Good afternoon, Maria, like the seven hundred constituents in the District of Columbia, I am appalled at these new developments in this high-profile case. I feel the justice system has to help us bring these criminals to justice and keep them there. I'm truly dismayed about the death of the young woman, Fatima Muhammad, who was brave enough to agree to testify against Kareemah El-Amin. My administration ..."

The more I looked at the clip, I started to remember the case. I was new to the force back in 2003. Had only been with the PG Police Department for about two years. A man had been killed near a deli on St. Barnabas Road and the other man had been kidnapped and found dead later. Dearaye James and Thomas Murphy. I remembered pulling up at the double body scene to secure it until the detectives got there. I also remember that a young woman from DC had been under investigation for the murders. Kareemah El-Amin.

"...DA Rosenthal, what can you tell us about the status of the government's case against Kareemah El-Amin, now that the government's star witness is dead?"

"Hello, Maria, we at the District Attorney's office have been diligently trying to bring this case to trial for months. Our case

wasn't strong from the beginning, but Fatima Muhammad strengthened it. Without Ms. Muhammad, it's going to be very hard to put this case in front of a jury. While working in conjunction with several law enforcement agencies in an effort to find out who poisoned Fatima Muhammad. At this time, I decline to comment on the status of the case because investigations are ongoing ..."

There was one final news clip icon on the screen. I moved the cursor and clicked on it.

"This is Maria Wilson of City Under Siege Fox News reporting from the DC Superior Courthouse. We're here live, anticipating the outcome of a hearing that will decide Kareemah El-Amin's fate. Accused murderer, Kareemah El-Amin, as we speak is waiting to find out if she'll still be prosecuted for three murders in the District of Columbia. Our sources inside the courtroom predict that Ms. El-Amin will not be inducted, due to a lack of evidence and therefore, she'll be released.

"Wait a minute ... I'm receiving information as we speak ... we've just received word that the District Attorney's office has dismissed all charges against Kareemah El-Amin. Yes, it's now been confirmed ... Kareemah El-Amin has been released from custody. She's on her way out of the courtroom now. She should be coming out of this door right behind me. Hold on ... folks ... here she comes now ... Ms. El-Amin? Ms. El-Amin ... can we ask you a few questions? Do you have anything to say to the people of DC? Ms. El-Amin ..."

I paused the newsclip just as the cameras panned in on Kareemah El-Amin as she left the courtroom surrounded by her defense team. The camera caught a specific angle of her face. It filled the entire screen. Again, it was undeniable. Kareemah El-Amin was beyond beautiful. She was breathtaking. Breathtaking and dangerous. I sat in the chair at CNN and thought about everything I'd read and heard and wondered if the murders at 6708 Deborah Drive were in retaliation for something Kareemah had done years ago. One person, possibly two, had walked into an expensive suburban home and killed two people in cold blood. Execution styles. I needed to figure out the who and why of the case. I logged off the computer, said goodbye to Keyona and left the building.

***

When I walked into my house, Mesha met me at the door dressed in only a low thong. She grabbed my hand and led me to the dining room.

"Sit down. Let me get your dinner," Mesha said and went to the kitchen.

I heard the microwave beep minutes later. Mesha returned with a plate of food and sat it down on the table in front of me. Grilled salmon, rice pilaf, broccoli with a cheese sauce on it and buttered biscuits. I picked up the fork and dug into the food. Mesha dropped to her knees and pulled my dick free. She put me in her mouth. There was no way I could eat while she sucked my dick. Putting down the fork, I gripped her head and pushed her further down onto the dick. I closed my eyes and thought about the woman from the computer screen. I thought about Kareemah El-Amin.

Anthony Fields

Chapter 25

Najee

Newark, NJ

I was in the Maxima and Gunz and Tye were behind me in the Expedition. I picked up my phone and called Gunz, then put the call on speaker.

"What's the deal, baby boy?" Gunz asked.

"Yo, you know I'm burnt out, son. Did anybody ever say whether Shahid and his organization was in the Nation of Islam, or if they are Sunni Muslims?"

"My shit kinda burnt, too, yo. I can't remember if it was said one way or the other, or if it was ever said. All I know is that they Muslim. Why? What do you have in mind?" Gunz asked.

"On North 13th Avenue, there's an Islamic bookstore there that be open late. I think it's owned by some Nation niggas," I said.

"In the little strip mall," Tye added. "There's a boutique next door to it that Shareema went to go get all of her hijabs from. I can't remember the name of it …"

"Hawa's Gorden," Gunz said. "It's about five blocks from where we are now."

"That's where I'm going. And you already know what I'ma do when I get there," I said.

"Naw, you can't be serious, Ock. Random Muslims?" Tye asked.

If I had been sane, I would have never made the decision I made. But my last remnants of sanity died with my sister. On the way back to Newark, I had already decided my course of action. And it was a plan I was sticking to, no matter who didn't like it. "Anybody can get it, son. Anybody!"

***

The door to the bookstore was locked, but I could see movement inside the store. From what I could see through the plate glass window on the door, there were two men inside. One near the cash register, wiping down the display cases and the other was at the far end of the store, restocking shelves. I rang the bell near the door. The locking mechanism clicked, and I pulled the door open. Inside the bookstore, I quickly noticed the man who'd buzzed me in was tall, had to be at least six three and stocky. He was an older man, but the absence of a mustache and beard made him appear younger. His salt and pepper hair was neatly brushed to the side of his head.

"Assalamu Alaikum, my brother. What can I get for you this evening?"

I pretended to scour the bookshelves for a minute.

"I need *The Sealed Nectar*, *How to Eat to Live* by Elijah Muhammad and some incense. Any flavor."

"Good choices, my brother," the stocky dude said and turned to get the books.

I pulled the Smith & Wesson four-fifth out of my waist and shot him. His body slammed into the shelves. I put a bullet into his back and the back of his head. He dropped like a sack of hot potatoes from the corner of my eye, I saw the second man try to flee. I took off in his direction. He disappeared through a door at the rear of the store. I caught up to the man just as he reached the back door. He was fumbling with the locks. In a futile attempt to save his life, the man turned to face me.

"Please, … let me make it. I have a family…"

"So do I," I replied and upped the four-fifth. "Today, you get to see if there really is a mothership in the sky, with Elijah Muhammad on it." I blew the man's brains out of the back of his skull. As I walked back towards the entrance to the bookstore, I pulled the baseball cap down over onto my head and exited the store. As I walked over to the Maxima, I could see Tye getting into the backseat of the Expedition.

My next destination was the halal spot on Rockland Terrace where Yasir had been snatched from. I called and told Gunz that.

"I'm positive them brothers are Sunni Muslims, Naj," Gunz said.

"I guess you didn't hear me when I said earlier that anybody can get it. Somebody in there might've known ya and called them niggas that snatched him. I'm crushing any and everybody, Muslim and Kaffir. Allah can sort it all out on the day of Yama Ki Yama."

"That's blasphemy, Ocki," Gunz replied. "But I'm with it."

I disconnected the call. Ten minutes later, both vehicles pulled into the parking lot of the Crescent Moon. Me, Tye and Gunz walked into an almost full halal eatery. This time I pulled two four-fifth handguns. Gunz and Tye pulled guns, too. We killed everybody in the halal spot. Everybody.

***

St. Michael's Hospital

"Sorry, I never told you /all that I wanted to say/now it's too late to hold you/because you've gone away/so far away/never had I imagined living without your smile/feeling and knowing you hear me/keeps me alive/and I know you're smiling down on me from heaven/like so many friends we've lost along the way/I know that eventually we'll be together/one sweet day ..."

The words to the Boyz II Men and Mariah Carey's song, "One Sweet Day" played in my head as I identified my sister's body. An immense feeling of sadness overwhelmed me and threatened to make me hurt

l. Tears flooded my eyes and fell as snot ran down my nose. I cried hard and long. Salimah's body lay on a metal gurney. A simple white sheet covering her nakedness up to her neck. A scar on her forehead that hadn't been there before her death, was the lone blemish on an otherwise too-perfect face.

Salimah had been shot once in the back of the head, so I had been told. The bullet had exited the front of her face through her forehead. I stared down at the lifeless body of my sister and the photo Carlos showed me of Salimah and me came to mind. I thought about the identical smiles on both of our young faces. Realization set in then, I would never see that smile again. Suicidal thoughts crossed my mind. The guns in my waist becoming heavier to alert me to their presence. Either one of the four-fifths could be the instrument that could take me to wherever Salimah had gone to in death. An image of myself pulling a gun, putting it into my mouth and pulling the trigger also crossed my mind.

Shaking my head, I cleared it of the crazy thoughts I was seeing. Killing myself wasn't an option, I told myself mentally. I couldn't let my enemies win in that fashion. Wiping tears from my eyes, I thought about the big mistake I had made. I was never supposed to have let Mu's wife live to tell the story. In my cockiness and arrogant state that night, I never even thought about the people Mu was connected to. I never thought about them because I didn't know about them.

I had left Hafizah alive, daring her to talk to cops. A mental error on my part had produced a disastrous result. My revenge move against Mu was the direct cause of my sister's demise. All because I'd failed to kill Hafizah Kareem. Then something that Carlos told me came to mind …

"According to my source, Kareem was killed then robbed. But his wife Hafizah was spared. She was spared by the man who'd taken the cocaine, but not by the Shahid organization. She was killed in her hospital room days later."

Hafizah Kareem had been killed anyway, but not before telling Muhammad Shahid I was the person that killed Mu and took the coke.

"I'm sorry, sis. I fucked up," I said aloud, hoping wherever Salimah was, she could hear me. "I was supposed to have killed Mu's wife, but I didn't. And that's what got you … taken away from me. But I'ma make a lot of people pay for your … for you being gone. Some people have already paid with their lives. There will be a lot more blood running in the streets before I'm done. Rest well, baby girl, I'ma mourn you until I join you, which may be soon. I love you, Limah. I love you."

I wiped out the tears in my eyes again and my resolve stiffened. Muhammad Farid Shahid was rumored to be a well-connected, powerful man. But he was a man, nonetheless. He could feel pain. He could bleed. He could die. His family as well. I pulled my phone out and called Carlos.

"Najee, how are you holding up?" Carlos asked as soon as he answered.

"I'm holding. I just identified my sister's body." My voice broke despite my attempts at being strong. "I want Muhammad Shahid's blood. I want his whole organization's blood. Tell me something good."

"I'm still waiting on the info to come in. As soon as it does, I'ma get it to you. You want blood. You shall have it. I promise you that."

"I appreciate it, yo. Holla back."

***

In the hospital parking lot, Tye leaned on the side of the Maxima, Gunz on the side of the Expedition. They both looked at me as I approached. The parking lot was well lit, I could see their faces well. Pain was etched across their faces. I assumed that it was because of my sister. I was wrong.

"More bad news, baby boy." Gunz said.

"What can be worse than Limah?" I asked.

"I didn't say worse. Just more bad news. Niggas forced their way into Hasan's mother's crib and killed everybody inside. Haleem and his man pulled up as they were leaving. They sparked it out and killed one of the niggas, but they both got hit. Haleem died at the scene, but his man is fighting for his life at Mercy."

"Ha's ma dukes ... Anessa ... the kids?"

"From what I was told. Everybody, yo," Gunz told me.

"Same niggas that hit Haleem was ..."

Gunz shook his head. "Muslims, baby boy. The nigga they killed, kufi jalebeeyah ... just like the ones who snatched Yasir?"

"And that ain't all of it, fam," Tye piped in. "Speaking of Ya, niggas went to his house, too. Killed his father and girlfriend. They killed the family cat and the dog in the backyard. Executions, yo. Straight executions."

"Muslims, too?"

Tye and Gunz both nodded their heads.

"Somebody put them niggas on Ya. But me, you and Ha, they knew about. Carlos said Shahid sent them pictures of us. Their intel on us …" a thought hit me. "If they hit Hasan's family and Yasir's family …" That's as far as I got before we all ran to our vehicles and pulled off out of the parking lot.

***

Since Gunz's house was closer, I followed the Expedition to his house. As soon as we pulled onto Market Street, the scene in front of us was unmistakable. From 9th Avenue, all the way to Market Street, yellow crime scene tape lined the area. Marked and unmarked Newark police cars were everywhere. The Expedition pulled to the curb and Gunz hopped out. He ducked under the crime tape and darted down the street to his mother's house. He was met and swarmed by a sea of cops. I sat in the car and watched the scene play out. It was sad to see. Once Gunz dropped to his knees and covered his face, that was enough for me. I pulled away from the curb.

I raced the Maxima towards Ridgewood Avenue and knew exactly what I'd find. The scene on my grandmother's street mirrored the one on Market Street. Unlike Gunz, I stayed in the car. There was no need for me to exit the vehicle. I could see from where I was parked that cops were all over my grandmother's house. Without being told, I already knew that Marinda Santiago was dead. She lived alone. And although we weren't close, she was still my grandmother. Still my mother's mother. Still my blood. Her death called for vengeance.

I thought back to my early years on Ridgewood Avenue in the house my grandmother bought when she left Washington, D.C., in

1980. I remembered all the interactions between my mother and my grandmother. Their relationship strained, due to my mother's change of religion. I remember all the pork chops my grandmother tried to force on Salimah and me after my mother died. The Christian lifestyle Miranda Santiago tried to impose on us had caused me and Salimah to flee as teenagers.

But no matter her character flaws, Miranda Santiago had been punished enough. She'd suffered through the loss of her husband and two sons. Then the loss of her last remaining child, my mother, who'd died on a ferry. To lose her two grandchildren to the streets had to have been rough. She didn't deserve to be killed for no sin of her own.

"Rest in peace, Grandma. Give Granddad, H.J, Cheo, my mother and Salimah a hug for me."

Anthony Fields

Chapter 26

Angel

Carl H. Moultrie Superior Court

Washington, D.C.

"El-Amin, c'mon. Time for court. Time for court," the U.S. Marshal said as he opened the door of the holding cage in back of the courtroom.

I was led into the courtroom. The galleries were packed with people who'd come to find out the fates of their loved ones who'd been arrested the day before. I saw the man sitting at the defense table but didn't recognize him. I was seated next to the man, who was writing something onto a piece of paper.

"Hey, kiddo," the man said and turned to face me.

I looked into the face of Jay Alexander Williams with a confused look. "Jay?"

"Don't look so happy to see me," Jay replied.

"Where did … where did you …?"

"Where did I come from? Good question. Just flew in from the West Coast last night. Our mutual friend sent me here to represent you. He wants you out of jail, pronto."

"Carlos wants me out of jail? Pronto? Why? And how does he even know where I am?" I asked in rapid succession.

"Don't know. Don't know. Don't know. All I know is that the big kahuna sent me here to work my magic and that's what I plan to do. Relax, you should be a free woman in a few minutes, we'll talk more later."

***

"Doug Barne, for the government, Your Honor. We are requesting a seven-day B1-A fold for the defendant. Kareemah El-Amin escaped prosecution in the courthouse several years ago when the lone witness against her was killed while in the Witness Protection Program. Kareemah El-Amin was charged with multiple murders and weapons offenses. The government believes now, as it did then, that this defendant is a very dangerous woman. One who is a serious threat to the community. Kareemah El-Amin was arrested yesterday in a high crime area with a loaded firearm. We respectfully ask this court to remand this defendant on the B1-A hold."

"Defense Counsel Williams, the court will hear you now," the judge said.

"Thank you, Your Honor. The defense opposes such an egregious, dereliction of law ..."

Jay Alexander Williams argued vehemently for the courts to release me, but the woman judge sided with the government. And just like that, I was headed to the D.C. jail for the second time in my life.

***

I was back in the holding cage behind the courtroom when the big door opened and in walked Jay.

"Things evidently didn't go as planned. I'm sorry, Kareemah. The case law that Doug Barne argued about the B1-A hold was archaic and antediluvian, but it worked. Add that to the fact that Judge Sherah is a former prosecutor, who's obviously sympathetic to the U.S. Attorney's office. I called our friend and told him what happened. He's not too happy about the outcome. I told him what you asked me earlier. I was told to tell you he's coming to visit you."

"Visit me? When? Why?"

"Those are more questions I can't answer. I'm just a puppet on a string. You already know that. He says 'do this' and I do it. He says 'go there' and I go. Give me a break, would you?"

"You're right, Jay. I'm sorry. Finish what you were saying."

"I was told to tell you to expect a visit. Same as twelve years ago. He says you would know what that means. D.C. jail stopped housing females about ten years ago. They moved all the women and juveniles across the way to the Central Treatment facility. So, you'll be able to talk to our friend freely and ask him all the questions you asked me."

"Thanks for the heads up, Jay. I appreciated it."

"It's the least I could do, since I failed at getting you out."

"You did your best," I assured Jay.

"But my best wasn't good enough. I'll talk to you in a few days, kiddo. I'll come to see you after you visit with our friend. Okay?"

"Okay. Take care, Jay."

"Take care, Kareemah."

***

"… twenty-five to life is real/I get a body, take one right to jail/I know what it's like in hell/I did a stretch in a trifling cell/What you know about twenty-three and one/locked down all day underground never seeing the sun/visits stripped from you never seeing your son …"

The D.C. Department of Corrections van was nearly empty. Only two other women were on it with me. The van smelled of corn chips and old bologna sandwiches. I sat back in my seat, handcuffed to a belly chain and shackled and couldn't believe the recent turn of events. In the last thirty days, I'd been shot, lost my boyfriend, stood over my murdered mother and cried, killed my uncle. My daughter had been kidnapped, and now I was on my way to jail for a loaded gun. I listened to the Beanie Sigel lyrics on the throwback edition of the WPGC 95.5 morning show and felt each word. I thought about Jay Alexander Williams showing up out the blue to defend me.

Having been sent by Carlos, I couldn't figure out his angle, his motive. I hadn't seen or heard from Carlos in over ten years. And he suddenly makes his presence known while in the middle of a blood feud with Najee. He has to know my connection to Najee, who's obviously his enemy. And yet he sends Jay to free me.

"He wants to kill me," I inadvertently said aloud.

The woman seated near me whipped her head around and looked at me like I was crazy. I rolled my eyes at her. She looked away quickly. Thinking about my impending visit with the notorious drug czar who was at odds with the man I loved, made me nervous. Thinking about Carlos Trinidad brought on thoughts of his daughter. My daughter, Aniyah. I knew that while my daughter's heartbeat was strong inside me, there was one heartbeat that ceased to exist in me. Grief clenched at my heart, knowing my mother's heart no longer beat.

As tears came to my eyes, the van I was in turned onto Massachusetts Avenue, the D.C. jail and CTF quickly came into view. Both behemoth buildings looked like fraternal twins that had suffered a lot of abuse. I couldn't wipe my eyes the way I wanted, so I let the tears fall. Again, I pondered my current situation. The gun that was found in the BMW was the murder weapon used to kill Uncle Samir. In my grief-stricken state, I forgot to get rid of it. I wondered how long it took for law enforcement to match a specific gun to the bullets pulled from a person in a murder case. It couldn't be long. The one thing I was sure of was that I needed to be out of CTF when that happened. I'd have a better shot at coordinating my defense from the street.

***

Central Treatment Facility

"Strip, ladies," the female CO announced. "Act like we your husbands and boyfriends. Don't be bashful. We need you to take everything off. Everything. We see ass, pussy and titties, all day, every day. You ain't got nothing we ain't never seen. That includes venereal disease, etcetera. If you got crabs, don't trip, we got plenty of de-lice spray. You got gonorrhea in your pussy, we got plenty of penicillin. If you got a rash on your nasty ass, it can't penetrate these gloves we got on. Having a herpes outbreak? We got some cream for you! Got abscess on you and there's blood and pus oozing out, we don't give a fuck. We gon see it. We can't wait to see it. We gon search every cavity you got. It's gon feel like rape. So, ladies, please don't try to be slick. We love slick bitches. We got special shit for you slick bitches ..."

***

After going through the whole intake screening process, I was assigned to one of the two female units. As soon as we walked into the unit, the female CO said, "which one of you is El-Amin?"

"That's me," I told her.

"Aight, baby, put your shit in forty-eight cell, then come back down here. You got a social visit."

***

I walked into the visiting hall and saw people all over the phone. I saw a man sitting alone. He looked up at me and waved me over. His disguise was a good one, but his Hispanic features were unmistakable. His dark, unruly, curly hair was peppered with gray. Carlos Trinidad had to be in his early fifties, but disguise or not, he was still a specimen of physical attractiveness, sexy as hell. I walked over to him. He stood and embraced me. He kissed my cheek. Was that the infamous kiss of death?

"You haven't changed much over the years, Angel. Still a very beautiful woman," Carlos said as he broke our embrace.

"And you're still, tall, dark and handsome. Bill, is it?" I asked.

"You can call me Bill. I see you remembered. Always paid attention to detail. That's something I've always liked about you. Sit down."

I sat down in a chair across from Carlos. He pulled his seat up closer to me.

"You sent Jay to represent me. Thanks are in order, I guess."

"No need for that. Listen, let me get right to the reason for my visit. I know everything, Angel. Years ago in a Denny's on Benning Road, I told you I was like God, all knowing and all powerful. Well, that's almost true, still." Carlos smiled a sheepish, boyish smile. It was disarming and alarming at the same time. "Obviously, I know all about you and Najee. His belief that whoever fired those shots at y'all outside of your store in Southeast ..."

"I know who that was now. I didn't then, but I do now."

"You know who was in the black Escalade?"

I nodded my head. "I'll tell you after you finish telling me why you're here."

"Fair enough. As you know, Najee believed you were shot by bullets that were meant for him. Those bullets he thought were fired by my associates."

"Yeah, but ... how do you know that?"

Carlos smiled again. "You warned Najee not to start a war with me. Told him he couldn't win. His ego got in the way, he got mad and left you. After that he initiated his attack on my business."

"Ya talked to Najee?"

Carlos nodded his head.

"How?" I asked, incredulous. "Your man captured Najee? Ya killed him, didn't you? Carlos, please tell me that you didn't kill Najee!"

"I didn't kill Najee," Carlos said.

My shoulders sagged in disbelief. There was no way Najee was still alive. "You didn't kill Najee. One of your men did."

"Najee's not dead, Angel. I came here to tell you that, and to tell you why he's not dead. Najee Bashir is my son."

I couldn't believe what I'd just heard. But then an incident from the past rushed to mind. I had walked into Denny's one day and saw Najee sitting in a booth. I remembered thinking to myself how much Najee resembled Carlos. "You're lying. How can Najee be your son?"

"Why would I lie? Najee's mother's name is ... was Maria Santiago. She was my girlfriend when she got pregnant with my son. With Najee. In the streets, Maria heard whispers about some murders I committed. Those whispers were confirmed when a man appeared in our living room one night and spoke to me about those murders. Maria was there. She heard my admissions, became afraid of me. She left me and fled to New Jersey. To Newark, the city where her family was from. I had no idea where Maria had run to.

She met Nadeem Bashir after she got to Newark. Already pregnant. Najee's sister Salimah was Nadeem's only child."

"You just told me Najee's mother's name, his sister's name and the man he called his father's name. You must be telling the truth," I conceded.

"I am. Najee has a friend named Gunz—"

"I know that. I met him before in Newark. He's over-protective of Najee."

"My people abducted Gunz. He was the one that told me you had nothing to do with Najee's moves against me. He called Najee and we arranged a meeting. We all met at a restaurant and talked. I had known for weeks that Najee was my son. How? Because I was sent a photograph of Najee, by a man named Muhammad Farid Shahid. Apparently, Najee killed a man named Muqtar Kareem—"

"I don't mean to keep cutting you off, but just so you'll know, I was there. I was in Newark when everything happened. I was with Najee the day men tried to kill him as we left a restaurant in New York. One of those men told Najee that Muqtar ... Najee called him Mu ... that Mu had sent them to kill Najee. Najee had considered Mu a friend. He felt betrayed. I was with him the night he went into Mu's house and killed him."

"Najee never told me you were there, but since you know all that and you were there, then you know Najee took fifteen thousand kilos from Muqtar, right? And that was the cocaine you helped Najee move in D.C. without my consent."

"I'm not gonna lie about that. I helped him get the cocaine here by truck, I helped him settle in and then move the coke. My connections were still good. I'm guilty of that."

"Well, those fifteen thousand kilos didn't belong to Muqtar Kareem. They belonged to Muhammad Farid Shahid. His organization has been looking for Najee for the last nine months. Since Kareem was murdered and the cocaine was taken. But they had no idea where Najee or the cocaine was. Najee made a mistake by leaving Kareem's wife alive. She told Shahid the person who'd killed her husband and took the coke was Najee. Shortly thereafter, she was killed. By Muhammad Shahid's people. When I learned of the influx of cocaine in D.C. I wanted to trace its origin.

"Word got to Shahid that the cocaine was here in D.C., along with Najee. They reached out to me for permission to come here and get Najee. I refused that request. Not because I knew who Najee really was, because I didn't. I told them no because I didn't want other men from another organization running around my streets. When Najee brought his war to me, I reached out for info on Najee. That's when Shahid sent me the picture of Najee. I took one look at that photo, and I knew Najee was my son."

"Can't fuckin' believe it." That was all that I could say.

Carlos laughed. "You sound just like Najee. He said the exact same thing."

"I can only imagine. Where is Najee now?"

"I'll get to that in a moment. Najee told me about your daughter. Our daughter."

I looked into Carlos's eyes, and they seemed to penetrate my soul. "Najee got a big ass mouth, don't he?" I said and exhaled. "It's true. We share a child, Carlos. I got pregnant the night we got busy in the sauna at Bally's. I never told you about it, because I was afraid of what your reaction would be—"

"Najee told me all of that. I can understand your reasons for not reaching out to me. It's okay. No need to explain anything else. But where is Aniyah now? I need to see her, hold her."

My eyes watered immediately. "Before I answer that, I have to tell you some other things. Fill in some blanks. I already admitted to you that I killed Tony Bills and why. Well, Tony's daughter, Honesty—"

"I remember her. Tony brought her around a few times," Carlos said.

"Almost killed me and the baby. I was about seven months pregnant then. One of the stylists who worked for me left her purse in the shop. She came back for it and found me on the floor bleeding to death. She got me to the hospital in time to save the baby and me. It's the only reason that I am alive today. Me and Aniyah. While in the hospital recovering, my uncle Samir told me he was going to kill Honesty. I believed him. Told him all I knew about the teenager and her mother, Tina.

"But my uncle couldn't do it. He couldn't kill a young girl. He came to the hospital, and he lied to me. Told me that he'd killed Honesty. Again, I believed him. Fast forward nine years later. I was watching a graduation on TV. Michelle Obama was speaking. I heard the name Honesty Phillips, then saw her face. I couldn't believe it. I had thought the girl was dead. Thought Uncle Samir had killed her. I knew then that he lied to me. I got upset. Decided right then and there I had to kill the girl. The woman. I couldn't chance the fact that she'd come for me again.

"I learned her mother still lived in the same house in Kettering, M.D. I went there looking for Honesty. I found her mother there. I killed her. I don't know why I did it. I just did it. On impulse. Then I texted Honesty from her mother's phone and told her to come home. About thirty minutes later, she did. I tried to kill her. She had a gun. She tried to kill me. After shooting it out with Honesty, I fled. Got paranoid, thought maybe Honesty would tell the cops I killed her mother. So, I left town. Went to Newark, where my family lives. My cousin Aminah introduced me to Salimah, Najee's sister. I met him later. There was an instant attraction. We hooked up and became a couple. That's what led to me being there at Mu's house, the night Najee killed him and took the coke. I went and got the U-Haul and helped him load all that damn coke into it. Remember earlier when you mentioned the black Escalade and the shots being fired from it?"

Carlos nodded.

"I hadn't remembered after getting shot, but I wish I had. It was Tony's daughter Honesty in the Escalade firing those shots."

"How do you know that?" Carlos asked.

"Because I do. The Escalade belonged to her father. Tony loved that truck. He drove it often. The night I killed Tina Brown, when I left the house after shooting it out with Honesty, I saw the Escalade parked in the driveway. It wasn't there when I first got there. That meant Honesty had to be driving it. I'm sure of that. She found out where my store was and brought me a move. Those bullets fired that night wasn't meant for Najee. They were meant for me. When Honesty figured out I had survived the attack, she went to my mother's house and killed my mother—"

"Are you serious? She killed your mother?"

A new set of tears welled up in my eyes and fell as I nodded my head. "Night before last. My mother always kept Aniyah. To keep her safe. I went there to check on them, I found my mother in the living room, on the floor. Shot in the face. I went looking for Aniyah. Her bed was empty, and she was gone—"

"Gone? Gone where?"

I wiped at the tears falling down my cheeks. I shrugged. "Don't know. But I know Honesty took her."

"But how … how do you know Honesty took her?" Carlos asked.

"She left a letter taped to Aniyah's mirror, in her room. She told me she killed my mother and took my daughter. Said I'd killed her mother and father and now we were even."

Carlos's face changed to a look I'd never seen before. One of anger and pure evil. His eyes went dark. "So, you're telling me that Tony's daughter—Honesty—has my daughter?"

I nodded.

"Do you think she's killed her?"

I completely broke down then. Made a scene in the visiting hall. People's eyes zoomed in on me and Carlos. I quickly gathered myself. Shrugged to regain my composure. I shrugged again. "I don't know. But I don't think so. I think I'd feel something if she did."

"If Honesty has touched a hair on my daughter's head, I will personally kill her and every remaining relative she has left. "Do you know where is? Where she might be?"

Chapter 27

Carlos

"I don't have a clue. I been looking for her ass since I read the letter she left on the mirror. I only knew of one address for her. Her mother's house on Benedict Court. In Kettering. I went there immediately," Angel told me.

"And she wasn't there, huh?"

"If I had caught her there, I'd be in jail for a murder, not a gun. Naw, she wasn't there. Nobody was there. The house looked like it ain't been lived in for months. After leaving there, I just drove around. Forgot all about the gun in my purse. That's when I ran the red light and ended up here."

"Yeah, Jay told me all of the details of the gun case—"

"Carlos, wait," Angel interrupted, "There's more to the story. I never told Jay everything. When I saw my mother laying there dead with bullet holes in her head ... I lost it. Then I discovered Aniyah was missing. I blamed my uncle, the one I told you about earlier. Samir was supposed to have killed Honesty as a fourteen-year-old. She was never supposed to grow up. Had he just admitted to me that he couldn't kill that little girl, I would have gotten out the hospital and did it myself. It would have been too easy to kill her. By lying to me, that put me behind the eight ball and jeopardize my life. I called my uncle Samir to my mother's house and killed him."

"You killed your uncle? Samir?" I asked.

Angel nodded her head. "I blamed him for everything."

I couldn't believe what I was hearing. Although I'd heard of the work Angel had put in, it was a different thing to hear her say certain things. I was sitting in front of the one woman whom I considered the living personifications of me. Angel was a ruthless, natural-born killer. A vindictive one. She was heartless. Just like me. Our lives had taken a similar path. Angel felt betrayed by her uncle, so she killed him. I'd felt betrayed by my aunt, so I killed her.

"After I killed my uncle," Angel continued, "I left. Drove around trying to figure out where Honesty might be. I ran the light.

The cops got the gun out my purse. That's the gun that I killed my uncle with."

"Shit!" I muttered.

"Shit is right. Once the cops in Maryland connect that gun to the murder at my mother's house, my ass is awaiting trial again."

"We'll see about that," I assured Angel. "I still have friends in high places. We made DNA disappear before, a gun should be even easier. First, we need to find Aniyah. Then I'll deal with your gun case. You got a seven-day hold, I should be able to accomplish both tasks before your next court date."

"That's what's up, but what's good with Najee? You haven't said nothing else about him other than that he's your son."

"Najee is back in Newark."

"Back in Newark? Why?

"The Shahid organization killed his sister—"

"What? No! Salimah? Salimah's dead?"

I nodded. "Killed her the night Najee and I met at Live! Casino. About two days ago. And you already know that he's crushed and out for blood. He left for Newark the same day he found out. Then he got there ... yesterday and got hit with more bad news. Muhammad Shahid's men killed his grandmother—"

"Najee's grandmother?"

"Yeah. They killed Najee's grandmother, Miranda, Gunz's mother and grandmother, his friends Yasir and Hasan's family and some other people."

"Damn! Fuck and shit! I know Najee's fucked up about that."

"You already know what he's on. I tried to talk to him but he's stubborn, just like me."

"All this shit happening like this ... this shit is crazy. My mother, you being Najee's father, dudes killing his sister, Aniyah is taken, I'm in jail ... this shit feels like a *Lifetime Movie*."

"If something happens to my daughter, it's gonna turn into a horror movie."

***

As I climbed into the backseat of the Maybach, I spit out the putty that stretched my gums. I removed the fake nose and glasses. I pulled out my phone and sent a text to three different women.

"Where to, boss?" my driver, Enrique asked.

"Take me home, Enrique," I replied.

I made a call. An international call. The phone on the other end rang five times.

"Carlos. How are you, my friend?" Pedro Escobaro answered the call.

"Pedro, I need a favor. I need some information," I told him.

"Tell me what you need, Carlos. I will do what I can to get it."

"Are you familiar with a man named Muhammad Farid Shahid?"

"I am. Works with the Sinaloa's. You need info on him?"

"I do. I need anything you can find on him. It's urgent."

"I'll call you as soon as I have what you need."

"Thank you, Pedro."

"What are friends for, Carlos? Goodbye."

***

My margarita cocktail was shaken, not stirred. It was fruity, yet spicy. Just the way I like it. Thoughts of a little girl I never seen flooded my mind. I sat on the couch in the study vexed. Moments later, two women entered the study. One was Dorothy Benigan, and the other was a woman from my past who I hadn't seen in a while. The woman was petite. Her skin the color of caramel. She'd grown dreadlocks that were dyed a light brown. They accented her hazel eyes. I stood up and embraced her. "Latesha, it's been a long time."

"I agree, Carlos," Latesha Gerrison said.

"Thank you for coming on such short notice."

"How can I ever refuse you? You called, then texted. I come."

"How's the new job? Never figured you for a CIA type."

Latesha broke our embrace. "What are you drinking? I think I need a good drink."

"Here, take mine," I said and handed Latesha my cup.

"The CIA is okay. Never thought I'd join up myself. Always thought I'd be an actress or something. Especially since you had me playing all kinds of different roles. The last time I was around you, I was your niece, right?"

I smiled and nodded. "Your role was important, though."

"Important, huh? Bullshit. Women will do anything in the name of love. You had my ass locked up at the D.C. jail for almost a year and a half."

"Like I said, it was important. Nevertheless, I need you again," I told her.

"Anything but that. I love you, Carlos, but I'm not going back to that dirty ass jail," Latesha stated emphatically.

"Don't need you to. What I need now are your resources. Yours, Dorothy's and Susan's." I looked over at Dorothy.

Dorothy smiled. "I'll do whatever. I talked to Susan. She's in a meeting that she can't get out of. So, it looks like it's just us. What do you need?"

"Information. I need everything you can find out about two people. Everything."

"Who?" Latesha and Dorothy said in unison.

"Muhammad Farid Shahid and Honesty Phillips. And I need that info yesterday."

Chapter 28

Angel

"El-Amin, go ahead and move into 22 cell," the fat, man-like CO said. I didn't want to take anything out of the cell. I felt like I needed all new sheets and clothes. Holding my nose, I gathered my stuff out of 48 cell and moved to 22 cell. The woman in 48 cell had been homeless. Her feet, pussy and breath smelled like her ass. Pure shit. I couldn't believe a human being could smell so bad. There was no way I was staying in that cell. I was in 22 cell, making up the bed on the top bunk when my celly walked in. She was cute in a tomboyish kind of way. She had a low-boy haircut with waves spinning. She had a beautiful skin tone and pretty white teeth.

"The lunch trays just came in, celly," the woman announced.

"I don't want that shit. You can have my tray," I told her.

"Say less," she said and walked out of the cell.

After making the bed completely, I climbed in the bunk. Everything Carlos had told me was on my mind. I couldn't believe how bad things could be in one year. Salimah was dead. I imagined Najee somewhere in Newark killing behind his sister's death. Salimah was the lifeblood that ran through his veins. Without her, he was empty inside. I could hear his animalistic roar as he unleashed murder and mayhem on all who stood in his path that led to total annihilation. Najee believed in mass destruction that would equal retribution.

I thought about everything Najee had said about his grandmother. The good and bad. To think somebody killed her to get back at Najee was crazy. According to Najee, there were twenty degrees of separation between him and Miranda Santiago. Apparently, he was wrong. I thought about the families of his friends. I had never met Hasan or Yasir, but I had met Gunz. I remembered my first impression of Najee's man. I hated him. He'd threatened me at the airport the day me and Najee was leaving to go on our trip that formed our bond. Our love. I thought about the eyes that I'd seen on Gunz's face. They always told the story. His eyes told me that he meant every word he said when he threatened me. I could now imagine the pain he had to be in about the loss of his mother and grandmother. Two generations lost in one senseless act. Things were all bad in Newark, New Jersey and about to get worse.

"You sure you don't want none of this shit?" my celly asked as she entered the cell carrying two dark brown food trays. "It's chicken salad, macaroni noodles and applesauce. It ain't the best, but you get used to it."

"I'm good. I will never get used to jail food. I might not never eat that shit."

"Oh, yeah? You gon starve then ... What's your name, celly? So, I can stop calling you celly."

"Kareemah. But you can call me Angel."

"Say less. Hope you don't mind me asking, but I gotta know who I'm in a cell with. What you in here for, Angel?"

"I'm on a seven-day hold. But my charge is CPWL."

"A seven-day hold? For carrying a pistol without a license? Fuck you had, a Tommy gun? A street sweeper?"

I shook my head. "I had a Glock forty."

The woman sat the two trays down on the desk and sat down to eat. "Never heard of them giving nobody a seven-day hold for no simple gun charge," she said between bites of chicken salad. "They usually let you go on PR. Unless you on paper or something. You on some kinda supervision?"

"Naw, none of that shit."

"This your first time in jail?"

"It's my first time at this jail. I was at the D.C. jail in '03 for some murders. But I beat all that shit," I said and locked my arms beneath my head.

"In 2003? For some murders? Oh, shit! You're *that* Angel?" The woman stood up and turned to face me.

I sat up and braced myself for some kind of an attack, but none came.

"Oh ... my ... gawd! Kareemah El-Amin. Also known as Angel. Bitch, you are a real live street legend around here. They had stories about you in the *DON DIVA*, the feds magazine and in ASIS.

Some white dude named Seth Fersanti wrote a book about D.C. and you was in it. Real talk. You are like the Griselda Blanco of D.C. I was out Maryland, locked up on a body when you was doing your thing in the streets, but I always heard your name. I read about your case in the newspapers. Muthafuckas killed your little sister, and you went HAM. I remember that shit like it was yesterday. The government dismissed your charges and you walked right out of the courtroom on their ass. Your best friend ... the hot bitch ..."

"Fatima."

"That's right. Fatima Muhammad. She got poisoned while in the Witness Protection Program. Damn! I can't believe it's you. I'm in the fuckin' cell with Angel ..."

"Stop what you doing ... uh?"

"Bay One. My bad, Angel, should've been told you my name when you first moved in. My government joint is Bayona Lake, but I been Bay One since I was a kid."

"Aight, Bay One ... you need to stop what you doing. I ain't nobody special. I'm just Kareemah from ward seven. Born and raised right up the street from the projects."

"Which projects?" Bay One asked.

"Pick one. Simple City, Eastgate or Benning Park."

"Modesty is a good character trait to have, Angel. I love it, but we both know the truth. Never admit to anything that can be repeated against you in court. My stupid ass had to learn that the hard way."

"Why you say that?"

Bay One finished up one tray then moved it to start in on the next one. She walked over to the sink and drank from the spigot. She wiped at her mouth, then said, "I been here for a few years. I was fighting a body myself. That's what I came in on. I'm from the projects. Arthur Capers. A dude I raised up in the hood, he killed my daughter. She was my only child. I got her name tattooed right here." Bay lifted her dark blue uniform shirt up over her sports bra.

I could see the tattoo imprinted over her heart. It said, "ESHA (heart pic) I LOVE YOU.'

"My daughter's name was Ronesha, but we called her Esha. The dude I raised ... TJ ... he killed my daughter for reasons that only he knew. He took my baby away from me and crushed everything inside me. She meant the world to me. I caught his ass a couple weeks later when he least expected it. In the second court near Seventh Street. I killed him in front of everybody. Nailed his ass to the concrete."

"As you should have," I remarked. I would've done the same thing if somebody killed my daughter." I thought about myself standing over Honesty's body after shooting her dead.

"But what I didn't know," Bay One continued, "was that a detective was looking for TJ to arrest him for murder. Not my daughter's murder, but some other bodies. He was sitting in an unmarked car nearby watching TJ. He watched me kill TJ. Then he arrested me. He ended up being the only eyewitness against me on the case. That's how I got here. But listen to this. Once I got here, I started catching the pack. Dope, weed, pills, strips ... shit like that. The COs kept raiding my cell, so I knew that there was a rat in my mix.

I automatically assumed it was this wild bitch named Tika. Mytika Lemons. The bitch was always in the police face and sitting in the office with them and shit. I got mad one day, tricked her into the cell and killed her ass. Right across the hall in the other female housing unit. The only person that knew I did it was Gloria. This bitch Gloria Dunbar was locked up on a body. Stabbed another bitch to death on Nelson Place off of Minnesota Avenue. Come to find out the bitch was a real live killer. She was facing time in Maryland and Virginia for multiple murders. Bitches back then compared Gloria to you. Bitch had everybody fooled. She contacted the government and told them I killed Tika."

"Get the fuck outta here!" I exclaimed.

"Real talk. Cooked my ass. And the fucked-up part is that I killed Tika because I thought she was the rat and all the time, the rat was Gloria. The whole time Gloria was smoking all my weed and then dropping notes to the C.O.s, telling them I had the weed."

"Damn!" All I could do was shake my head.

"I copped to Mytika's murder. Either that or face off against Gloria in court. They gave me ten years for that."

"So, what happened with the other beef? The charge you faced for the nigga that killed your daughter?"

"I copped to that, then took my cop back. Ended up beating that shit," Bay One said and smiled.

"How the fuck you do that with a detective as the eyewitness?"

"I caught a helluva break. The detective that was on TJ's line was also on Khadafi's line …"

"Khadafi? I heard that name before."

"I'm not surprised. Everybody's heard his name. Either in the streets or on the news. That was a vicious young nigga, Angel. Bullshit ain't nothing, his body count will make both of ours look like light shit. Ain't nobody fuckin' with him. Sean Branch, Antone White, Wayne Perry, Kevin Grey, Rodney Moore, Tony Hammond … none of them niggas ain't got more bodies than Khadafi. Nigga been crushing shit since he was like eleven or twelve. He watched two niggas kill his mother when he was seven years old. Two crackheads lied on his mother and told these two niggas that she stole their stash of drugs. Fucked him up. By the time Khadafi was thirteen, he'd killed all four of them … the two crackheads and the two niggas … Rick and Moody. All he did was kill.

"Until he went to jail at sixteen and did ten years in prison. He came home after that and started killing again. The detective tried to arrest Khadafi out Maryland one night. He wasn't having it. They shot it out and both ended up in the hospital. As fate would have it, the cop died from his wounds and Khadafi lived. Just like that, the eyewitness on my case was gone. That's how I beat the case."

"That's crazy. You talking about you caught a helluva break. Helluva break is an understatement. Khadafi saved you from doing thirty years to life."

"Yeah, he did that … but I can't pat him on the back," Bay One said.

"Why not?" I asked.

"Because his gangsta ass pulled a Gloria Dunbar on a muthafucka …"

"Huh? What?"

Bay One nodded. "You heard me right. He pulled a Fatima Ma-hammad. He … Khadafi was facing a rack of time for the detective's murder out Maryland. Then, D.C. wanted to charge him with some shit. That nigga broke under pressure and testified against one of his friends. A good dude that had killed a rack of niggas who killed his daughter."

I swung my legs off the bed. "I remember that. A girl got killed at a gas station, after attending a funeral for her boyfriend. The girl's father killed seven people on Alabama Avenue, then killed a rack of other people. All the murders happened in my neighborhood. The dude they charged with it was named Anthony or something …"

"Antonio. His name was Antonio 'Ameen' Felder. I know because I helped him out. I got on the stand in his trial and told the jury that Khadafi was lying on Ameen. Me and another dude named Kilo. It worked. Ameen beat that shit. Walked right out the courtroom, just like you did back in the day."

"That's what's up. I wonder what happened to him?"

"Who, Ameen?" Bay One asked.

"Yeah," I replied.

"Don't know. But Khadafi's bitch ass is out Maryland somewhere doing three years. He'll be home soon. Killing and getting money again. Niggas gon act like he ain't never told on nobody. You know how that shit goes. This new generation is fucked up. No morals. No principles. I got almost three years in on ten. I'm waiting for the feds to come and get me now. I'm tryna go out the feds, get married to my girlfriend Lisa and then finish this last five years. After that, I'm getting the fuck out of D.C. The city done changed too much. I done changed too much. My daughter gone. Ain't nothing left for me here. Fuck D.C. And the land they got from Maryland and Virginia to build it on."

"I feel you, Bay One," I said and laid back down. "I feel you."

Bay One grabbed both now empty trays and left the cell. But her last words remained.

"Fuck D.C. and the land they got from Maryland and Virginia to build it on …"

How many times had I thought about leaving D.C., but never left? I thought about my plans to leave D.C. and go to L.A. I wanted to be a celebrity back then, a movie star. I fancied the glitz and fame. Wanted to see the credits roll on the big screen with my name in them. I want my name in bright lights. These were the foolish dreams of a teenager. Dreams that faded away once I touched the first fifty bricks of cocaine Carlos Trinidad fronted me.

I thought about my life and how different things would be had I just took on a different path to stardom. Had I never pulled that gun from under the bed and killed Tony. My sister would still be alive. Fatima would still be alive. My mother would still be alive. My uncle Samir would still be alive. But on the flip side of all that, my daughter would have never been born, and I would not have met Najee Bashir.

"Fuck D.C," I muttered to myself. Then fell asleep.

Anthony Fields

Chapter 29

Honesty

"Your name is beautiful, Aniyah. What does it mean?"

"My name means Angelic, yet majestic in Arabic. My mommy picked it out."

"Is your whole family Muslim?" I asked Angel's daughter.

"Umm hum. Everybody on my mother's side is. I don't know about my father's side because I never met him or anybody on his side. He's in Puerto Rico. Mommy says that she's going to take me to Puerto Rico one day to meet him."

Not if I can help it. "That's good. Are you pretty good in school, Aniyah?"

Aniyah popped a Chick-fil-A chicken tender into her mouth after dipping it in sauce. All the little girl ate was Chipotle and Chick-fil-A. "I think I'm a great student. Everybody likes me. My grades are always A's and B's, which reminds me, I've missed a few days. They are probably worried about me."

I looked down at my chicken sandwich that was untouched and getting cold. "What school do you go to?"

"Islamic Village Learning Center. In Southeast. I'm in the fourth grade. The principal ..." I saw Aniyah's lips moving, but I tuned her out completely. My mind was elsewhere all of a sudden. I'd had Angel's daughter for two days and had yet to speak to Angel. I'd bought the girl a prepaid iPhone 4 just to be able to call her mother, but as of yet there'd been no answers. Why? Where the hell is Angel? And why is she acting like she doesn't want her daughter back?

I imagined a frantic Angel at home somewhere, pacing the floor, worried about her young daughter. I imagined her grief as she dealt with the death of her mother, and the fearful uncertainty of the fate of her child. Surely, Angel had to believe I'd kill her daughter just as easily as I'd wash my clothes. Angel had to know that. I think I proved that the day I tried to kill her in her salon. I saw her belly was big with child, but I didn't care. All I cared about was killing the woman who'd killed my father.

I thought about my father. Anthony Jerome Phillips. Also known as Tony or Tony Bills. Images of my father came to mind. He was a very handsome man. A beautiful smile, a warm, bubbly personality, a smooth mocha complexion and dark wavy hair. I remembered all the intimate moments I'd shared with my father. All the times he kissed me and told me how much he loved me. He called me his twin. I thought about the days leading up to my moment. The moment when I'd finally get my chance to kill Angel. I was calm, I planned out a strategy and I saw it through. I never wavered in my position or in my aim. But still I failed. My failure then on that day, essentially cost my mother her life. An irrefutable fact that I had to live with every day.

Trigger's slurping the dregs of soda from his Chick-fil-A cup snapped my reverie.

I looked in his direction. He must've felt me looking because he turned to lock eyes with me. Then his eyes fell on Aniyah. He rolled them with femininity and went back to devouring his meal. Trigger was adamant about getting rid of Aniyah. The forty-eight-hour deadline he'd set had been renegotiated after a marathon round of bomb head, wet pussy and tight ass that could coax life out of a dead man. But that didn't mean I still didn't have to hear him complain all the time ...

"We gon end up on America's Most Wanted, fuckin' with your crazy ass, True. Muthafuckas don't care about a few murders. That shit happens all the time. All day, every day. But when you start fuckin with them kids, that's some whole other shit. That's why they made Amber Alerts and shit like that ..."

"Aniyah," I said, rising from the table. "Why don't you call your grandma's phone back. Then dial your mother's phone again and see if one of them answers."

"Okay," Aniyah replied, pulled out her cell phone and dialed a number. After a while, she ended that call and dialed another. Seconds later, to my dismay, she ended that call as well. "Nobody's answering. Either my mother or my grandmother usually always answer their phones."

I cleared my food and Aniyah's from the table. "Is there anybody else that you can call that might know where your mom is?"

"Uh ... my uncle Samir and Hasan, but I don't know their numbers by heart. I know the number to my school. Want me to call there?"

"No, baby. Not the school. We don't want the principal and teachers to worry about your mother and grandmother. Let's just go and play *Call of Duty* some more and hopefully one of them will call us back soon."

Aniyah loved playing *Call of Duty* on the Xbox. "Yeah. let's do that."

***

"This shit is getting strange," I told Trigger an hour later.

"Newsflash, this shit been strange, True," Trigger replied. "I told you that from the beginning."

"I know you did, but things were different then. I never envisioned being at a stalemate like this. I'm starting to feel like I've done all of this for nothing. Angel is missing in action. We ain't gaining no ground. I'm starting to question myself and second guess myself too much."

"I been questioning this and second guessing this stupid ass shit. It made a little sense at first. But as the days go by, it's making little sense at all to stick with it."

I jumped on the couch and laid back, covering my head and face with a towel. "Aaaarghhhh! I can't believe this shit. Angel, where the fuck are you?"

Anthony Fields

Chapter 30

Det. Mitch Bell

Prince George's Police Department

"Mitch, what're you eating for lunch?"

"You?" I muttered. Then aloud, I said, "Whatever you trying to eat, Sandra, but it's on me."

Sandra Smith was P.G. County's best version of Nicki Minaj in a police uniform. All the men in the department had tried to bag Sandra, but all had failed. "Shit, that's even better. I was thinking Panera Bread, but since lunch is on you, I'm thinking Olive Garden. Their 'never ending pasta bowl' lunch sounds good right now."

"You eating in or taking out?"

"I take lunch in about forty minutes. And all this week, my lunch break is an hour break. So, it's really up to you," Sandra said.

The phone on my desk rang. I picked it up. "Forty minutes is good. I'll be finish what I'm doing by then. We can go there and eat in," I told Sandra, then answered the caller. "Hello?"

"Mitch, hey, it's Joel Cohen." Joel Cohen was a homicide detective in D.C. "I heard you've been inquiring on my end about Angel."

"Angel? What Angel? Can't say that"

"My bad, Mitch. You know her as Kareemah El-Amin. But here in D.C, we know her as Angel."

"You're right, Joel. I forgot about that nickname. I gotta case out here that happened recently. House in Clinton. Victims were her mother and a man we've just identified as her uncle. DNA evidence puts her on the scene the night of the murders, but it doesn't appear that she lives there. I don't think she's the killer, but I'm just doing my due diligence. Maybe something from her past resurfaced. Or somebody. Catch my drift?"

"Drift caught and that's the reason for the call. I consider myself one of the foremost leading authorities on serial killers in the District of Columbia and our girl Angel definitely fits that bill. So, if it turns out that someone did kill Angel's mother and uncle ... the murder rate in the city and beyond is about to be sky high."

"You think so?" I asked.

"I know so," Joel replied. "Let me fill in a few blanks for you, Mitch. I been in this homicide department for over twenty-three years, and I have never seen or heard of another case like hers. I sat in on the proffer sessions when her friend Fatima Muhammad got arrested and flipped. Poor woman was scared to death of Angel. Tried to string us along at first, you know, tell us about the murders, but mitigate Angel's role in them. Since Fatima Muhammad's prints were found at the tourist home where the murders happened, there was enough leverage to threaten her into coming clean.

"The stories we heard in that interview room was never released to the public. Had the case went to trial, a lot would have been revealed, but it didn't, so the details were never exposed. What you're about to hear is exclusive from my mouth to God's ears. This chick Angel makes John Muhammad and his Malvo look like choir boys. Wanna hear it?"

Joel had definitely piqued my curiosity. "After putting it like that, how could I not want to hear about her?"

"Angel's father was her first victim," Joel started.

"Her father?"

"You heard me. Her father. Abdul Khaliq El-Amin. Turns out the good brother was a devout Muslim by day and a super pervert, pedophile by night. He had been raping Angel since she was about nine or ten years old. One day, Angel comes home to find her father attempting to rape her sister. Angel decides she has to save her younger sister from their father. She concocts a plan and tells no one but Fatima Muhammad.

"Angel lures her father to Anacostia Park and stabs him to death. She was fifteen years old. Case goes unsolved. She literally gets away with murder. A few years later, Angel goes off to college in North Carolina. Forget which one. But she meets a guy. A basketball player. Popular guy. Good with the ladies. The guy takes her innocence that she's reimagined, then spurns her. Angel lures the guy to a roof on campus and sexes him. Then she pushes him off the roof, killing him. She leaves school and moves back to D.C. Once she's back here, she decides that she wants to move to L.A. and become a movie star. But she doesn't have the money to support herself in California while waiting to be discovered.

"She puts herself in a position to meet a guy. A guy who's rumored to be this big-time drug dealer. Guy with plenty of what she needs. Money. According to Fatima, Angel hooks up with the guy and they maintain a two-year-long relationship. Then ... boom ... one night, she kills him. Shoots the man in the fuckin' head and pretends like burglars did it. She makes off with drugs and over a million dollars in cash. Instead of taking the money and leaving, Angel decides to hook up with the dead man's drug connect. A name we all know ..."

"Carlos Trinidad," I blurt out.

"Correct. But how did you know that?" Joel asked.

"Read that part in the newspaper. Go on with the story, please."

"After convincing Carlos Trinidad to provide her with drugs, Angel politicks all over the city. Lining up most of her murdered boyfriend's clientele. Somewhere along the way two brothers, twin brothers actually, came into the picture. She sells them drugs. Kilos of cocaine. At some point, she became sexually involved with one of the brothers. Dearaye James. His twin brother was Deandre. Then for some reason, Angel dumped Dearaye and starts to mess with the brother, Deandre. The jilted lover, Dearaye, gets mad and sends hired killers to kill Angel and his own brother ..."

"Damn!" I interrupted. "No offense, Joel, ... and excuse my language, but her pussy must have gold lined in it. Sending killers at your own twin brother over some pussy? I couldn't imagine it."

"No offense taken, buddy, and I agree with you completely. The hired killers kidnap, rape and kill Angel's sister ..."

"The one that she killed her father to protect."

"That's the one. Angel only had one sister. Angel snaps after the death of her sister. She puts up a lot of money, and hires killers of her own to find the killers of her sister. Again, according to Fatima Muhammad, Angel orders the killings of over thirty people. Some of the murders she carried out herself. Her hired killers, two local dudes that were cousins, Andre 'Stink' Richardson and Mark 'Boochie' Murphy found out the identities of all the people involved in the death of Angel's sister. Two men were the ring leaders, Dearaye James and Thomas "Tommy Gunz" Murphy. Angel gets Stink and Boochie to kidnap both men. Then she strangles one and blows the other's brains out. Angel goes on to order more killings. The other people who were a part of the whole plan and whoever took part in her sister's deaths. Stink and Boochie did their jobs well. After all of that was done, Angel turned her attention to the two hired killers ..."

"Stink and Boochie."

"Glad to see that you're paying attention. Wanting no ties that could lead back to her and her murderous rampage, Angel lures the two hired killers to the Tourist Home on Talbert Street in Southeast. There she kills both killers and a woman who worked at the Tourist Home. Fatima Muhammad witnessed everything. She was arrested a week later at the home of her boyfriend, a guy that was under investigation by the FBI and ATF for drugs and guns. That's how she ended up in our interview room in the first place. Everything that Ijust told you is what Fatima told us. Do you know the rest of the story?"

"I do. Fatima Muhammad was going to connect the dots for prosecutors here in Maryland after she testified against Angel in DC. I remember that. But she never got a chance to testify because she was killed while in the witness protection program. Poisoned."

"Now, I see why you made detective your first time up. Seriously though, since beating the murders, we've heard virtually nothing from her. It was as if she dropped from the face of the earth. Well, except for the fact that she got shot in 2005."

"Somebody shot Angel in 2005?"

"Yep. And it appeared to be someone she knew because the Salon ... she was shot in her salon ... was closed for the day. Whoever the shooter was, Angel opened the door and let them in. She was shot four times and almost died. Someone found her at the shop ... one of the stylists who had left something there ... and got her to a

222

hospital in time to save her and the baby. Angel was like seven or eight months pregnant when she was shot."

Angel was pregnant when she was shot in 2005. I quickly did the math in my head. As the photos all over the house in Clinton came back to me. In almost every photo of Naimah El-Amin, there was a little girl. The little girl as a baby up until what appeared to be the present days before her death. The young girl appeared to be about nine or ten years old in the photo. It made perfect sense to me now. The young girl was Naimah El-Amin's granddaughter. Angel's daughter. I was half listening to Joel and still thinking about all that I'd just heard when another thought hit me. Something that I'd read in the newspaper articles at the CNN building, something that Joel had said. "Joel, sorry to cut you off, but what was the guy's name that Angel hooked up with? The guy she ended up killing and taking his drugs and the million cash?"

"That would be Tony Bills. His government name as Anthony J. Phillips."

Anthony Phillips. Anthony Phillips. Where had I heard that name before? I racked my brain until it came to me. A cold case murder from last year. A case where a woman had been killed. In her home, by an alleged intruder. The woman's daughter came home and encountered the intruder after the intruder had killed her mother. The daughter had retrieved a gun from somewhere in the home and shot at the intruder. A shoot out ensued. But the intruder had gotten away, unharmed. The details came back to me in waves. The woman who had been killed was Tina Brown. Her daughter's name was Honesty Phillips. I was one of the investigating detectives called to the scene in Kettering, MD. I thought about the surreal nature of what we'd been told that had happened. The evening I talked to Honesty Phillips played in my mind …

"I walked into the house using the garage entrance. I called out to my mother but received no reply. I was frozen with fear. I remembered that my father kept a gun hidden in the house …"

"Stop right there, Honesty. You said your father kept a gun hidden in the house?" Able Voss asked.

"Yeah."

"And what is your father's name? Where is he? We need to contact him."

"Anthony Phillips. My father's name was Anthony Phillips. But you can't contact him, though."

"And why is that?" I asked.

"Because he's dead. He was killed twelve years ago ..."

The evening I listened to Honesty Phillips tell her version of the story about an intruder killing her mother didn't make sense. There were enough holes in her story to sink it in a river of doubt. Weeks later, Able Voss and I interviewed Honesty Phillips again. This time at the police station. Her story that day basically mirrored the one she'd told us the night of the murder.

"I got the gun out and went down the hall. I walked in on the intruder standing over my mother."

"Okay, let's focus on the intruder for a minute, Honesty. When you reached the living room where your mother was, there was a person there, right?"

"Yes."

"And what was he wearing?"

"I don't recall. I just know the clothes were dark."

"Did you see any shoes?"

"No."

"Who fired the first shot? You or the intruder?"

"He did. Then I returned fire."

"Do you think your mother may have known the intruder?"

"I don't think so."

The reason I ask is, we checked out every door that leads into your house. And all the windows. We found no signs of a forced entry. That tells us your mother knew the person and let him in, or the intruder had a key. Either way, it leads us to believe this was not a random murder."

"... that she owns all sorts of property and is strictly legit. Woman has turned into Oprah Winfrey."

"Question, Joel, do you figure Angel for killing her mother and uncle?"

After a brief pause, Joel replied, "I can't say either way, Mitch. Wouldn't put it past her. She did kill her father, didn't she?"

"Yeah, well she had a good reason for that. Pervert fuck was raping her and her sister. There's nothing I've seen so far that suggests she killed them."

"Well, Mitch, your guess is as good as mine. Good luck figuring it out. Just thought I'd call and give you the rundown on Angel, since Donovan Baker told me you called this morning making inquiries. It's been fun, bud, until next time. You take care."

"You, too, Joel. And thanks for the history lesson. It was interesting and necessary. Have a good one." I placed the receiver onto the phone hook. I leaned forward and, on a whim, decided to type Kareemah El-Amin's name into the system again. As soon as I put the name in completely, a ping sounded. An alert.

According to the newest entries into the WIAAC system, Kareemah El-Amin had been arrested in D.C. a couple of nights ago. Traffic violation. Her vehicle was searched, and a loaded handgun was found. I looked at the date of the arrest and the time. Apparently, Kareemah had been arrested hours after the estimated time of the murders at her mother's house. And we know for sure she had been there that night. The vomit told us that. And she'd been arrested with a gun. I needed to see that gun. I stood up and grabbed my coat.

"Sandra, I'm gonna have to take a raincheck on that lunch," I called out. I gathered my things and left the station.

Anthony Fields

Chapter 31

Najee

1291 Vailsburg Terrace, Newark, NJ

Gunz walked into the spot on Vailsburg with bloodshot red eyes that told the story of his murderous intent. His clothes were disheveled, his hair unbrushed, his beard even looked different. And it hadn't even been twenty-four hours since I'd last seen him. I was leaned up against the wall when our eyes locked. Without saying a word, I understood where my partner's thoughts were. It didn't have to be communicated for me to know what he wanted. Our wants were the same. Vengeance. One of the seven deadly sins. And we wanted it in abundance.

***

"At the end of the day, even though I been in D.C. for a minute, the bricks are always and will always be home. Even when covering my face with dirt. And everybody in this room is a part of my team." I looked around at the faces of the men assembled in the room. Every face somber, yet attentive. Tye sat in a chair on the wall and Gunz stood next to him observing every face present. There was a traitor in the room. Gunz knew it and I knew it. We'd have to flush him out and that would take some time. Goo, Shotgun, Bebe, Rah Rah and Killa were all spread out around the living room, sitting or standing.

"We took a lot of losses recently and I'm not accustomed to losing. I just lost my sister and I'm fucked up about it. I'm fucked up about Gunz losing his mother and grandmother. I'm fucked up about Ya and his family. About Ha and his family. His little brother Haleem was one of us. His sister Anessa was us, too. I'm fucked up about my grandmother, Yo. None of the people I just named should be dead. None of 'em. But they are and I gotta … we gotta make it as right as we can. Y'all remember what we did after we found out who was behind Hasan's death? Well, this is about to be that times ten. I need to lace everybody's boots before I get any further. So, we'll all be on the same page. Last year when we were at the Casino in AC, I recognized Bones and Jim Jim from Spruce Street. They brought us the move that killed Hasan. We smoked three of them niggas and y'all know the rest. Okay, but here's what y'all don't know. Last year, niggas tried to body me, but I wasn't in the car ..."

"Supreme was in the Bentley. He got murked behind the wheel," Shotgun said.

"Yeah, that's right, but a few days later, the same niggas tried to get me outside of Justin's over the bridge in New York. I was prepared for the move. Defense became offense and all that. Before I killed one of the niggas, Yo, he told me that it was Mu who had sent them at me both times. Then it all made sense ..."

"Mu? Mu that was fuckin' with Limah?" Rah Rah asked.

"Yeah, that Mu. He wanted me out the way so that he could put niggas in key positions to take over Spruce Street and Brick towers."

"But that couldn't have ever happened," Goo added. "Especially not in the Towers. How the fuck was he gonna do that?"

"Your guess is as good as mine. But he thought he could do it. I know that for sure, because he admitted it."

"Mu's bitch ass admitted that to you, son?" Killa asked.

I nodded. "Yeah, right before I blew his muthafuckin' brains out."

"Damn, yo! That was your work? I heard Mu got crushed in his house, but I had no idea that was you!" Bebe exclaimed.

"You wasn't supposed to know it was me. Nobody knew that it was me. Well, not nobody. Only one person knew that I killed Mu. The one person who witnessed me do it. His wife."

"His wife? I thought Salimah was wifey," Shotgun said.

"Salimah was wifey, but Mu still had a real wife at home. Hafizah. Even though Mu was fuckin' my sister I knew he was married. I knew where he really lived, although he acted like he was living with Limah. But he didn't know I knew that. I trusted Mu, but I didn't trust Mu. If that makes any sense. It was my business to know his business when he didn't think I knew his business. And knowing his business saved my life. I was gon kill his wife the night I went to his house, but for some reason, I decided to let her live. I threatened her about the cops and all that, then I bounced. But not before taking all the coke and money Mu had at home. Instead of sticking around, I left for D.C. took everything with me."

"That's crazy, yo," Bebe commented. "Limah told us that you went to D.C. chasing a bitch. Some bitch named Angel."

I smiled, despite of myself. "Limah thought that, but that wasn't true. After killing Mu, I needed a change of scenery for a minute. I took the coke to D.C. and bubbled." There was a pyramid of small duffle bags on the floor by the bar. I walked over and tossed one to Rah Rah, then Bebe, Shotgun, Goo and Killa. "In D.C., I got fat while my team starved. Today, I'm making amends. In each one of them bags I just gave y'all is a quarter mill ..."

Somebody whistled.

"Cut the bullshit, yo," Killa said and unzipped the duffle. "Damn!"

"That's a gift from me to my men," I told the room. "Consider it me breaking bread."

"It's almost April, yo ..." Bebe said. "So, this gotta be an April fool's joke."

"You wasn't bullshittin," Goo said as he opened the bag and flipped through the bills.

"Muthafucka killed my sister and my grandmother, yo. Do it look like I got time to be bullshittin?" I hissed.

"My bad, yo," Goo apologized. "I didn't mean no disrespect."

"It's two-fifty in each one of them bags," I continued. "And if we make it through the next week or so, there's plenty more where that came from."

"The rap game was good, huh, son?" Killa said.

"Naw! Yo, the coke game was good. So ... where was I? Oh, yeah ... Mu was connected to some serious Muslim niggas. A nigga named Muhammad Shahid ..."

"I heard of son, yo," Bebe offered. "My pops came out of the Nation with him. They call him Farid ..."

"That's him," Gunz said, coming off the wall. "What else you know about him?"

"Not much. Just that he should be in his fifties now and that he was raised in the fruits of Islam. Back in New York somewhere. Him and Pops. Then he left the Nation and started his own Masjid in Brooklyn. Near Fulton Street in Bed-Stuy. Pops was fuckin with him hard but then they fell out. After they fell out, pops came back here to Newark. That was like twenty years ago, I think. Last I heard from Pops and his men talkin' about son, they said that the good brother, who was the Imam at one time, he turned into a drug king-pin. Started selling dope and coke to everybody in New York."

"I need to get up with your pops, yo. Later," I told Bebe. "Mu was connected to that nigga and his organization. I killed Mu and took money and coke that belonged to him. His people are respon-sible for all the murders mentioned earlier. My folks, Gunz's folks, Yasir's folks, Hasan's folks, all died because Muhammad Shahid couldn't find me. Somebody gave them niggas our names, our fam-ilies names. They snatched Ya …"

"Ayo," Bebe interrupted. "Are you sure about that part? About them snatching Ya? Word on the street is that Ya had beef with them Crazyville niggas and some Grape Street Crip niggas …"

"The niggas that snatched Ya from the halal spot wasn't Crips, yo. They were Muslims. Niggas had on Kufis and jalebeeyahs. Since when Crips start wearing shit like that?"

"True dat, true dat, but all I'm saying is that we can't jump the gun …"

Bebe was starting to get on my fucking nerves. "Jump the gun? Jump the hun?" I exploded. "I'm way past jumping the fuckin' gun. I been killing shit …" I pointed at Gunz and Tye. "We been killing shit since we stepped back into the city yesterday evening. All the murders that's been all over the news this morning, that's our work! Fuck you mean … jump the gun? This nigga Muhammad Shahid is fucked up about me killing Mu …"

"Naj, bruh, Mu been dead … what? Ten months? All the recent deaths of everybody's people just happened. Why would he … why would they wait …"

"Today is Friday," I said, interjecting and dismissing Bebe's words. Friday is Jumah. The assembly. The gathering of the Muslims. We got eight Masjids in New Jersey. One in West ward on Irvington and Garden State parkway. South ward got two. One in Clinton Hill and the other across from Seth Boyden. North ward got one on 4th Avenue near Grafton. East ward got one that's near Riverview Courts. The last three are here in the Central ward. Al-Nur is between Springfield and Clinton. Masjid Al-Islam is on High Street …"

"Wait a minute, yo … Naj, you buggin' out, yo," Bebe interrupted again." Are you saying that we targeting Muslims, yo? I'm Muslim. You Muslim …"

My anger took control of me. My anger and my thirst for blood and vengeance took over as I pulled the gun from my waist and shot Bebe repeatedly. I walked over to his body as it fell over and hit the floor. I put a bullet in his head. "I been killing Muslims since yesterday. Targeting and killing 'em. Fuck you talkin' bout?" I screamed at Bebe's corpse, then shot him again. I looked around the room with death in my eyes.

"If somebody in this room feels some kinda way about what I just did to Bebe, speak up right now! We can handle it however y'all wanna handle it. Somebody in this fuckin room is a traitor! How do I know that? Because only the people in this room knew that Yasir was the only person alive who knew Salimah moved out in the suburbs and where. When them niggas … Shahid's men snatched Ya … they knew that he knew. They tortured my nigga, and he broke. He took them to my sister's house. They killed Ya, my sister and some Blood nigga name Drama. And somebody in this room also told them niggas where our families lived.

"They had to because I haven't lived with Grams for almost twenty years. There was no connection from her to me. None. And for all I know, the traitor might've been Bebe. He said his pops know them niggas. He tried to throw me … throw us off their trail. He protested against my plan. So for that, he's gone and we still here. These niggas killed my sister, yo, and I'm all the way disturbed about it. I'm fucked up. And the only thing that calms my nerves is killing. This shit I'm on ain't up for no debate." I paused to see if anyone had anything to say. When nobody spoke, I continued my spiel.

"Islam is a beautiful religion, yo. I'm not at war with Islam. I'm at war with the muthafuckas that say they practice Islam but they do shit that Islam forbids. Feel me? This shit I'm on is bigger than religion. Bigger than Muslims, Nation niggas and Christians. Anybody can get it. My bullets for everybody. Even niggas in this room that get in my way. Mu was Muslim. He knew that Hasan, me … a lot of us is … was Muslim. But that didn't stop him from putting the wheels in play that led to Ha's death. Mu did that shit, yo. He was behind that shit the whole time. Islam didn't stop Mu from sending niggas for my head. So, it didn't stop me from chopping off his. This nigga Muhammad Shahid been on my line for almost ten months.

"Why he didn't come for our families sooner is anybody's guess. Something I'll ask him before I kill him. That nigga is Muslim. His organization is full of Muslims. Them niggas don't give two fucks about any of us being Muslim or our families being Muslim. So, why should I care about killing Muslims? I'm on my 'Philly niggas' shit. Them niggas go to the Masjid, pray in the ranks together, leave the Masjid and kill each other the same day. That's what I'm on. Whoever in this room ain't on what I'm on, can take their bag of money and bounce. You can take Bebe's money, too. Take it and bounce and there ain't no love lost. I'll just know we ain't fuckin' with each other the way I thought we was.

"I'ma say this shit one last time … Limah didn't do nothing to them niggas, yo. Grams didn't either. Mrs. Minnis and Granma Pearl ain't do nothing to them niggas. Yasir's family and Hasan's family ain't do nothing to them niggas. I did. But they killed all the people I just named, anyway. So, I'ma return that bloodshed in spades. We … me, Gunz, and Tye … ain't gon stop killing until we satisfied. So, Goo, Shotgun, Rah Rah and you too, Killa … if one of y'all wanna leave, leave now! Leave!"

I waited for someone to speak or stand up and leave. No one did.

"So, like I was saying before I was so rudely interrupted," I shot Bebe's dead body again. "We got eight Masjids in the city. If we pair off"

"We can't pair off, baby boy!" Gunz said. "You killing Bebe left us a man short."

"Yeah, son, you right. Y'all pair off, I'ma go dolo," I replied.

"Can't let you do that, fam," Tye said.

I looked over at him. My eyes filled with emotion. "It ain't up for debate, yo. We all got two Masjids to hit. And not a lot of time to get there. Kill muthafuckas, but not too many. Just a couple at each one. Only men though. No women and no kids. Let the brothers who die today find out if paradise is real."

"What about Bebe, yo?" Killa asked.

"What about him?" I replied, voice filled with venom.

"We just gon leave his body right here?"

"Why not?" I answered Killa. "He ain't going nowhere."

***

By the time I got to Masjid Muhammed, Jumah was already in session. The Imam's Khutbah could be heard blasting through speakers positioned all over the building. I parked the Maxima and waited for victims. I had no second thoughts about what I had come to Garden State Parkway to do. It was the qadr of Allah that someone died that day. I was there to fulfill destiny.

Anthony Fields

Chapter 32

Aziz Navid

"Often labeled as the sixth borough due to its close proximity to New York, Newark is undoubtedly the Garden State's largest metropolis. The nation's third oldest city is known for its cultural centers of state and its endless arts and entertainment options. With the occurrence of gentrification and the city's plans of renovating its downtown area, together with rebuilding within the surrounding communities. Newark's nickname of Brick City seems to be less relevant as numerous neighborhoods are being torn down. But today, Newark is again a part of the national news cycle and not for any of the things I just mentioned.

Newark is again the most dangerous and murderous city in the nation. In the last forty-eight hours, Newark has experienced its largest rise in homicides since the early two thousands. There have been over forty people slain in the city. Local authorities have called in the FBI hours ago to investigate possible hate crimes against the city's largest population of Muslims. Last night, several Islamic businesses were targeted, and several people were killed at those businesses. Earlier today, Islamic worshipers were ambushed and brazenly attacked outside of the city's eight mosques. Seventeen people were killed as they left Friday religious services. Newark police believe that anti Muslims hate groups are responsible for the attacks ..."

"Papa," my seven-year-old daughter, Azizah said as she leapt into my lap.

I lowered the volume on the TV's news broadcast. "Hey, ZiZi," I replied and hugged my only child tight. I tickled her side and made her giggle.

"Papa, I helped Mama cook your dinner."

"And what is it the two of you cooked, ZiZi?"

"A Malaysian dish called 'yakiniku don buri.' Fried eggs, roasted vegetables, basmati with toasted cumia, sauteed mushrooms, chicken and um ... shellfish."   .

"Sounds delicious, but what is a don buri?"

Azizah smiled. "Papa, duh ... don buri means bowl in Japanese."

"That's right. You are a very smart girl, ZiZi."

The cell phone on the table vibrated. I moved my daughter to reach it. Grabbing the phone, I saw the screen and recognized the caller. After hearing of the deaths of so many Muslims, my heart ached with implication. I wondered if the killers were the men I sought. Deep inside, a quiet rage simmered. But looking at my daughter, who I considered my heart manifested into human form, I couldn't help but to soften. "ZiZi, go and tell Mama that Papa is ready to eat. To fix my plate and put it on the table in the dining room. And I would love it if you and Mama would eat with me."

"Okay, Papa," Azizah replied and darted down the hall.

"Hello?" I said as I answered the call. I listened to the caller confirm my earlier assumptions. I frowned and disconnected the call. I dialed Muhammad Shahid's number.

"Assalamu Alaikum," Muhammad greeted me in Arabic.

"Walaikum Assalam," I said, returning the greeting. "Sorry to bother you, Ocki, but I figured you'd want to hear the latest news."

"What news, Aziz?"

"Najee is back in Newark. And according to my source, he's pissed off about his family and the families of his friends."

"As he should be. That's predictable. What else?"

"You were right about how to get Najee here, but you said nothing about what he'd do once he got here. Or how you want me to respond."

"What has our friend Najee done since he's returned to Newark?" Muhammad asked.

"He's learned it was you who ordered the deaths of his grandmother and sister. His friends know it was us who killed their families, to include Yasir Rahman, his family and Hasan Sharif's family. Since yesterday, Najee has been sending a reply to our message to him. In blood. He's targeting Muslims all over the city. At restaurants, bookstores, boutiques, Masjids ..."

"Masjids?"

"Yes, Masjids. Since you are in New York, you don't get the local news here. But you can go online and read about what I'm telling you. The police here in Newark think there is an active hate group targeting Muslims. They've called in the FBI. We hit Najee and his friends and now they're hitting back. I never expected him to go after the innocent Muslims ..."

"Aziz, we've had this conversation before. At times of war, there is always collateral damage. It's necessary ..."

"You sound just like my wife," I mentioned.

"Nadia Navid has always proven to be very wise. She's a good wife."

"Nevertheless, I created the lanes for us to recoup the fifty million dollars we lost on the keys that Najee stole. We replaced that shipment with many others. My question to you now is this ... at what point does this all end?"

"Muqtar was a lieutenant in my organization. His life was ours to protect. We failed. His wife Hafizah was my first cousin and I had to have her killed to silence her. This is no longer about the money that was taken or the drugs Najee took. This is about the slight. The disrespect. All the blood that was shed in anger. This ends when Najee Bashir and all of his friends are dead," Muhammad Shahid said and ended the call.

Shaking my head, I dialed another number. "Assalamu Alaikum."

"Walaikum Assalam," Khitab answered.

"Are we close to getting up on Najee's camp?"

"My source is afraid to reveal exact whereabouts. His friends are not hard to find, but Najee is. He's spontaneous, unpredictable and crafty. He's smart, paranoid, impulsive, merciless and he has unlimited resources in the streets. The city of Newark fears him, I'm told."

I listened to Khitab's assessment of our common enemy. "That makes Najee a very dangerous man."

"I agree, Ocki," Khitab concurred.

"I've been told Najee is behind the recent attacks on Muslims all over the city. We need to find him and kill him. Cut off the head of the snake ..."

"And the body dies shortly thereafter. I heard about a candle-light vigil that's scheduled for later this evening, in the projects where Najee and his friends are from. To remember his sister and friends. I'm told Najee will be there somewhere."

"Good. take Amir and Minister Rico with you there. If you find him, kill him. And his closest friends too."

"And if he's not there?" Khitab asked.

"Kill some people anyway," I told him. "He sent us a message. Send one back."

To Be Continued...
Angel 4
Coming Soon

Angel 3

Turn The Page for A Sneak Peek at If You Cross Me Once 2

Anthony Fields

If You Cross Me Once 2

Chapter 1

Quran

Near the Woodley Park Zoo, was 3321 Connecticut Avenue, a sixteen-story, high rise condominium building. The neighborhood was expensive, inhabited by mostly affluent whites that walked up and down the street with no cares. One block over, there was a Neiman Marcus department store and a Saks Fifth Avenue. Sean Branch and I sat in the Dodge Journey Caravan near a gas station across the street.

"Kenneth Sparrow lives in that building?" I asked, pointing at 3321.

Sean nodded his head and then went back to wherever his thoughts were.

"He gotta be the only black muthafucka that lives in this neighborhood."

"Probably is," Sean said and looked at the building. "A rat that lives near a zoo. Ain't that some shit?"

"All I wanna know is, who the fuck he knows to even get into a building like that."

"He knows all the prosecutors and detectives in the city, it don't surprise me that he lives there. Probably got a witness protection voucher or some shit like that. I heard that that nigga got the bag now, too. So, maybe he paid his way in. Or let the cracka that own the building fuck him. Ain't no telling, slim. Them rat niggas be resourceful than a muthafucka. You still smell that body that was back there?"

"Hell yeah, I still smell that shit. Shit stinks like shit. You actin' like you don't smell that shit. That's why I got my window down."

"I gotta get this joint detailed, then. I thought you had your shoes off."

I laughed at that. "Shid, nigga, if anything, that's your breath smelling like that."

Sean cracked up laughing.

"Seriously, though, what's your plan? How we gon get in there to Kenny Sparrow?"

"Just fall back, youngin, you gon see in a minute."

I did exactly what Sean said. I fell back. Leaned back rather, in the passenger seat and thought about Zin. no matter where I was or what I did, I couldn't shake Zin from my thoughts. My cell phone vibrated. I thought that it might be Zin. It wasn't. It was KiKi Swinson. "KiKi, what's up?"

"Hey, Que. Ain't nothing up, I was just missing your sexy ass. Were you busy?'

"Kinda sorta. But I can talk. I miss you, too. When can I see you again?"

"I'm flying out to L.A tomorrow," KiKi said. "Got a meeting with some people from *Netflix* about turning one of my books into a movie. I'ma be gone for a week, then I'll be back on the East Coast. Either I can pit stop in D.C., or you can come down to Virginia Beach. It's up to you."

"Right now, it's looking like a pit stop, but in a week things might look different. By the time you ready to fly back this way, I'll know for sure. That good with you?"

"Of course, it is. No worries. Whatever you want, Que."

"I'm glad to hear about the book to movie thing. You gon be in the movie? I ain't never fuck nobody who been in the movies."

"Well, you just might get that chance, baby. Stay tuned," KiKi said seductively.

"Which book is they tryna do for the movie?"

"*Candy Shop.* the one I did with Wahida Clark."

"Wahida Clark? She's the one that put out that *Ultimate Sacrifice* for my homie, right?"

"Yup. Damn, you still remember that book, huh? You must've really liked it."

"How could I not? It was in my city, written by a real nigga and raw. I'm waiting on the other parts so I can read them. But anyway, congrats on the movie thing. You gon kill the meeting. Hit me when you on your way back."

"I will. Be safe, baby. Bye," KiKi said and ended the call.

I turned to Sean. "When you was doing that time, did you read any of them urban novel joints?"

Sean nodded. "I read too many of them joints. In the early two thousands, them joints was getting a nigga through. I was in the hole a lot and niggas was ordering them joints and sending them to me. They were cool when Dutch came out. *B-More Careful*, *Larceny* by the homie Jason Poole, all them Al-Saddiq Banks joints, *True 2 the Game*, joints like that. I was fuckin' with them joints heavy, but then them joints got watered down real fast. I was reading so much trash, I decided to write one."

"Write what? A book?"

"Yeah. It was easy. I put my mind to it and got it done."

"Stop what you doing, slim. Talkin' bout you wrote a book."

Sean picked up his phone and did some finger moving, then he passed the phone to me. On the screen of his phone was Amazon.com and a picture of a book called "Money, Murder and Mayhem. The book was written by none other than Sean Branch.

"Damn, slim, you wasn't bullshittin.' You really wrote a book." I passed Sean his phone back. "I'ma cop that joint asap. That's crazy. The notorious Sean 'Teflon' Branch is really Sean Jerome Dickey."

"Hey," Sean said and frowned. "That nigga's gay."

"My bad, slim. My bad. You ever read the 'Ultimate Sacrifice' series?"

"Of course, I did. All five of them. I'm waiting for part six. The dude that wrote them joints is my man."

"You know, slim, too, huh?"

"We been around each other in a few spots out the feds. Good dude, youngin. Real live stand-up man, although niggas tryna salt him down. But salt kills snails, not men."

"Niggas tryna salt him down, how? I asked curiously.

"This new generation is fucked up, youngin. They can't think past go. Young niggas don't understand defenses. There's a disconnect between my era and yours. In my era, you could put the body on a dead man. It made sense. You put the body on the dead man because he's dead. He can't face prosecution, go to jail, there's no harm that can come to him. But young niggas today say that that's hot. To them, everything dealing with old principles is hot. But ain't none of this new shit they doing 'hot.'

Getting on *Facebook* Live and *Instagram* live and calling out niggas' names ain't hot to them. Telling everybody on *Instagram* live that y'all hoods beefing and who killed who. Telling niggas to pull up and then flashing all kinds of guns, ain't hot. Saying on *Facebook* that John John and Tay Tay killed their man 'Dawg Pound' so they gon spin the block around Lincoln Heights ain't hot. The feds look at all that social media shit. They might as well tell the cops. Feel me?"

"I feel you, slim. That dumb ass shit ain't never proper."

"These niggas hit a lick and then post pictures of them and their man with all the money and guns, wearing the same clothes that they hit the lick in. When they get bagged for the lick, they don't say their man was hot for posting the pictures. Why? He got them knocked off."

"You right about that." I agreed.

"I been killing niggas since I was twelve years old. Majority of them was rats. That makes me a certified rat hunter. Just like you. You killed your own brother for telling on a nigga. How gangsta is that? That proves that you believe in the Omerta, the code that says no snitching allowed. The code that we live by is this, you become a rat when you debrief and make statements, written and videotaped, signing affidavits implicating niggas in crimes that can send them to jail. Setting niggas up for the feds wearing wires ... all that shit makes you hot. To me, it's the intent. In Buck's situation ... my man that wrote the *Ultimate Sacrifices* ... he got on the stand and testified on his own behalf.

"He denied all the allegations that the government put on him and his men. Remember when I said earlier that dudes don't understand defenses? On the stand, Buck said that the drugs found in the barbershop wasn't his. He said that he didn't know who they belonged to. His co-defendant was beefing with Buck because it came out that Buck thought he was a rat. He put out there that Buck's defense was hot and niggas ran with that.

"But how? He never implicated nobody."

"I just told you that niggas out here totally fucked up. Everybody is hot but them. Niggas' logic twisted. Check this out. Niggas running around saying what Buck said was hot. Repeating what some coward ass nigga named Lennell Tucker, his co-defendant, said. When did it become cool to let cowards and suckas slander good men who been tried and tested, and stood up under every situation threw at them?"

What Sean was venting about made a lot of sense. Shit really was fucked up.

"Young niggas think what Buck did was 'hot', but they love Tupac. Tupac wasn't hot to them. He got robbed and shot at that studio, he immediately implicated Biggie, Puffy, Lil Cease and others. He got on the radio and said it. Said it on TV and in magazines. His case was being investigated by NYPD and back then, NYPD was all over all that shit. They questioned them dudes because of what Tupac said. And that ain't hot to them. T.I. got on the stand for the prosecution in Ohio, something about his man getting killed. He didn't point at the shooters. But he told the court the defendants left the club and got into a green Tahoe. When asked did he see who shot his man, he said no, but that the bullets came from the green Tahoe. That's hot. But niggas love T.I.

"Take the nigga Ray Lewis, the football player. Everybody, especially all the Baltimore young niggas love Ray Lewis. Ray Lewis got caught up in a murder. He said he didn't witness the murder and he never saw the defendant stab the victim. But he turns around and says he was with the defendant the day before the murder, when he purchased the knife from a sporting goods store. The knife was the murder weapon. He put the murder weapon in the defendant's hand. How the fuck that ain't hot? All this shit is twisted …"

Sean's phone vibrated. He looked at the phone and then the rearview mirror. "About time." Sean turned back to me. "Here's how we get to Kenny Sparrow, right here."

Before I could say a word, a woman walked up to the Caravan. Sean let his window down. "Trina, what's up, babygirl?"

The woman was stylishly dressed, but her face reminded me of a Muppet. Whichever one you envisioned she was it. She leaned into the window and hugged Sean. "I can't believe they finally let your crazy ass out of jail. Welcome home, Sean."

"I'm definitely glad to be home." Sean said and reached into his pocket. He pulled out a wad of money and passed it through the window to the woman. "I need you to order some food. I'ma bring it to the door. You let us in, then bounce. You know the routine."

"Just like old times, huh? You ain't gon never change. Kenny's dick game is garbage. Gimme about twenty minutes and then come up. He lives on the sixth floor. Apartment 614."

"Got it."

"Good. See you in a few," Trina said and left.

We watched her go to the entrance to the building and minutes later get buzzed in.

"You trust her, slim?" I asked Sean. "She can be trusted not to tell after they find Kenny dead?"

Sean smiled at me. "Do you know who that is?"

"You called her Trina. So, I guess she must be Trina."

"That ain't just any old Trina, youngin. That's Trinaboo."

I had heard a lot about the notorious Trinaboo since I was young. She was a legend in the city. For a whole lot of reasons. "Oh, yeah. I guess her name and rep makes her trustworthy, huh?"

"Naw, Que. What makes her trustworthy is fear. Trina knows exactly who I am. Exactly what I do. Been doing. She knows her daughter Tierra, and her son lil Mike gon die, if she ever crosses me. Trina knows I'ma kill everybody she loves if she talks. Her fear of me will keep her mouth closed."

"Muthafuckas be saying that she got that HIV shit."

"They been saying that shit since the early nineties and she ain't dead yet."

"You fucked her before?" I asked Sean.

The look on Sean's face was demonic. "I wouldn't fuck Trinaboo with somebody else's dick."

***

"He's in the bedroom. No gun that I saw. He's worn out sexually and don't suspect shit. My part is done, right?" Trinaboo said after opening the apartment door.

Sean and I were dressed in Papa John pizza uniforms. We entered the apartment.

"Yeah. You can go," Sean told Trina.

In a flash, the woman known as Trinaboo was gone through the door. I locked the door behind her.

"What did you get on that pizza?" a man's voice called out from the bedroom.

"Cheese … all rats love cheese," Sean mouthed to me and smiled.

Sean put down the empty pizza box and pulled his silenced handgun. I pulled mine as well.

He led the way to the bedroom. The door was ajar. Sean pulled it open.

Kenneth Sparrow was laid out on the king-sized bed with burgundy satin sheets. The sheet was pulled up to cover his nakedness to the navel. "I'm hungry as shit." His eyes were closed.

"I wish I had food for you, homie. It would be your last meal."

At the sound of Sean's voice, Kenny Sparrow's eyes popped open. "Sean? What the fuck?"

"What the fuck is right, Kenny. It's been a long time coming, but a change has come."

"Fuckin' bitch set me up."

I laughed at that. The doomed man sounded like D.C.'s infamous former Mayor Marion Berry after he was caught at a hotel smoking crack cocaine.

Sean pulled out latex gloves and put them on. "I been waiting eighteen years for this day."

To Be Continued…

Lock Down Publications and Ca$h Presents assisted
publishing packages.

BASIC PACKAGE $499
Editing
Cover Design
Formatting

UPGRADED PACKAGE $800
Typing
Editing
Cover Design
Formatting

ADVANCE PACKAGE $1,200
Typing
Editing
Cover Design
Formatting
Copyright registration
Proofreading
Upload book to Amazon

LDP SUPREME PACKAGE $1,500
Typing
Editing
Cover Design
Formatting
Copyright registration

Anthony Fields

Proofreading
Set up Amazon account
Upload book to Amazon
Advertise on LDP Amazon and Facebook page

***Other services available upon request. Additional
charges may apply
Lock Down Publications
P.O. Box 944
Stockbridge, GA 30281-9998
Phone # 470 303-9761

Submission Guideline

Submit the first three chapters of your completed manuscript to ldpsubmissions@gmail.com, subject line: Your book's title. The manuscript must be in a .doc file and sent as an attachment. Document should be in Times New Roman, double spaced and in size 12 font. Also, provide your synopsis and full contact information. If sending multiple submissions, they must each be in a separate email.

Have a story but no way to send it electronically? You can still submit to LDP/Ca$h Presents. Send in the first three chapters, written or typed, of your completed manuscript to:

LDP: Submissions Dept
Po Box 944
Stockbridge, Ga 30281

DO NOT send original manuscript. Must be a duplicate.

Provide your synopsis and a cover letter containing your full contact information.

Thanks for considering LDP and Ca$h Presents.

NEW RELEASES

THE BRICK MAN 4 by KING RIO
HOOD CONSIGLIERE by KEESE
PRETTY GIRLS DO NASTY THINGS by NICOLE GOOSBY
PROTÉGÉ OF A LEGEND by COREY ROBINSON
STRAIGHT BEAST MODE 2 by DE'KARI
ANGEL 3 by ANTHONY FIELDS

Anthony Fields

3X KRAZY III

STRAIGHT BEAST MODE III

De'Kari

KINGPIN KILLAZ IV

STREET KINGS III

PAID IN BLOOD III

CARTEL KILLAZ IV

DOPE GODS III

Hood Rich

SINS OF A HUSTLA II

ASAD

RICH $AVAGE II

By Martell Troublesome Bolden

YAYO V

Bred In The Game 2

S. Allen

CREAM III

THE STREETS WILL TALK II

By Yolanda Moore

SON OF A DOPE FIEND III

HEAVEN GOT A GHETTO II

By Renta

LOYALTY AIN'T PROMISED III

By Keith Williams

I'M NOTHING WITHOUT HIS LOVE II

SINS OF A THUG II

TO THE THUG I LOVED BEFORE II

IN A HUSTLER I TRUST II

By Monet Dragun

QUIET MONEY IV

EXTENDED CLIP III

THUG LIFE IV

By Trai'Quan

THE STREETS MADE ME IV

By Larry D. Wright

IF YOU CROSS ME ONCE II

ANGEL IV

By Anthony Fields

THE STREETS WILL NEVER CLOSE IV

By K'ajji

HARD AND RUTHLESS III

KILLA KOUNTY III

By Khufu

MONEY GAME III

By Smoove Dolla

JACK BOYS VS DOPE BOYS II

A GANGSTA'S QUR'AN V

COKE GIRLZ II

By Romell Tukes

MURDA WAS THE CASE II

Elijah R. Freeman

THE STREETS NEVER LET GO II

By Robert Baptiste

AN UNFORESEEN LOVE III

Anthony Fields

By **Meesha**

KING OF THE TRENCHES III

by **GHOST & TRANAY ADAMS**

MONEY MAFIA II

LOYAL TO THE SOIL III

By **Jibril Williams**

QUEEN OF THE ZOO II

By **Black Migo**

VICIOUS LOYALTY III

By Kingpen

A GANGSTA'S PAIN III

By J-Blunt

CONFESSIONS OF A JACKBOY III

By Nicholas Lock

GRIMEY WAYS II

By Ray Vinci

KING KILLA II

By Vincent "Vitto" Holloway

BETRAYAL OF A THUG II

By Fre$h

THE MURDER QUEENS II

By Michael Gallon

THE BIRTH OF A GANGSTER II

By Delmont Player

TREAL LOVE II

By Le'Monica Jackson

FOR THE LOVE OF BLOOD II
By Jamel Mitchell
RAN OFF ON DA PLUG II
By Paper Boi Rari
HOOD CONSIGLIERE II
By Keese
PRETTY GIRLS DO NASTY THINGS II
By Nicole Goosby
PROTÉGÉ OF A LEGEND II
By Corey Robinson

Available Now

RESTRAINING ORDER **I & II**
By **CA$H & Coffee**
LOVE KNOWS NO BOUNDARIES **I II & III**
By **Coffee**
RAISED AS A GOON I, II, III & IV
BRED BY THE SLUMS I, II, III
BLAST FOR ME I & II

ROTTEN TO THE CORE I II III

A BRONX TALE I, II, III

DUFFLE BAG CARTEL I II III IV V VI

HEARTLESS GOON I II III IV V

A SAVAGE DOPEBOY I II

DRUG LORDS I II III

CUTTHROAT MAFIA I II

KING OF THE TRENCHES

By **Ghost**

LAY IT DOWN **I & II**

LAST OF A DYING BREED I II

BLOOD STAINS OF A SHOTTA I & II III

By **Jamaica**

LOYAL TO THE GAME I II III

LIFE OF SIN I, II III

By **TJ & Jelissa**

BLOODY COMMAS I & II

SKI MASK CARTEL I II & III

KING OF NEW YORK I II,III IV V

RISE TO POWER I II III

COKE KINGS I II III IV V

BORN HEARTLESS I II III IV

KING OF THE TRAP I II

By **T.J. Edwards**

IF LOVING HIM IS WRONG…I & II

LOVE ME EVEN WHEN IT HURTS I II III

By **Jelissa**

WHEN THE STREETS CLAP BACK I & II III

THE HEART OF A SAVAGE I II III

MONEY MAFIA

LOYAL TO THE SOIL I II

By **Jibril Williams**

A DISTINGUISHED THUG STOLE MY HEART I II & III

LOVE SHOULDN'T HURT I II III IV

RENEGADE BOYS I II III IV

PAID IN KARMA I II III

SAVAGE STORMS I II III

AN UNFORESEEN LOVE I II

By **Meesha**

A GANGSTER'S CODE I &, II III

A GANGSTER'S SYN I II III

THE SAVAGE LIFE I II III

CHAINED TO THE STREETS I II III

BLOOD ON THE MONEY I II III

A GANGSTA'S PAIN I II

By **J-Blunt**

PUSH IT TO THE LIMIT

By **Bre' Hayes**

BLOOD OF A BOSS **I, II, III, IV, V**

SHADOWS OF THE GAME

TRAP BASTARD

By **Askari**

THE STREETS BLEED MURDER **I, II & III**

THE HEART OF A GANGSTA I II& III

Anthony Fields

By **Jerry Jackson**

CUM FOR ME I II III IV V VI VII VIII

An **LDP Erotica Collaboration**

BRIDE OF A HUSTLA **I II & II**

THE FETTI GIRLS **I, II& III**

CORRUPTED BY A GANGSTA I, II III, IV

BLINDED BY HIS LOVE

THE PRICE YOU PAY FOR LOVE I, II ,III

DOPE GIRL MAGIC I II III

By **Destiny Skai**

WHEN A GOOD GIRL GOES BAD

By **Adrienne**

THE COST OF LOYALTY I II III

By Kweli

A GANGSTER'S REVENGE **I II III & IV**

THE BOSS MAN'S DAUGHTERS I II III IV V

A SAVAGE LOVE **I & II**

BAE BELONGS TO ME I II

A HUSTLER'S DECEIT I, II, III

WHAT BAD BITCHES DO I, II, III

SOUL OF A MONSTER I II III

KILL ZONE

A DOPE BOY'S QUEEN I II III

By **Aryanna**

A KINGPIN'S AMBITON

A KINGPIN'S AMBITION **II**

I MURDER FOR THE DOUGH

By **Ambitious**
TRUE SAVAGE I II III IV V VI VII
DOPE BOY MAGIC I, II, III
MIDNIGHT CARTEL I II III
CITY OF KINGZ I II
NIGHTMARE ON SILENT AVE
THE PLUG OF LIL MEXICO II

By **Chris Green**
A DOPEBOY'S PRAYER
By **Eddie "Wolf" Lee**
THE KING CARTEL **I, II & III**
By **Frank Gresham**
THESE NIGGAS AIN'T LOYAL **I, II & III**
By **Nikki Tee**
GANGSTA SHYT **I II &III**
By **CATO**
THE ULTIMATE BETRAYAL
By **Phoenix**
BOSS'N UP **I , II & III**
By **Royal Nicole**
I LOVE YOU TO DEATH
By **Destiny J**
I RIDE FOR MY HITTA
I STILL RIDE FOR MY HITTA
By **Misty Holt**
LOVE & CHASIN' PAPER

Anthony Fields

By **Qay Crockett**
TO DIE IN VAIN
SINS OF A HUSTLA
By **ASAD**
BROOKLYN HUSTLAZ
By **Boogsy Morina**
BROOKLYN ON LOCK I & II
By **Sonovia**
GANGSTA CITY
By **Teddy Duke**
A DRUG KING AND HIS DIAMOND I & II III
A DOPEMAN'S RICHES
HER MAN, MINE'S TOO I, II
CASH MONEY HO'S
THE WIFEY I USED TO BE I II
PRETTY GIRLS DO NASTY THINGS
By Nicole Goosby
TRAPHOUSE KING **I II & III**
KINGPIN KILLAZ I II III
STREET KINGS I II
PAID IN BLOOD **I II**
CARTEL KILLAZ I II III
DOPE GODS I II
By **Hood Rich**
LIPSTICK KILLAH **I, II, III**
CRIME OF PASSION I II & III
FRIEND OR FOE I II III

Angel 3

By **Mimi**

STEADY MOBBN' **I, II, III**

THE STREETS STAINED MY SOUL I II III

By **Marcellus Allen**

WHO SHOT YA **I, II, III**

SON OF A DOPE FIEND I II

HEAVEN GOT A GHETTO

Renta

GORILLAZ IN THE BAY **I II III IV**

TEARS OF A GANGSTA I II

3X KRAZY I II

STRAIGHT BEAST MODE I II

DE'KARI

TRIGGADALE I II III

MURDAROBER WAS THE CASE

Elijah R. Freeman

GOD BLESS THE TRAPPERS I, II, III

THESE SCANDALOUS STREETS I, II, III

FEAR MY GANGSTA I, II, III IV, V

THESE STREETS DON'T LOVE NOBODY I, II

BURY ME A G I, II, III, IV, V

A GANGSTA'S EMPIRE I, II, III, IV

THE DOPEMAN'S BODYGAURD I II

THE REALEST KILLAZ I II III

THE LAST OF THE OGS I II III

Tranay Adams

THE STREETS ARE CALLING

Duquie Wilson

MARRIED TO A BOSS I II III

By Destiny Skai & Chris Green

KINGZ OF THE GAME I II III IV V VI

Playa Ray

SLAUGHTER GANG I II III

RUTHLESS HEART I II III

By Willie Slaughter

FUK SHYT

By Blakk Diamond

DON'T F#CK WITH MY HEART I II

By Linnea

ADDICTED TO THE DRAMA I II III

IN THE ARM OF HIS BOSS II

By Jamila

YAYO I II III IV

A SHOOTER'S AMBITION I II

BRED IN THE GAME

By S. Allen

TRAP GOD I II III

RICH $AVAGE

MONEY IN THE GRAVE I II III

By Martell Troublesome Bolden

FOREVER GANGSTA

GLOCKS ON SATIN SHEETS I II

By Adrian Dulan

TOE TAGZ I II III IV

LEVELS TO THIS SHYT I II

By Ah'Million

KINGPIN DREAMS I II III

RAN OFF ON DA PLUG

By Paper Boi Rari

CONFESSIONS OF A GANGSTA I II III IV

CONFESSIONS OF A JACKBOY I II

By Nicholas Lock

I'M NOTHING WITHOUT HIS LOVE

SINS OF A THUG

TO THE THUG I LOVED BEFORE

A GANGSTA SAVED XMAS

IN A HUSTLER I TRUST

By Monet Dragun

CAUGHT UP IN THE LIFE I II III

THE STREETS NEVER LET GO

By Robert Baptiste

NEW TO THE GAME I II III

MONEY, MURDER & MEMORIES I II III

By **Malik D. Rice**

LIFE OF A SAVAGE I II III

A GANGSTA'S QUR'AN I II III IV

MURDA SEASON I II III

GANGLAND CARTEL I II III

CHI'RAQ GANGSTAS I II III

KILLERS ON ELM STREET I II III

JACK BOYZ N DA BRONX I II III

A DOPEBOY'S DREAM I II III

JACK BOYS VS DOPE BOYS

COKE GIRLZ

By Romell Tukes

LOYALTY AIN'T PROMISED I II

By Keith Williams

QUIET MONEY I II III

THUG LIFE I II III

EXTENDED CLIP I II

By **Trai'Quan**

THE STREETS MADE ME I II III

By **Larry D. Wright**

THE ULTIMATE SACRIFICE I, II, III, IV, V, VI

KHADIFI

IF YOU CROSS ME ONCE

ANGEL I II III

IN THE BLINK OF AN EYE

By **Anthony Fields**

THE LIFE OF A HOOD STAR

By Ca$h & Rashia Wilson

THE STREETS WILL NEVER CLOSE I II III

By K'ajji

CREAM I II

THE STREETS WILL TALK

By Yolanda Moore

NIGHTMARES OF A HUSTLA I II III

By King Dream

CONCRETE KILLA I II III
VICIOUS LOYALTY I II
By Kingpen
HARD AND RUTHLESS I II
MOB TOWN 251
THE BILLIONAIRE BENTLEYS I II III
By Von Diesel
GHOST MOB
Stilloan Robinson
MOB TIES I II III IV V VI
By SayNoMore
BODYMORE MURDERLAND I II III
THE BIRTH OF A GANGSTER
By Delmont Player
FOR THE LOVE OF A BOSS
By C. D. Blue
MOBBED UP I II III IV
THE BRICK MAN I II III IV
THE COCAINE PRINCESS I II III IV V
By King Rio
KILLA KOUNTY I II III
By Khufu
MONEY GAME I II
By Smoove Dolla
A GANGSTA'S KARMA I II
By FLAME
KING OF THE TRENCHES I II

Anthony Fields

by **GHOST & TRANAY ADAMS**
QUEEN OF THE ZOO
By **Black Migo**
GRIMEY WAYS
By **Ray Vinci**
XMAS WITH AN ATL SHOOTER
By **Ca$h & Destiny Skai**
KING KILLA
By **Vincent "Vitto" Holloway**
BETRAYAL OF A THUG
By **Fre$h**
THE MURDER QUEENS
By **Michael Gallon**
TREAL LOVE
By **Le'Monica Jackson**
FOR THE LOVE OF BLOOD
By **Jamel Mitchell**
HOOD CONSIGLIERE
By **Keese**
PROTÉGÉ OF A LEGEND
By **Corey Robinson**

BOOKS BY LDP'S CEO, CA$H

TRUST IN NO MAN

TRUST IN NO MAN 2

TRUST IN NO MAN 3

BONDED BY BLOOD

SHORTY GOT A THUG

THUGS CRY

THUGS CRY 2

THUGS CRY 3

TRUST NO BITCH

TRUST NO BITCH 2

TRUST NO BITCH 3

TIL MY CASKET DROPS

RESTRAINING ORDER

RESTRAINING ORDER 2

IN LOVE WITH A CONVICT

LIFE OF A HOOD STAR

XMAS WITH AN ATL SHOOTER